Belonging

Murray and Tidswell Paranormal Investigations

Book Three

J.E. Nice

First published in Great Britain in 2020 by Write Into The Woods Publishing.

A CIP catalogue record for this book is available from the British Library.

ISBN 978-1-912903-22-1

Cover design and typesetting by Write into the Woods.

Brush for Ruby's headers from www.valhalla-vania.com

www.writeintothewoods.com
www.jenice.co.uk

The Last War Series:
Matter Of Time
Despite Our Enemies
In My Bones
With A Scream

Murray And Tidswell
Paranormal Investigations:
Beginnings
Becoming
Belonging
Bewitching
Bedevilling

No Masters Or Kings:
No Masters Or Kings
In Feverish Haste

Find them all at www.jenice.co.uk

JOIN US IN THE WOODS
for news, early access and freebies at
www.jenice.co.uk

For all the witches reading this.

1
Erica

It was early, too early, but this couldn't wait. Stomach churning, Erica knocked on Jess's front door. After what felt like an age, the bulk of Marshall approached, visible through the glass, and the door opened. A fluffy brown, black and white face appeared first, straining to reach Erica with wide brown eyes and a pink tongue flopping out. Marshall held Bubbles the puppy back by her collar.

'Ric? Everything okay?' he asked sleepily. Erica blinked, trying to keep her eyes on his face and not on his broad bare chest, which was hard considering she was eye level with his nipples.

'Yeah, hi, sorry, did I leave my phone here last night?'

'Oh. Erm.' Marshall looked behind him and then gestured for Erica to come in. She closed the door behind her and Bubbles pounced on her. Erica gave her a distracted cuddle and fretted for a moment.

If she were her phone, where would she be.

'Ric? What are you doing here?' Jess wandered down the stairs in a white dressing gown. 'Where's Ruby?' she asked Marshall over Erica's shoulder.

'Watching cartoons.' Marshall stretched, looked between Jess and Erica, and decided he was no longer needed. He disappeared into the living room where the sound of high-pitched talking could be heard from the television.

'What's up? It's not the woods, is it? Or your gran?' Jess reached the bottom of the stairs.

'No, no. Did I leave my phone here last night?'

'Oh, okay. Oh.'

Erica did a double take at Jess.

'Oh what?'

'Nothing. I, erm, I think I saw it in here.' Jess led Erica into the kitchen and began lifting up pieces of discarded wrapping paper left on the side from the previous night's party. 'Here. This is it, right?' She held up a phone and Erica exhaled in a rush.

'Oh, thank god.' She took it from Jess, grinning. 'I was so scared. It's like losing a limb, isn't it.' She hugged the phone to her chest for a moment and then checked the screen.

She held her breath.

In one second the events of the last week rushed through her mind before crashing, smashing to pieces. With trembling fingers, she opened the message that displayed as a notification and then looked up at Jess.

She hesitated at Jess's wide eyes.

'Did you know?' she murmured, her voice strained against the pain in her chest.

Slowly, Jess nodded.

'I saw it last night. I was going to tell you. I was. But you were so happy with Alfie. You've only just gotten together and we were only just finished with the demon and I didn't want to do anything to... I mean, I didn't want to...'

'Have you read it?'

'No. I didn't touch it. I swear. I just saw it when your phone beeped.'

She had to read the message. What if he was in trouble?

Taking a slow breath and sitting down at Jess's dining table, Erica read the message in full.

Hi. It's Rick. Not your Rick. It's future Rick. I know I said I wouldn't come back but I need your help. It's urgent. Please get in touch on this number. I need to see you. Please.

It wasn't enough. She needed more.

Two months ago, she would be calling him before she'd finished reading the message, but now?

Erica stared at the words.

It's urgent.

I need to see you.

I need your help.

Only the day before, Erica had sat in her car on Jess's driveway and silently begged Rick to come back to her, and here he was. Her prayer had been answered, hours too late. Or was it minutes too late? Only seconds had passed between her uttering her wish to the universe and Alfie tapping on the window, bringing her back to reality.

Erica looked up at Jess.

'I don't know what to do,' she murmured, holding out her phone so that Jess could read the message.

Jess scanned the words.

'I hate to say it, Ric, but—'

'You're going to tell me to listen to my heart, aren't you? To listen to my gut. You're going to ask me what I *want*.' Erica gritted her teeth. 'I'm so sick of this,' she muttered, taking her phone back and walking towards the front door. 'I'm so sick of making all the decisions. Why can't someone just tell me what to do.'

'Okay then. Call him. Right now, before you leave, call Rick and ask him to meet with you,' came Jess's voice from behind her.

Erica stopped and looked over her shoulder before glancing down at her phone.

'No? Okay, then go back to Alfie. Right now. Delete that message and go back to bed with Alfie.'

Erica sighed.

'He says he needs my help.'

'He's a grown man from the future, Ric,' said

Jess. 'He can find help from somewhere else. If you want Alfie, stay with Alfie.'

Erica slid her phone into her pocket and held up a hand to Jess in defeat.

'It's going to have to be my decision, isn't it?'

'Sorry.' Jess nodded, holding out her arms and embracing her friend in a tight hug. 'Let me know what you do and if you need me there.'

Erica hugged her back, her phone burning into her jeans.

2

Rick

Rick took his eyes from the road to glance down at his phone. The screen was black, dormant. It had been less than twenty-four hours since he'd messaged Erica, less than twenty-four hours since he'd arrived back in the past. He'd done quite well, considering. He'd bought a phone, he'd messaged Erica, found himself somewhere to stay for the night and just picked up a rental car which he was now weaving through Bristol traffic, heading for the motorway.

Once he was on the M32, what then? Where was he going? If he didn't make a decision soon, he'd be heading towards Wales or Cornwall, neither of which were ideal at this time.

Not yet.

He needed Erica to respond first.

He should have stayed in the coffee shop, but being inactive was making things worse. He needed to be moving, he needed his momentum to keep up with his whirring thoughts. Even if that meant driving round and round Bristol.

Rick smiled. It had been a long time since he'd driven these roads. Cars were pretty much banned in the city centre in his time, but now memories of taking his driving lessons around the edges of the city poked away at him.

He'd put himself into such a dangerous position, coming back here. More dangerous than the last time. This time, he wasn't here in an official capacity, this time it wasn't for work. He wasn't chasing someone, he had no clear mission and no clear date to return to his own time.

This visit was something else, and, again, it meant sharing a time with another version of him.

Nearly three months had passed since Rick had asked Erica to find him in her time, to ask him out on a date, to take a chance on him. He wondered if she'd found him yet?

What if he'd said no?

A thought niggled at him. The same thought that had been niggling at the back of his mind for the best part of two weeks now.

If Erica had found him, asked him out and he'd said yes, was that the reason why things had happened the way they had?

There was a suspicion playing on Rick's mind, one that he was loathe to admit, that Erica hadn't searched for him. That she had decided against looking for him, maybe deciding to let fate do its thing.

Of course, the other option was that she had found him but had decided against asking him out. That was the thought Rick couldn't bring himself to form clearly in his mind. That was the option that he didn't want to exist.

What if Erica had rejected him?

He had to find her, he had to talk to her.

The next turning off the M32 would lead him to her family's home. Rick smiled, remembering her parents' Labradors. How old would they be now? There would still be two of them, the old one would still be alive. What was her name again?

What if Erica had rejected the idea of finding him? He doubted she would take kindly to him turning up at her family home. He'd have to talk to her parents, as much as he liked them, he'd have to explain himself to more than just her.

No. It had been less than twenty-four hours.

He needed to be patient.

Where then?

Rick came off the motorway, waiting in a queue to go around the large roundabout and return to the motorway heading back the way he'd come. Back into the city.

There was one other place where Rick could go with the assurance that Erica was likely to turn up, but it was risky.

As he followed his memory and then signs to the

Victorian cemetery, Rick wondered if explaining himself to Erica's parents wasn't actually the easier option.

Erica

Erica chewed on her lower lip as she pulled into the cemetery, easing her car to the back and parking up. Without thinking, she climbed out of her sky blue Mini Cooper, slammed the door, locked it with a beep and headed towards the café. Her eyes automatically scanned the trees and gravestones as she crunched over the gravel.

In a few months the leaves would start to turn, a mist descending between the gravestones, but for now the trees and grass were full and lush. Birds sang above Erica's head and the sun beat down over the chapel as she walked past, up the steps and into the café.

There were a few people already inside despite the early hour. An older couple drinking coffee and eating croissants, a younger couple discussing something in hushed tones – Erica smiled, wondering if they were there to discuss their wedding –

and someone sitting in the corner, a large newspaper covering their face as their coffee went cold.

Erica was greeted by the staff, she came in regularly enough to be known by name, and she ordered her coffee to go, handing them her bamboo cup.

After a moment's deliberation, she ordered a brownie to go with it.

'For later,' she lied with a smile. Truth was, she needed a kick and the sugar might help her think through Rick's message and its implications.

Leaving the café, she made her way through the cemetery and settled on the grass beside a gravestone. Taking a sip of her scalding coffee and flinching from the heat, Erica waited.

'Bit early for that, isn't it?' came a man's voice as she broke off the corner of her brownie.

'Not when you're having the day I'm having,' she told her grandfather as he sat beside her. Popping the brownie piece into her mouth, she brandished it at him. 'Sorry I can't share,' she said around the mouthful.

The spirit of her grandfather studied her.

'Why is it a bad day?'

Erica sighed.

'Last night was Jess's birthday party.'

'It didn't go well?'

'It went very well. You'll be pleased to know that Alfie and I are...well...'

Her grandfather smiled.

'I know. He told me.'

Erica swallowed her mouthful and stared at him.

'He came and told you that we'd gotten together? Isn't that a little...weird?'

Her grandfather shrugged and the blurred vision of his gravestone that Erica could just make out through him rippled.

'Maybe a little. I suppose you could say we've become friends, though. He used to moon over you, Ric. You should have seen him this morning. Such a spring in his step. If he hadn't told me, I would have guessed. I'm happy for you both, truth be told. You know I am. That is...you are happy, aren't you?'

Erica broke off another piece of brownie.

'I was,' she mumbled. 'I think. I don't know.' She sighed again. 'To be honest, I thought you might be a little unbiased about this Alfie and Rick situation. But you're not, are you? You're the same as Gran, you're on the fae's side. The only unbiased one is probably Jess and she just told me to do what I wanted to do, which doesn't really help at all even though she's right.'

Her grandfather leaned back as the words spilled from her. His eyes widened a little at the mention of Rick's name.

'Rick? As in, that fella from the future? The policeman?'

'My future husband the time travelling detective, yes.'

Her grandfather whistled through his teeth.

'You're still debating about talking to him even though you're with Alfie? I do hope you're not giving Alfie hope where there isn't any.'

Erica rolled her eyes without thinking.

'I'm not contacting Rick. Rick from this time, present day Rick. I saw him, we met, and nothing happened. There was no spark, no interest, no nothing. And then, just before I went into Jess's party, I just wished... I wished for future Rick to come back. He's the one I wanted but I knew that wouldn't happen and then Alfie was there. And there is a spark with him and I do want him. And then this morning I got this.' Erica found the message on her phone and held it up for her grandfather to read. Being dead, he no longer needed his glasses, but smartphones weren't much of a thing when he was alive, so reading from a small screen was a strange concept to him. He narrowed his eyes, holding his nose up as he read the message.

'This is from...?'

'Future Rick, Granddad. Rick from the future, the one I had the spark with, the one I had the connection with, the one I wanted. He's back and he needs my help and I don't know what to do.'

'What does he need your help with?'

'I don't know. I haven't replied yet.'

Her grandfather ran a hand down his face.

'Does Alfie know?'

'No.'

'And you came to me?' He smiled. 'That's very sweet of you.'

'Like I said, I thought you'd be unbiased.'

'I just want you to be happy, Ric. Your grandmother and your mum and dad just want you to be happy. None of us are biased.'

Erica looked at her grandfather and raised an eyebrow. He lifted his hands in defeat. 'Okay, maybe we're a little biased. Alfie's a good one and he can keep you safe. And I imagine your mum and dad will say the same about a policeman.'

Erica took a big bite of her brownie out of despair.

'But ultimately, it's about what makes you happy, sweetheart. That's all we want for you, however that looks.'

Erica nodded as she chewed.

'I guess,' her grandfather continued, looking away and into the depths of the cemetery. 'If I had to try and help you decide, Alfie understands the family. You know...the witch side of things. Probably better than me, or your dad or this Rick fella. And he does love you. Fae love hard, I know, but that means that he'll protect you. He'll keep you safe. And you love him, don't you?'

Erica glanced sideways at her grandfather.

'I don't know.' Erica took a swig of her cooling coffee, movement in the trees to the side catching her eye. A figure was walking the path. Erica checked her positioning. A woman sitting beside a gravestone, sipping her coffee, mourning her loss. Whoever it was wouldn't be able to see her grandfather beside her. If they could see him, Erica would be furious. It had taken her years to be able to see and hear him, it was taking her far too long to learn her craft. Part of that was her mother's doing, keeping her shielded from the spirits and fae who were such a part of her grandmother's life, despite her grandmother's best efforts. Mostly, though, it was Erica's doing. All she had wanted as a teenager was a normal life, to grow up, get good qualifications, have a career, maybe meet someone, fall in love, settle down.

Erica hugged her knees. Rick said they'd had that, in the future, in his future. They were married and settled with a child. She still ran the paranormal investigation agency with Jess, but she was in love, she had a family, she was a mother and a wife with a mortgage. And maybe a dog. She smiled, lost in the imagery of it.

The figure on her peripheral vision hadn't moved on. The sight tugged her out of her daydream. Although merely a silhouette against the morning light, she could tell it was a man and he was watching her, a newspaper hung loosely at his side. Erica frowned. Was it the man from the café? Or someone else having a morning stroll around the cemetery?

Her grandfather took a deep breath of air, a habit

of filling his lungs that he'd never lost, even in death.

'I always loved summer mornings here,' he murmured. 'I would get up early and leave Minerva asleep in bed to come here and tend to the grass and flowers.'

Erica turned away from the watching figure so that he wouldn't see her lips move.

'I prefer autumn.'

Her grandfather's brow creased at her low voice, until he peered over her shoulder and spotted the man on the path.

'He's watching you,' he murmured.

'I know.'

'Do you know him?'

'No idea. I can't really see him.' Erica didn't dare turn to look again. 'He's probably just wondering why a woman is sitting next to a gravestone drinking coffee and talking to herself.'

Her grandfather chuckled.

'Let him wonder,' he told her. 'So, will you be contacting this Rick?'

'I have to, don't I,' Erica murmured. 'He needs my help.'

Her grandfather gave another shrug.

'So? He can find help from somewhere else.'

Erica shuffled her position, her hips were beginning to hurt. Stretching her legs out in front of her, she pulled up some grass between her fingers. Her grandfather watched her. 'You have to do what you have to do,' he murmured. 'And if you help this Rick, that doesn't mean you owe him anything, or you have to be anything to him. You know that, don't you?'

Erica blinked and then laughed.

'You know, I think I'd forgotten that.' She looked up at her grandfather. 'Thank you.'

He beamed at her and then nodded in front of them.

'Are you going to tell him?'

Erica followed his gaze and saw Alfie approaching slowly. As her stomach flipped pleasantly, she reminded herself that she was in her thirties. Still, she allowed herself a moment to appreciate the sight of him. His curly brown hair that was in need of a cut, his muddy jeans with his hands shoved deep into the pockets, and crisp white shirt unbuttoned at the top. Just under his eye and across his cheek was the silver scar, the tell-tale sign that Alfie had placed himself between a demon and Erica only a few days ago. She caught his eye and he smiled that easy-going charming smile of his, picking up the pace.

'Hope I'm not interrupting,' he said as he reached them, giving Erica's grandfather a nod.

'Not at all,' said her grandfather, standing and brushing off his hands despite nothing being able to stick to them.

Alfie was studying Erica and despite that smile still plastered to his lips, his eyes had grown hard.

He knew, she realised. She didn't know how, she never knew how, but he knew.

Erica stood up, brushing the grass from her backside and downing the last of her coffee.

'Want a drink?' she asked him.

Alfie studied her a moment longer without responding and then slowly turned his head to the man still on the distant path, newspaper in hand, watching them. The two men stared at one another and then, with the slow movements of someone forced, the watcher walked on, turning his back on them.

Alfie looked back to Erica, his gaze still hard.

'Come on, I'll buy you another.' He held out his hand and she took it, glancing over her shoulder to the man walking away.

'See you later, Granddad,' she murmured.

'Take care, love,' came her grandfather's voice on the soft summer breeze.

Alfie squeezed Erica's hand as he led her back towards the café and she trotted to catch up and walk beside him.

'Are you okay?' she murmured.

'Of course.' He lifted her held hand and pressed it to his lips. When he looked back to her, his blue eyes were soft again and he dropped her hand, wrapping an arm around her waist.

She noted he didn't ask her the same question.

4

Jess

Jess Tidswell reached into the bottom of the last large box and pulled out the final piles of clothing, chucking them on the bed.

'This is really it?' she called out.

Marshall poked his head around the door and inspected the boxes from where he stood, which wasn't difficult considering how he towered over her.

'Yup.' He disappeared again.

'Why don't you have any clothes?' she shouted after him.

'I do!'

'This isn't enough for a grown man.' Jess surveyed the piles on the bed with her hands on her hips. 'And there I was, worried about where we were going to put all your stuff.'

'Nah, I'm easy.' Marshall carried another box into the bedroom as if it weighed nothing, placed it on the floor and then scooped Jess up into his arms. 'I just waltz into your life, slip into your home and you're none the wiser.'

Jess laughed, wrapping her arms around his neck.

'I think I noticed.' She pulled him down for a kiss. 'But yeah, now that you mention it, it's almost like you meticulously planned all of this.'

'I did,' Marshall told her with a grin. 'I saw you moving in, fell madly in love with you, noticed your fence was broken and your kid liked worms and the rest was easy.'

Jess hesitated. It was so easy for all that to be true.

'Did you see me moving in?'

Marshall gave her his lopsided smile and kissed the end of her nose.

'Nope. First time I saw you was that day Ruby accused me of murdering worms through the fence. You had your arms full of shopping and your hair was a mess and you were the most beautiful woman I'd ever seen. I had no idea that Ruby would accuse me of such crimes, though.'

Jess beamed up at him.

'I told Erica I thought I was in a porn film.'

This time Marshall hesitated.

'You what?'

'Single mother moves into a new house and starts fantasising about the handyman next door? Come on. It practically writes itself.'

'And it's porn is it?'

Jess ran her fingers down Marshall's broad chest.

'Isn't it?'

Marshall caught her hands and kissed her hard.

'Mummy?'

It was a sound that would once have made Marshall and Jess jump away from one another, but not anymore. Not now that Marshall had moved in, even if he wasn't completely unpacked yet. He was part of the family, he was Jess's missing piece and Jess would no longer feel guilty about kissing him so hard in front of her daughter.

'Yuck!'

'Okay,' Jess murmured, pushing Marshall away and revealing Ruby in the doorway holding a book. 'What can I help you with, oh beautiful child of mine?'

Ruby grinned, wiggling a front tooth with her tongue. 'Don't do that,' Jess warned. 'You're too young. That tooth isn't allowed out until you're five.'

Ruby laughed and threw herself between her mother and Marshall.

'And when are you five?' Marshall asked, leaning down and lifting Ruby into his arms, swinging her up.

'Soon,' she said breathlessly, laughing as Marshall placed her standing on the bed. She bounced a little until with one gesture Jess stopped her.

'These are clean clothes.' Jess warned her. 'No bouncing on the bed.'

'How soon is soon?' Marshall asked.

Ruby lifted up a finger.

'One week!' she yelled.

Something hit Jess's knee and she looked down to find Bubbles, their five-month-old Bernese mountain dog, at her feet, tail wagging and banging against Jess's legs.

'Oh, good, now we're all in here.'

Bubbles cocked her head up at Ruby and then growled. They all stared down at her in shock. The puppy barked. One fierce, guttural bark straight at Ruby.

'Bubbles!' Jess scolded.

Bubbles whined and sat down. After a moment of them continuing to stare at her, the dog nudged Jess's hand with her nose.

'Okay, you're forgiven,' said Jess, stroking the dog's ear. 'What was that about, huh?'

'So, how long is one week?' Marshall asked, turning back to Ruby.

'Seven days!' Ruby erupted into fits of giggles as Marshall lifted her up again, spun her around and placed her next to Bubbles.

'So, that tooth can come out in seven days?' Marshall looked at Jess who shrugged.

'Let's see it if lasts that long,' she said, ruffling Ruby's hair and then Bubbles' ears.

'Mummy? Can we read this?' Ruby held up the book. Its spine was barely clinging on to yellowing pages and the cover bore a title Jess had never heard of. It had been given to Ruby as a present by one of Jess's aunts. It was sweet that her aunt had thought to give Ruby a present for Jess's birthday party, even if it was an old, musty, falling apart present. Jess had wondered if it was worth something but Ruby had insisted that the book belonged on the bookshelf in her bedroom and Jess could hardly argue with her.

'Not right now, love. Let's read it tonight, yeah? Before bed. Right now, I'd like you to do something for me, okay?'

Ruby looked up at her with the eagerness of a soldier awaiting her first orders. 'Go put that book back on the shelf, carefully, and then go around the house and count all of the moving boxes that still have stuff in them. Let me know how many are left. Okay? Ready? Go!'

Ruby ran back out onto the landing, was in and out of her room in seconds and then trotted down the stairs, Bubbles hot on her heels.

Jess wrapped her arms around Marshall and held him tight.

'One week until this house is filled with five-year-olds.' She buried her face into his t-shirt. Marshall laughed, stroking her back.

'And then she'll go to her dad's for the weekend after,' he reminded her. 'Just think, one week of craziness, one week of normal and then we'll have quiet for a whole weekend just the two of us.'

'A whole weekend to sleep.' Jess had already closed her eyes, breathing Marshall in.

'We can't sleep the whole weekend,' he rumbled in her ear, sending a shot of thrill through her. She looked up at him.

'You've never had a house full of sugared-up small children, have you?'

Marshall laughed but Jess caught the hint of fear in his eyes. She smiled, the warmth in her chest spreading. It was so long since she'd felt this happy, even considering when she and Marshall had first met. That had been mixed with the thoughts of him deciding against her, leaving her, using her, although she knew deep down he never would.

Now, he was hers. His property was being mixed with hers. He was about to put up with a child's birthday party, not just because he wanted to share Jess's bed but because he loved Ruby too.

Jess caught her grinning reflection in the bedroom mirror.

'What the hell? You didn't tell me I looked like crap.' She moved closer to her reflection and ran a finger over the heavy bags beneath her eyes.

'You look beautiful. You always do.'

Jess shot Marshall a look.

'Thank you, but these bags are not beautiful.'

Marshall sighed.

'Well, you haven't been sleeping. That'll change

soon and those bags will go. Probably after Ruby's party,' he mused, rubbing a hand over the stubble on his chin. He watched as she started to organise the piles of clothing on the bed. 'Did you have more bad dreams last night?'

Jess didn't stop. She continued refolding Marshall's t-shirts and jumpers, placing them in the drawers she'd prepared and working out how many hangers she needed.

'Yeah.'

Marshall moved to help her.

'It's only been a few days,' he said quietly. She looked up at him, meeting his eyes.

'It's okay. I mean, it's not. I'm not getting any sleep and I've got a nearly five-year-old to look after and a business to run, but you're here now and, like you said, it's only been a few days since...' Jess took a deep breath, willing the visions of the red-eyed demon away. 'The dreams will stop. And if they don't, I'll...I don't know, I'll get help. Counselling, or whatever.'

They stared at each other for a moment, neither wanting to say the specific words out loud.

'Do you... Maybe...' Marshall started.

'I'm not giving up the business, Marshall,' Jess told him. 'This was a demon, it wasn't a spirit. I've told Erica I'm not getting involved in anything other than spirits from now on. She's agreed. It's fine. We're fine. It's only been a few days.'

A few days since Jess had faced the demon in the

woods, a few days since she'd helped the fae, Erica and her grandmother banish the demon back to where it had come from, a few days since their new friend Emily had told her to protect her family from such things.

It wasn't long enough for the nightmares to stop, Jess knew that. But she'd been tired before the demon had taken a hold of her local woodland, now she was exhausted.

One night's good sleep, that would probably make all the difference.

It would be wonderful if that night could be tonight but Jess knew the reality was that she'd probably have to wait a whole week after Ruby's birthday. A whole weekend alone with Marshall and Jess was likely to spend it asleep.

She sighed as she hung up a pair of Marshall's jeans, pausing to smile at the fabric. It had been a long time since she'd handled a man's laundry. She rubbed her fingers over the denim. This was the first time she'd handled the clothing of a man she loved, or at least a man she loved this much.

'You all right?'

Jess blinked and looked up at Marshall.

'I love you.'

He grinned and pulled her over, kissing her and wrapping his arms around her tight.

'Love you too,' he murmured, giving her a quick grope as if expecting Ruby's voice to cut through the moment.

'Mummy?'

Marshall chuckled as Jess ducked out of his grip and threw a jumper back to him.

'Finish unpacking,' she called over her shoulder, pausing to blow him a kiss. 'What's up, sweetheart?' she asked Ruby as she walked downstairs and entered the living room where Ruby was sitting on the sofa.

'There are three boxes, Mummy.'

'Really? Three?' Jess rubbed at her head. That was more than she'd thought. 'Okay. Thank you, love.'

'Mummy? Can we take Bubbles for a walk?'

'Of course. We'll all go, but not for a bit.'

'Can we go in the woods?'

A chill ran over Jess.

'Erm. Not yet, no.'

'But we haven't been in the woods in ages. Years,' Ruby whined.

It had been a week, but Jess wasn't in the mood for that argument.

'I know, baby. Maybe soon.'

'Bubbles misses the woods,' Ruby told her.

'Yeah? Did she tell you that?'

Ruby nodded and Jess studied her daughter.

'How about some cartoons while me and Marshall finish unpacking, then we'll all go for a walk. Yeah?'

'Okay.'

Jess put the TV on and found the right channel,

leaving her daughter transfixed on the screen as Bubbles climbed on the sofa and snuggled up.

Instead of going back upstairs to Marshall, Jess found herself in the kitchen, staring down at her laptop on her dining table. This wasn't the time to do any work, but something had brought her in there. Out of habit, she flicked on the kettle and listened to the water boil. Staring past the kettle, her gaze landed on a box still sitting in torn wrapping paper from her birthday party. Quietly, Jess reached for the box and opened it.

There was the silver knife Emily had given her, along with the note. Jess wondered where she was now, what the werewolf hunter would be facing next. Alongside the knife were the charms Minerva had given her. Jess lifted them up in turn, examining them in the daylight.

Would these help with her nightmares?

She would have to ask Minerva. Erica's grandmother had also mentioned doing a cleanse of the house once Marshall had moved in. Would that help too?

Jess ran her fingers over the silver blade. What good would this do her? She had to keep it where she could get it if needed but out of Ruby's reach. She'd be arrested if caught with it, surely. This wasn't the movies, she couldn't keep it in her boot, or her sock, or her bra. Wasn't that the fashion now? To keep your phone and money in your bra? Is that where young werewolf and demon hunters were keeping their weapons? Jess shook her head. That wasn't going to happen.

She placed everything back inside the box, closed it and pushed it behind the kettle. The box settled into place beside a smaller box which Jess pulled out. Lifting the lid, she ran her fingertips over the tarot cards inside.

A quick glance at the hallway told her no one was coming looking for her. She carried the tarot cards to the table and sat down, gently shuffling the cards and closing her eyes.

What will help me sleep? she asked. What will help me sleep?

She folded the cards, stacking them and restacking them before one last shuffle.

What will help me sleep?

With a deep breath, Jess revealed the top card of the deck.

Her stomach dropped.

It had been a day since Minerva had gifted her the cards, there hadn't been enough time to learn them but the artwork of the tall tower ablaze didn't inspire positive reassurance. Jess reached for the booklet that had come with the cards and found the illustration.

The Tower.
The Tower is a solid structure but is built on a rocky foundation and a strike of lightning is all it takes to bring it down.

Jess stared at the card, wondering if it would be rude to burn the entire pack.

'What the fuck?' she muttered, shoving the card back into the pack and slamming the box lid back on. The box was thrown onto the worktop as she jogged up the stairs to fetch Marshall.

What did that card mean? That her new family would come crashing down? That her tower was about to fall?

She walked into her bedroom and threw herself into Marshall's arms.

'What's up?' he hugged her back, kissing the top of her head.

'Ruby wants to go for a walk. Come on,' Jess said after a moment, taking Marshall's hand and leading him downstairs.

Neither of them noticed the door to Ruby's bedroom opening slightly as they passed.

5

Ruby

The walk with Bubbles had been uneventful. There had been no woods or trees or even squirrels to chase after. Bubbles hadn't been allowed off lead and there was no ball to throw. It had been what Ruby liked to call a pointless walk.

She hoped this wasn't a sign of things to come. Nothing much had changed since Marshall had moved his boxes into the house, other than her mum and Marshall being too busy to do anything fun. Her mum had told her it would be over soon. Soon, it would be the end of school, the start of the summer holidays and Ruby's birthday.

It couldn't come fast enough, as far as she was concerned.

Since September, which was years ago, she'd watched her new friends turn five one by one and grow up while Ruby was left behind. Yes, she put her hand up in class more than the others and yes, she mostly got glowing praise for her work, but it was time for her to grow up. She wanted to be five now.

One more week. Seven days.

Ruby followed Bubbles from the kitchen and up the stairs into her mum's bedroom where Marshall had gone back to folding clothes.

Boring.

She watched him, smiling as he flashed her a grin.

'All right, kiddo?'

She nodded, eyeing the bed.

'You glad I'm moving in?'

Again, Ruby nodded. She was glad. It would be nice to have Marshall there when her mum was working or was busy or had to dash off for some reason. Ruby wouldn't feel in the way if Marshall was there to keep her company, without her mum having to call Marshall or take her to Erica's house.

Not that she didn't like Erica's house. She loved it there. It always smelled delicious and there were two other dogs to play with. But being with Marshall was better.

'There's a boy in my class who has two dads,' Ruby said.

'Oh, yeah?' Marshall glanced at her as he placed the last of his clothes away.

'Yeah. I told him that I've got two dads now and a mum. So, I win.'

Marshall laughed, sending happy thrills through

Ruby. He opened his arms to her and without thinking she walked into them for a hug. Had his eyes been wet? He wouldn't let her pull away to look.

'That's lovely,' he said, giving her another squeeze before letting her go. 'You have a lot of people who love you, Rubes. I'm very proud to be one of them.'

Ruby grinned up at him. His eyes were definitely wet.

'Me too. And you living here means we can have more adventures, doesn't it.'

It wasn't a question. It was a statement, a fact. Marshall had no choice in the matter.

'Of course. What would you like to do?'

'I want to go back to the woods.'

Ruby frowned as that was met with silence. Marshall's smile had gone. Had she upset him? 'Why can't we go back to the woods?' she asked quietly.

Marshall lifted her up to sit on the edge of the bed and then sat beside her, his weight making her fall into him.

'We'll be able to go back there soon. It's just... some scary things happened around there recently and we need to make sure it's safe to go back.'

'What scary things?'

'Nothing for you to worry about. It's all over now.'

'So, it's safe to go back?'

'Yeah, but your mum needs to make sure. That's all.'

Ruby nodded.

'These things always take time.'

Marshall gave her a strange look with his usual, warm lopsided smile but Ruby just shrugged, hopped off the bed and walked into the hallway and her bedroom.

She stopped in the centre of the room, her stomach twisting and tears filling her eyes. She wanted to scream Marshall's name but something stopped her. Her breath came quick and then, suddenly and with no explanation, the feeling lifted and everything was as it should be.

6
Erica

'It's weird, being back, isn't it?' Jess rang the bell to the hotel, looking around.

'Yeah. Like nothing ever happened. It's weird that it all happened so fast.' Erica kept her eyes on the door, watching the figure behind the glass getting bigger.

Mrs Wilder, her blonde hair scraped back and her face a little pink, welcomed them with a smile and allowed them in.

'Sorry for the state of me,' she told them. 'We're moving a couple of rooms around in preparation for a coach party. They're arriving tomorrow and they're interested in the idea of ghosts. I don't suppose we could move our meeting up? It'd be great to have something to offer coach parties immediately.'

Erica blinked and looked to Jess for help.

'Of course. We can have the meeting today, if you

like? I think we're available?'

'We can sit down when me and Jess are done,' Erica agreed, her mind catching up. 'I'll let Jess go and we can go over the marketing side of things.' Jess shot Erica a look. 'It's mostly all on my laptop, nearly finished anyway.'

'You don't want me there?' Jess murmured as Mrs Wilder became distracted by a member of staff.

'I cover the marketing, remember? You deal with client management.'

'And you deal with the spirits,' Jess reminded her. 'You're one up.'

'You can stay if you want. I thought you might want to get back to Marshall and Ruby.'

'He's at work and she's at school.' Jess shrugged, then narrowed her eyes at her friend. 'And you're avoiding something, aren't you? It's Rick isn't it? You're avoiding Rick. Have you not messaged him back?'

Erica pursed her lips, thankful that Mrs Wilder chose that moment to bring her attention back to them.

'Sorry about that. That would be wonderful. I can spare an hour or so, if that's long enough. Here's the key, you can go up. Come and find me when you're done. Oh, would you like a drink? Tea? Coffee?'

'No, I'm all right, thanks,' said Jess, taking the key and starting up the stairs.

Erica paused. Jess was in a hurry and it wasn't so

she could talk to a spirit. Erica was going to have to face this at some point. She gave Mrs Wilder a smile.

'No, thanks. I'll have a coffee when we're chatting through the marketing, though.'

'Of course. Can't wait to hear how you get on,' the hotel manager called over her shoulder as she rushed to get back to work.

Erica took a deep breath and followed Jess up the stairs.

She found her friend at the door to the haunted hotel room, waiting for Erica. Without a word, Jess let them in and they entered slowly.

Erica waited a moment but felt nothing. That didn't mean anything, though.

'Anything?'

Erica shook her head.

'Maybe she's done. What if she's gone?'

'Then she's gone,' said Erica gently. 'I told you, there's more than one spirit here. And there's always going to be a chance that Mrs Wilder will be disappointed.'

'She could always lie, I suppose. It's not like she'd be the first to lie about a haunting for profit.'

'No, in fact she'd be following a long line of successful con artists.' Erica caught Jess's eye. 'It'll be fine.'

The hotel room hadn't changed since they'd last been in there only a few days ago. Erica placed her bag on the made bed and did a slow circuit of the room, searching for cold spots or areas where the air changed. She found nothing.

Jess wandered to the middle, having thrown her bag on the bed, and fumbled with the Dictaphone. Erica took out an electric thermometer and placed it on the dressing table before giving Jess a nod. Jess hit record.

'Hello. I don't know if you're still here, but if you are, it would be lovely to talk to you again.' Erica paused, gathering herself. 'We wanted to thank you for helping us and warning us. You probably already know that the demon is now gone. The woods are safe again. We wouldn't have figured it out as quickly without your help.' That wasn't necessarily true but Erica was grateful to the spirit anyway. 'If you're still here and you'd like to, we'd like to get to know you. If you have the energy. Can you talk to us? If you can, what's your name?'

Jess left a long gap before she hit stop and rewound the tape to play it back. They listened to the recording of Erica's voice and then the static that followed. With a sigh, Jess hit record again.

'It's okay if you don't have the energy,' Erica told the room. 'Maybe you can contact us in another way. Make the air cold. Drop the temperature in this room. Can you do that?'

They waited and after a while, Jess stopped the tape and listened back to it. Again, there was nothing. Erica checked the thermometer. The temperature remained steady and Erica deflated.

'Come on,' she murmured. 'Give us something.' She nodded to Jess to try again.

'Mrs Wilder, the hotel manager, is happy you're here,' Erica told the room. 'She wants to know who you are. We want to know who you are. What's your name?'

With a pre-emptive sigh, Jess rewound the tape and played it back.

'What's your name?' came Erica's recorded voice.

'*Lizzie*,' came a woman's voice through the static.

Jess and Erica stared at each other with wide eyes and Erica jumped as Jess whooped. Erica gestured to her to keep recording.

'Thank you, Lizzie,' said Erica, unable to keep the grin from her face. 'I think you mentioned this last time. Did you live here?' She left a gap, gesturing to Jess to keep recording. 'Did you die here?'

Jess rewound the tape and played it back.

'Did you live here?' came Erica's voice.

After a long pause came, '*Yeess.*'

'Did you die here?' came Erica's voice.

The static that followed was long as they strained to make out a voice. Lizzie the spirit hadn't replied. Was it too painful to talk about, or had she run out of energy?

'Thank you, Lizzie,' Erica said into the room. Rummaging in her bag, she pulled out the motion sensor light they'd used before. She placed it on the bed between her and Jess. 'Remember this, Lizzie? It senses when you're close. You can turn the light on and off, remember? Turn the light on for yes, leave it off for no. Do you understand?'

Jess laughed as the light flickered on.

'Hang on,' she murmured, rushing to close the curtains and create a little darkness in the room. 'Okay. Go on.' Jess sat on the other side of the bed to Erica and they both watched the light.

'Did you grow up here?' Erica asked.

The light flickered on and then off.

'Brilliant. Before it was a hotel?'

The light flickered on then off. Erica looked up to find Jess grinning, spellbound by the light. 'I know this must be a difficult topic, Lizzie, but did you die here?'

The light came on and stayed on for a moment.

'I'm sorry. Was it natural causes?'

The light stayed off. Jess shot Erica a look.

'Lizzie, did someone kill you?'

The light stayed off and both Erica and Jess exhaled in a rush.

'Was it an accident?'

The light came on.

Erica couldn't ask what had happened using this system, it would take too long to discover the whole story. An accident resulting in a death must have made the local press.

'Research,' Erica told Jess. 'That's what you do.'

Jess nodded and gave her a thumbs up, not

wanting to interrupt the spirit.

'Do you want to stay a part of this hotel, Lizzie? I can come here and keep talking to you. Others may want to meet you.'

The light came on and flickered before going off.

'I think that's a maybe,' said Jess.

'That's okay. It's early days. Thank you, Lizzie. Do you like talking to us in this way?'

The light came on and went off.

'Good. That's good. We'll do this first thing next time. Thank you, Lizzie. We'll be back again soon. Will you be here?'

The light came on and stayed on for a moment before going off. Jess sat up straight and pointed to behind Erica where the closed curtains fluttered just long enough for Erica to spot them.

'Thank you, Lizzie,' Erica murmured, smiling as she shut off the motion detector. 'Well, there you go. Let's find out more about you.' She looked up at Jess as she placed the motion detector box back into her bag.

'I'll go home and do some research, see what I can find. You're going to go see Mrs Wilder?' asked Jess.

'Yup. If she wants to do ghost tours, what do I say? Do we offer that? Is that me or you or both?'

Jess ran her fingers through her hair thoughtfully.

'I suppose it depends. We could hire an actor. Or, if we'll be talking to Lizzie, then it should be us, shouldn't it? How often would it be though?'

Erica nodded.

'I'll find out what she wants and we can give her some options. Hey, Jess, regular client.'

They high-fived each other which would have made Erica cringe a few months ago but now she was too happy to care.

'So, why haven't you called Rick back?' Jess asked as Erica slung her bag onto her shoulder. Erica hesitated.

'Because.'

'Because of Alfie?'

'Yeah.'

'Fair enough.'

'Is it? Rick said he needed help. I could just help him.'

'That's true. Helping him out doesn't mean you're agreeing to marry him. Unless that's what he needs help with.'

'Yeah.' Erica struggled with her thoughts.

'But you don't know if you can resist him?' said Jess with a smirk. Erica gave her a look and then walked into a patch of cold air.

'Oh, now you're all ganging up on me,' Erica murmured with a smile. 'I know I can stay with Alfie if I help out Rick and yes, I have self-control, thank you very much. But how do I explain it to Alfie?'

'Honestly, Ric? If he doesn't trust you, then what's the point?'

Erica sighed.

'It's not about trust, though, is it?' she murmured, mostly to herself. 'Alfie's always said I'm not really meant to be with him. He knows it, he's so sure. And I don't want to hurt him.'

Jess glared at her.

'You're seriously going to let a man tell you what you want?'

Erica bristled.

'Well. No.'

'And do you want to help Rick? Or at least talk to him?'

Erica stared off into space for a moment while the voices in her head argued.

'Yes? Maybe? Does it have to be now though? What sort of timing is this?' She knew exactly what timing this was. She had asked Rick to come back to her and he had. She'd gotten what she asked for. She could hardly complain. But why couldn't he have arrived the second she'd asked for him or months later?

Erica puffed out her cheeks.

'Maybe I need to talk to Alfie.'

'Maybe.'

They said goodbye to Lizzie and locked the room door behind them.

'What about you?' Erica asked as they walked down the stairs. 'How's Marshall settling in?'

'It's like he's always been there. Except the boxes, which are still everywhere and if it wasn't for him making a fort out of them with Ruby, I'd be close to screaming.'

Erica laughed.

'He really is good with her, isn't he.'

'He is.' Jess gave a contented sigh that made Erica smile. 'He's good with everything.'

'I don't need to know. I already know too much.' Jess grinned, looking at Erica over her shoulder. 'I bet Alfie's good at everything too, though.'

Erica's cheeks burned. She tried to ignore them.

'Of course he is. All fae are. Apparently.'

'So your gran says. And how does she know?'

'Don't! I don't want to think about it.'

They reached the bottom of the stairs and Jess turned into the reception area, walking straight into Mrs Wilder.

'Oh, sorry!' said Jess as Mrs Wilder also apologised. Erica stayed on the bottom step, her cheeks still pink. Jess hoped Mrs Wilder hadn't heard their conversation.

'Are you done already? How did it go?'

Jess and Erica exchanged a smile.

'Very well, actually,' Jess told her.

'Your spirit is called Lizzie and she died in this hotel due to an accident. I don't suppose that rings any bells?' Erica asked.

Mrs Wilder's expression moved quickly from joy to sadness to joy again.

'Oh, the poor girl. No, I haven't heard anything like that. But this place has a long history. I know it was a home before the houses were knocked through to create a hotel.'

'Yes, she grew up here, before it became a hotel. Maybe she was part of the last family to use this as a house. Jess is going to go do some research, see what she can find, while we have that marketing meeting.'

'Wonderful. Yes, that would be great. You couldn't ask the ghost more?' Mrs Wilder looked at Jess who turned to Erica.

'No,' Erica told the manager. 'She doesn't have a lot of energy and I don't want to push her too much at this stage. The easiest way for her to communicate is with yes and no answers, and we need a little more information to get to the point of asking those types of questions. It's easier for everyone this way. But we'd like to come back with what we've found and talk to her again, if that's okay? You could come sit in with us, see for yourself.'

'Oh, yes, of course. Fascinating!' Mrs Wilder placed her hands together in a clap that changed its mind. 'I'll let you finish up. Come to my office when you're ready. I already have some ideas.' Mrs Wilder shook Jess's hand and left.

They watched her go, both grinning uncontrollably.

'I knew this business was a good idea,' Jess murmured. Erica raised an eyebrow at her. 'Oh, that reminds me,' Jess continued, her grin falling as the memory of that morning came back to her. 'Your gran mentioned doing a cleanse of our house when Marshall was in. Can you ask her about that? It'd be nice to talk to her too. I think I'm doing the tarot thing wrong.'

Erica frowned.

'Sure, I'll ask her. What do you mean, doing the tarot wrong?'

'I pulled a card this morning and it was… actually, it was horrible. Like now that Marshall has moved in, everything's going to fall apart.'

'It doesn't mean that. The cards are very open to interpretation and often it's hard to know what they're talking about until it's actually happened. Everything's going to be fine.'

Jess nodded and then, after a pause, looked up at Erica, her eyes wet. She swallowed hard.

'The nightmares haven't stopped yet, Ric,' she whispered.

Erica's gaze hardened and somehow Jess felt safe with her in that moment, as if Erica could banish the demon from Jess's mind.

'They will.' Erica placed a hand on Jess's arm and squeezed. 'You need time to process what happened. We all do. But everything's okay. You've got your man and your girl and they're not going anywhere. Go home, do the research but maybe take a moment to just enjoy what we've got right now. Your family and your home and a business that's starting to take off. Go home and take a moment.'

Jess threw her arms around Erica in a tight hug.

'Thank you,' she murmured, before turning to leave.

Sitting in her car, Jess stopped and took a deep

breath. Erica was right. Everything was okay, everything was going to be okay.

She started the ignition.

It would be better once Minerva had been round to cleanse the house. Then maybe she would finally relax enough for the nightmares to stop.

Pulling out of the hotel car park, her mind went back to Erica. She had to admit, she was hoping Erica would contact Rick sooner rather than later. It wasn't that Jess had any feelings about which man her friend should choose, which was a surprise even to Jess. The events in the woods had softened her to Alfie, and actually, if this world was as scary as Emily had made it out to be, maybe it would be better for someone like Erica to be with someone like Alfie. Jess wanted nothing more to do with the horrors of this world but it seemed to be Erica's life, whether she wanted it or not, and Jess knew that Alfie would be more than capable of keeping her safe. Hell, he'd put himself between the demon and Erica and had the scar to prove it.

Sure, future Rick could keep Erica somewhat safe but he couldn't do what Alfie could do. She would have to teach Rick about her world whereas Alfie was teaching Erica.

Wait.

Jess hesitated.

Was that a good thing or a bad thing? Rick could take Erica away from it all, which would keep her safe. But then they wouldn't have a business.

Jess shook her head and stopped at a red light, running a hand over her face. No wonder Erica was having trouble with this, just a few seconds of it was giving Jess a headache.

She put the radio on and turned the volume up to drown out the sound of her thoughts as she drove the rest of the way home.

The driveway was empty as she pulled in. Marshall must have gone to a job and Ruby was at a friend's house for another few hours. Jess unlocked her front door and walked into the house to silence.

She stopped.

'Bubbles?'

A whimpering came from the kitchen. Her stomach dropping, bowels loosening, Jess ran into the kitchen, leaving the front door open in her wake. The puppy was sitting on her bed, her ears flat, her eyes big. At the sight of Jess, Bubbles' tail gave a weak wag and the puppy ran to her, pressing up against her as Jess crouched to greet her.

'What's wrong, baby?' Jess wrapped her arms around the dog as Bubbles snuggled up to her. She was shaking, trembling under Jess's touch. Jess held her tight, feeling her over, watching for signs of pain or illness but there were none. 'What's happened?' she asked the dog. Bubbles licked the air between them in a kiss.

As Jess straightened, looking around the room, Bubbles leaned against her, her tail between her legs. Jess backtracked and closed the front door, still searching for clues as to what was wrong. Had someone broken in? Was something missing? Had Bubbles eaten something she shouldn't have?

Nothing seemed out of place although the puppy was following her closely, crying softly.

Jess pulled out her phone.

'Hey,' Marshall answered.

'Hey.' Her voice was loud in the quiet house despite Bubbles' whining. 'I've just gotten home and Bubbles isn't right. She's crying. I can't see anything wrong but it's scary, Marsh. I think I might need to take her to the vets.'

'Shit. Do you want me to come?'

'No, no. I'm sure it's fine. Maybe she's eaten something and has tummy ache. I'll let you know.'

'Okay. If you're sure. Stay in touch. Hope she's okay.'

'Yeah. Me too.' Jess glanced down at the dog by her feet. Bubbles looked back up at her, pleading with her although Jess had no idea what she wanted. She hung up the phone and called the vets who told her to bring in Bubbles immediately.

Grabbing the puppy's lead and her bag, Jess made for the door again.

'Come on, sweetheart.'

To her surprise, Bubbles shot out of the door. Jess watched her, frowning. 'Do you just need the toilet?' she asked. Bubbles looked over her shoulder to Jess and gave another whine. Jess led her to some grass but Bubbles only tried to drag her further from the house.

After a moment, Jess looked back to her house. A wave washed over her. The same feeling she'd experienced in the woods upon seeing the demon standing behind Erica. Fear and adrenaline and something utterly primal.

It was her imagination. It had to be. A leftover from the woods, her brain still recovering from the demon.

Jess put Bubbles in the car. The dog jumped in gladly showing no sign of pain. After a moment's thought, Jess went back into the house and, without allowing anything to convince her otherwise, found the protection charms Minerva had given her, still in the knife box on the kitchen top. She placed the large charm beside the front door as she walked out, locking it behind her, before stopping to fasten the other charm on the chain around her neck. Wondering if that was enough, she climbed into the car and started the ignition. Bubbles watched her before lying down with a sigh. Jess's stomach remained in a heavy knot as she drove to the vets, her fingers tapping against the steering wheel.

8
Rick

It made sense now. Pieces were falling into place. Could it be that simple? When time travel had first been given to the police, they'd been told that often the simplest explanation was the correct one. In fact, that was the general rule when it came to police work.

Erica hadn't gone looking for Rick, like she'd said she would. She'd gone after Alfie instead.

Of course, Rick knew who Alfie was. The man was the enemy, the dangerous shadow on the edge of his relationship with Erica when they'd first met. But in his timeline, in his world, Erica and Alfie had never happened. That had never been a thing.

Had it?

Had his Erica lied to him?

It didn't matter. Not anymore. What mattered was what happened next.

Rick approached the front door and knocked,

pushing his hands into his pockets and then taking them out, clutching them behind his back before dropping them and shaking them.

How did people hold their hands when they weren't police knocking on someone's door?

He didn't have long enough to figure it out. First came the sound of two dogs barking, which made Rick smile, then the door opened.

He was taken aback, but only for a moment.

'Mrs Murray?' he asked quietly.

Esther Murray, Erica's mother and his mother-in-law back in his own time, looked Rick up and down in a quick glance.

'Yes?'

'Hi. I'm Rick Cavanagh.'

He'd hoped that Erica had mentioned him to her mother, so that he wouldn't have to explain himself or prove himself. He almost sighed in relief as Esther's eyes widened a little in recognition of the name. Then they narrowed.

'Can I help you?' she said, a little uncertainly. From behind a closed door inside the house, one of the dogs was still barking.

'I hope so. I'm from the future and—'

'Erica isn't here,' Esther interrupted. She hesitated, evidently wondering whether to close the door in his face or not.

'No, I know,' Rick said quickly, before she had a chance to decide. 'I was wondering if I could talk to you. Or your mother.'

Esther cocked her head to the side.

'You know Minerva?'

'I did.'

Esther faltered.

'I can't just let you in. Not without Erica here. I don't want to...interfere.'

Rick's insides fluttered.

Please, he thought. Please.

'Did she tell you I messaged her?'

'No.'

'Well, I did. But she hasn't responded.'

Esther sighed and softened a little.

'Then I really can't let you in.'

'I need help, Esther. I understand if Ricci doesn't want to help me. I understand if she's changed her mind.' That was partially true. He did understand, sort of, but it didn't stop the pain and the anger. 'But if she won't or can't help me, then maybe you can? Or maybe Minerva?'

Esther chewed on her bottom lip as she considered this.

'I suppose it depends on what you need help with. I'm already a little in my daughter's bad books. Things are a bit tricky right now. I can't just go letting you back into her life without her permission. Have you tried calling her? See if she picks up? She's been busy lately. There was Jess's birthday party and then today they've been working at a client's.'

'Jess's birthday party,' Rick repeated under his

breath. That made sense. He'd messaged Erica on Jess's birthday so she might not have seen it immediately. But then what about when she'd been at the cemetery? Sitting by the gravestones, drinking coffee and presumably talking to her grandfather's spirit. What about when Alfie had come to her. She hadn't been able to take a moment between any of that to check her phone?

'Yes. Call her. Or come back tomorrow, once I've had a chat with her. I'm sorry. I really am.' Esther went to close the door on him and then stopped. The sound of tyres on gravel made Rick turn and they watched as Erica's sky blue Mini Cooper drove up to the house.

Erica

Erica sat behind her steering wheel and stared at Detective Sergeant Rick Cavanagh, from the future, standing on her front doorstep. He was just as she remembered. His hair a dark brown, he towered over her mother at six foot and wore the same long brown coat as when they'd first met. His blue eyes watched her. Her breath caught in her throat, her chest aching, her legs refusing to move.

Not now, not yet, whispered a voice in the back of her head. She wasn't ready. She hadn't decided how to play this.

What if Alfie found out?

Alfie already knows, said another voice.

Her mother opened the door wide, giving her an apologetic look. She had to get out. She could hardly put the car in reverse and drive away.

Could she?

She could go to Jess's. Or back to Alfie. No, both

would ask her questions, both would want answers. Maybe it was time that Erica got some answers.

Turning the ignition off, she climbed out of the car, slamming the door behind her and locking it without taking her eyes from Rick.

It was fascinating, just how different he was to the Rick of her own time. The present day Rick Cavanagh, who she'd briefly met only a few days ago, had almost looked past her. This Rick's gaze was intense. That look of love was still there, but it was mixed with something else. Fear, she realised, her stomach twisting, and anger.

His hair was dishevelled and his skin pale. A ball of nausea dropped into Erica's gut. What exactly did he need help with?

'Hi,' she managed to murmur as she approached.

'Hi.' Rick gave her a weak smile and then seemed to struggle. Had he been about to hug her? Whatever he'd wanted to do, he stopped himself.

Esther looked between them, trying to catch Erica's eye.

'It's okay, Mum,' Erica told her, giving her the best smile she could at that moment. Esther nodded and backed away, but left the door open.

'Do you want to come in?' Erica asked. Chances were, this wouldn't be a quick conversation. Rick nodded.

It turned out Esther had only moved behind the door and she quickly returned and allowed Rick in, bustling him through to the kitchen and seating him at the large dining table. Erica followed at a distance, placing her laptop bag down, before frowning at the closed living room door where the barking was coming from.

If Rick would one day be her husband, then he had to be okay with dogs. She opened the door.

The two Labradors spilled out, the puppy, Bramley, leaping at Erica, ricocheting off and bounding into the kitchen. The older one, Daisy, trotted out happily, tail wagging, and followed the puppy only after Erica had ruffled her ears.

'Hello!' came Rick's voice as Bramley jumped on him. Erica walked into the kitchen to find Rick between to the two Labradors. She stopped when she noticed the tears in his eyes. 'It's so good to see you too,' he told them, wrestling with the gangly black puppy while looking over to Daisy, keeping her distance. He noticed Erica watching him.

'I didn't know her for long,' he murmured, pushing Bramley away to reach out to the golden Labrador. 'I never really got to know her.' She sniffed at him, tail still furiously wagging, before turning away and taking to her bed. Bramley took that as permission to leap onto Rick again.

Erica smiled as Rick laughed.

There it was. That spark, that love, that connection that had been missing when she'd met present day Rick. How was it that she had it with this Rick and not her own?

Esther placed a cup of coffee on the table near

Rick and then wandered over to her daughter.

'Coffee?' she asked, almost breezily.

'I'm okay,' Erica murmured, still watching Rick with the young dog. Esther followed her gaze.

'Are you sure?'

Erica nodded.

'Not really. I don't know what I'm doing, Mum.' Erica locked eyes with her mother. 'What do I do?' she whispered.

'Find out what he wants,' Esther whispered back. 'Don't agree to anything yet. Whatever it is, tell him you'll think about it. Buy some time.'

Erica gave a nod, looking back to Rick.

'What about Alfie?' she murmured as quietly as possible.

'One thing at a time,' her mother told her, squeezing her hand. 'I'll give you two some space,' she told the room, moving to grab Bramley by his collar and drag him out. He started barking in frustration immediately.

'It's okay. We'll go outside. It's a nice evening. Come on.' Erica beckoned for Rick to follow her. They left through the back door and after a few moments the barking stopped.

Picking her way down the path, Erica led Rick through her parents' garden. Past the herbs that her mother tended and the shrubs and flowers her father grew, to the bench at the back, nestled beneath the tall trees.

Erica sat and found Rick gazing up at the

treetops, cradling his coffee cup.

'This is your grandmother's bench,' he murmured.

Erica watched him as he slowly sat beside her.

'It's actually my dad's bench, but I guess Gran has sort of taken it over.'

'The conversations I've had here,' he said, fondly stroking the wooden arm beside him before resting his cup on it. 'With you and your grandmother. Sure would be great to see her again.'

Erica stiffened. She didn't want to talk about a future that didn't include Minerva.

'Why are you here?' she asked.

Rick met her eyes and she softened, feeling the burning of tears forming. She blinked them away. How ridiculous it would be to cry at this moment, and for what? Because she had missed a man she hardly knew.

He gave her a sad smile.

'Because I'm lost.'

Eric frowned. What did that mean?

'Lost? In time?'

Rick laughed.

'No. In life. I should never have come here before. I shouldn't have chased Rachel, I should have avoided you at all costs. I ruined everything. It's all my own fault. Every bit of it. Rachel, you, my career.'

Erica blinked.

'You're going to need to slow down. Start again.'

Rick studied her eyes and then sighed.

'When I went back to my own time, you were gone.'

'I left you?' Erica's hand went to her heart.

'No. We just never got together. You were never my wife, we never had our son. We were never together.'

Erica bit the inside of her cheek.

'Oh.'

'And I couldn't understand it. I couldn't understand why. I just knew this was my fault. I'd been so stupid. Then I got fired. I lost everything. And I can't...' Rick looked down at his hands in his lap, gathering himself.

'Why did you get fired? Because of me? Because we met?'

'No.'

Erica waited until Rick looked up at her. He searched her eyes.

'Did you look for me?' he asked gently, afraid to hear the answer.

'I did.'

'But you're with Alfie,' Rick said. He clenched his eyes shut. 'You found me but you chose Alfie.'

'No, I...' Erica sat back, wondering how to word this. Rick wiped at his eyes. 'Let me explain. I found you. An hour after you left, I found present day you. It wasn't hard, but it wasn't you.'

Rick's shoulders sagged.

'I told you it wouldn't be me. I told you I

wouldn't be the same.'

'But I thought there'd be something there,' Erica blurted. Rick looked up at her. 'Some sort of connection. Some sort of spark. Like there was the moment I first met you. But there wasn't. There was nothing. You hardly looked at me. I was right in front of you and you didn't even see me.'

'That doesn't mean anything.'

'It did to me.'

'And it didn't occur to you that I did see you? That I went home that night thinking about you?'

'No! How could you? You didn't know who I was!'

'You were the beautiful woman outside the woods, in danger of getting arrested. The woman who stopped that creature. The woman who saved those kids.'

Erica froze, staring at Rick with wide eyes.

'You remember that?'

Rick nodded.

'Is that how we met?' Erica asked, swallowing on the bile rising in her throat.

'No.'

'Should I have gone after you? Is that why the future changed?'

Rick struggled.

'I don't know.'

Erica couldn't stop herself then. The tears came, slowly, one dripping down her cheek as her stomach churned.

'I wished for you to come,' she said quietly, not daring to look at him. 'Before Jess's party, I sat in my car and begged for you to come back to me. I didn't want the Rick who barely glanced at me. I wanted you. I wanted you the moment I first saw you. But I didn't want him.' She looked up and met his eyes. 'What does that mean?'

Rick smiled, leaning in to wipe her cheek with his thumb.

'It means I'm an idiot,' he murmured. 'I've always been an idiot. But you made me better.'

There was a pause as they both considered this.

'I'm sorry,' Erica breathed. 'I'm sorry I wasn't there when you went back. That we never met.' She wiped her cheeks on her sleeve. 'I'm sorry I messed everything up.'

'It wasn't you,' Rick whispered, his fingers in her hair now, stroking the tendrils that fell around her shoulder. 'It was me. This is all my fault. And I just want to fix it.'

'And you think coming back here and talking to me will fix it?'

Rick sighed.

'I didn't know where else to go.'

Erica sniffed and took a deep breath to hold back more tears.

'What can I do to help?'

'Well, for that I need to tell you the full truth.'

Erica's stomach twisted violently. There was more? She didn't think she could take more.

'Go on.'

'I went against procedure, coming back here to get Rachel. We're not allowed to go back in time and mess with our own timelines. I knew you'd be there. Hell, I'd already met Steve and Joe. One day, you hold a big birthday party for the business and of course they're invited. Steve was technically your first client. I'd heard the story. I knew the risks. And I shouldn't have been the officer going back to get Rachel.'

'Then why did you?'

Rick took a deep breath and closed his eyes.

'Because it was my fault that she went back in time. Because I made a mistake.' He opened his eyes and looked at her. 'Because I'm an idiot.'

'What did you do?' Erica asked quietly, unsure whether she wanted to know the answer. Images of Rick and Rachel kissing flitted through her mind.

'She threatened you and our boy one day. We were in the interrogation room, just the two of us. It was meant to be something quick. Admin stuff. She was angry, but I was used to that. Except I'd been having a bad day. Cases piling up, lack of sleep, loads of stress. We'd argued the night before. And then Rachel threatened the two of you and I knew she'd go through with it, given the chance. So, I lashed out. Not at her,' Rick added quickly. 'I just... I let the stress get to me. I guess I dropped my guard. She'd somehow managed to slip her cuffs. Before I knew what was happening, a chair had been thrown at me and I was on the floor, my time travel device was gone and so was Rachel.'

'Sounds like she'd planned that perfectly,' Erica told him. 'That wasn't your fault.'

Rick rubbed his face and Erica listened to the soft sound of his skin brushing over his stubble.

'I shouldn't have let my guard down. I shouldn't have been in there alone with her. You see, I had to go get her. I had to fix it. But all I did was ruin everything. I couldn't keep away from you. I never could. And by the time I realised I had to go to my boss, it'd been too long. And then when I went back to my time and you weren't my wife...and my boss fired me. Just like that, my whole life fell apart.' Rick held his hand over his mouth and brushed his thumb over his eyes, the muscles in his jaw and neck straining against the onslaught of tears he was holding back.

'How do you fix it?' Erica asked, leaning towards him. 'What can I do?'

'I don't really know,' Rick laughed. 'But there has to be a way.' He searched her eyes, leaning closer. 'I'm sorry I came here, but I didn't know where else to go. I have to keep you close to me, Ricci, otherwise I'm going to forget everything we ever had together.'

10

Jess let Bubbles out of the car and opened the front door. The dog, who had pulled her into the vets and demanded cuddles from the receptionist, became meek once more and let out a whine. Jess frowned and sat down on the open boot of her car, pulling out her phone and calling Marshall.

'Everything okay?'

'Not really,' said Jess. 'Vet gave her the all clear and I can see why. She stopped crying the moment she was in the car. She dragged me into the vets, licked everyone and she was so happy her tail nearly fell off.'

'So, she's okay? Nothing's wrong then.'

'Except that now we're home, she's cowering by my legs and crying again.'

That was the moment Bubbles attempted to get back in the car, but Jess was in the way. She fumbled the phone as Bubbles' bulk knocked it from her grip.

'You still there? What was that?'

'That was Bubbles trying to get back in the car. I'm worried, Marsh. Something's definitely not right.'

'Maybe she's hiding something. Like, the excitement of being around new people was enough to make her forget how ill she's feeling. Don't worry though, maybe it's just a bug. Or she's eaten something and it'll come out the other end. She probably just needs rest.'

'The vet did say to bring her back if she's still bad at home. She said they can do some tests.'

'There you go, then. I'll be home in a bit. Want me to go pick up Ruby so you can stay with Bubbles?'

'Yes, please. If that's okay.'

'Of course.'

They hung up and it was only then that Jess realised Marshall had called this place home. It had been a day since he'd officially moved in and it was already like he'd always been there. She smiled, pushing her fingers through Bubbles' fur, looking down into her large brown eyes.

'What am I going to do with you?' she murmured to the puppy. 'What's wrong, hmm? Are you what the tarot card was telling me? You're not leaving us, Bubs. I've finally got my family together and under one roof, and that's how we're staying. Okay?'

Bubbles snuffled Jess's leg, pressing up against

her.

'Good. Let's get you in. You were so good at the vets, you should have a treat. But what if you have eaten something?' Jess sighed. If only dogs could talk.

She closed the boot and locked the car, leading Bubbles into the house. The puppy stayed close but didn't whimper or cry this time. She followed Jess into the kitchen where Jess put the kettle on and dug around in the cupboard where they kept the dog food. She pulled out a small dental chew and asked Bubbles to sit. The dog, eyes fixed on the chew and seemingly everything else forgotten, sat and gladly took the treat from Jess, munching on it in the middle of the room.

Jess watched her, hugging herself tightly.

If Marshall was bringing Ruby home then that gave Jess more time. She needed to research the spirit named Lizzie, but then there was also some washing to sort and the downstairs needed vacuuming. The bin needed emptying and Marshall's empty boxes were piled up by the patio doors that led from the kitchen into the garden. Just past the patio doors was the shiny new fire burner that Marshall had bought her for her birth-day. It needed preparing, she thought, although she wasn't sure how. She'd have to ask Marshall. They could light it one evening and sit around it. She'd buy some marshmallows and they could toast them like they did in the movies.

'Do you need a walk?' she asked the dog. Bubbles swallowed the last of the chew, which admittedly hadn't been chewed much, and looked up at her, tail thumping.

But where would Jess walk her? She missed going to the woods. The walk was easy and had been relaxing. A way to take her mind off stressful things like one of her babies being sick, or pulling scary tarot cards, and a way of thinking it all through. Now, the idea of going back to walking between those trees left her nauseous.

Alfie may have told her the woods were safe now, but every instinct in Jess told her to stay away. Would the graffiti marks still be on the tree trunks? Did that girl's spirit still haunt the place?

Jess was okay working with spirits but that was one that she didn't fancy seeing again.

With a sigh, Jess made herself a cup of tea and settled at the small dining table. Bubbles watched, her tail drooping.

'We'll go in a bit,' Jess told the dog, placing her tea down to cool. After a moment's consideration, she fetched the box of tarot cards and pulled out the pack.

What if she drew another card that scared her?

But then, what if she drew something that gave her comfort?

Minerva had told her on her birthday that she was a witch and that tarot might be her strength. Something in Jess wanted that to be true so badly.

If she was a witch, then she fitted into Erica's family and not just because she was Erica's friend. If she was a witch, then she could offer more than business sense and negotiation to their paranormal investigation agency. If she was a witch, then she was something more than a mother and business owner. Erica was bad at tarot, as was Minerva. Only Esther had shown any sign of a gift for it but she preferred her herbs.

This could be something that was just Jess's.

She began shuffling the beautiful, thick cards. Closing her eyes, she asked them, 'What do I do now?'

The cards couldn't answer yes or no, so she couldn't ask if everything would be okay, which was the question burning away at her. At least this question would give her some direction.

What do I do now? She thought, over and over.

'What do I do now?' she whispered, before placing the pack down and revealing the top card.

Well, the swords weren't encouraging. Or were they?

Jess flipped through the book that had come with the cards and found this particular one. The Nine of Swords.

Worry. Fear. Nightmares.

Jess swallowed and placed the card down, unable to take her eyes from it.

Well, there you go. The cards knew. Maybe she did have a knack for them after all.

The book went on to suggest that heavy thoughts were weighing her down. Jess laughed at that. She needed to let the thoughts go, to break the negative cycle. Every time a negative thought presents itself, the book told her, replace it with a positive one.

Jess sat back and sighed.

That was exactly what she needed to do.

'Right,' she told Bubbles. 'Every time I think about the woods, I'll remember our walks there. Every time the demon pops into my head, I'll replace it with...erm...oh, the blinding light that sent it back to its own world. How about that?'

Bubbles looked up at her eagerly.

'Yes, yes, we'll go for a walk. But that's a good idea, right?'

Bubbles grumbled and then burst into a fit of barking. A moment later, there came a knock at the door.

'Good hearing you have there,' Jess told the dog, following her to the front door. Holding her back by the collar, Jess opened the door and froze.

Alfie smiled down at her and then met eyes with Bubbles. The dog silenced and sat down. Jess watched, wondering whether to be horrified or not.

'Erm, Erica isn't here?'

'I know,' said Alfie. 'I wanted to talk to you.'

'Oh, okay. I just promised Bubbles we'd go for a walk. You, erm, wanna come?' Walking with Alfie felt better than letting him in the house, until Jess remembered that he'd been in her house at her birthday party. That had been different, though. The house had been full and he'd been with Erica. In fact, he'd been unable to pull himself away from Erica.

'Sure.' Alfie started to turn away and then stopped, peering past Jess into her house. 'Is everything okay?' he asked.

'Yeah. Why?' Jess looked over her shoulder but only saw her hallway and glimpses into the kitchen and living room as usual. She studied Alfie's expression. Something like curiosity sparked his eyes, there one moment and gone the next.

'Nothing. Probably. Shall we?' Alfie beckoned her out of her own house. Jess clipped on Bubbles's lead, grabbed her keys and stepped outside, checking her phone was in her pocket and sparing a moment's thought for her abandoned cup of tea.

'Are we walking in the woods today?' Alfie asked without any sort of tone that suggested he'd been present during the banishing of the demon.

Jess glanced up at him.

'No. That scar looks good. Does Erica like it?'

Alfie smiled his usual charming smile and Jess looked away. There was something about the fae. Something intangible but irresistible. Even though it wasn't directed at her, Jess hated the effect Alfie's charm had on her.

'She does. It's not as bad as I expected. Eolande did a wonderful job of healing me, even though she couldn't get rid of it all. I'm sorry that your friend couldn't get the same treatment. Perhaps if she hadn't rushed off...'

'Yeah, well, Emily had somewhere to be.' And someone to run from, Jess added silently.

'So, why aren't we walking in the woods?' Alfie asked, making Jess's attempt at changing the conversation pointless. She sighed, pulling Bubbles back as the puppy tried to pick up the pace.

'Because I don't want to.'

Alfie watched her until Jess could no longer take it. 'Did you want to talk to me about something?'

'I did, but first I want you to tell me why you won't go into the woods. There's nothing there, you know. We banished the demon. It's gone. We checked. We removed the symbols, all of the markings left are meaningless. Mostly penises, truth be told. So, you know, not completely meaningless.' Alfie grinned to himself.

Jess rolled her eyes.

'I know. It's just...I still don't want to go back there.'

'Why not?'

Jess looked up into Alfie's eyes.

'Because I keep having nightmares and because it doesn't feel safe and because every time I even think about it I see that demon,' blurted Jess. 'All right? Happy now? Why did you want to talk to me?'

Alfie remained quiet for a moment, shoving his hands deep into his pockets as he strolled beside her. They stopped and started as Bubbles sniffed and then pulled Jess onwards.

'I think we should go back to the woods. Now. Come on.' Alfie turned away and started on the road towards one of the entrances into the woods. To Jess's horror, Bubbles started following, pulling Jess behind her.

'What? No! No, no, no. We shouldn't do that.'

Alfie didn't reply. He kept marching on and despite Jess putting all of her weight into it, she couldn't stop Bubbles from following him. 'What have you done to my dog?' she almost screamed.

Alfie turned back to her.

'Nothing. I can't help it if she loves me.' He blew a kiss to Bubbles and continued on.

They reached the entrance and Alfie finally stopped, facing the tree line. Jess and Bubbles stopped beside him.

There was bird song, the green still lush in the bright summer evening light. What Jess saw, however, were the shadows. What she heard was silence, and then the loud cawing of the crows that lived in a particular tree deep in the woods.

'How do you feel?' Alfie asked.

Jess's mouth was dry, her stomach churning, her legs fizzing as she moved from foot to foot.

'Fine. Can we go now?'

Alfie cocked his head.

'The gateway is closed, Jess. The demon is gone. There isn't anything in there that shouldn't be. Not even a spirit. No fae. Nothing supernatural at all. It's the woods you know and love. They're yours again. You just need to reclaim them.'

Jess watched the branches sway in the breeze and took a deep breath of the almost clean air.

Maybe he was right.

'The man who has Erica's heart has returned,' Alfie said softly, watching the trees. 'He's come for her.'

Jess looked up at him.

'I know.'

'I haven't had long enough with her,' said Alfie. Jess crumpled, her shoulders sagging. Then, she smiled.

'Ric's saying the same thing about you, you know. Awful timing, apparently. She doesn't know what to do. If that's any consolation. I don't know what she'll do. She might still choose you.'

Alfie smiled, but it wasn't his usual playful, charming smile. It was sad, hardly touching his eyes.

'She won't. She's not supposed to. I just thought I might get longer with her.'

'Sorry,' mumbled Jess, looking back to the trees. 'I wish I could help in some way, but this is up to Ric.'

'Has she said anything else to you?' Alfie turned to her.

'No. Like I said, she doesn't know what to do.'

Alfie gave a nod and brushed his hand over his

hair.

'Do you want to go into the woods?'

Jess took a deep breath.

'Maybe not just yet. Hey, when you were at mine, just now, you said it was *probably* nothing. Did you see something? Or...sense...something?' As afraid of the answer as she was, the words just fell out. She had to know.

Alfie's eyes glazed over.

'Perhaps.' He refocused and looked down at Jess. 'Talk to Erica. About your house. And while you're there, ask her again about me, and her heart. Tell her to talk to me.'

'Can't you tell her?'

Alfie avoided Jess's gaze and she resisted the urge to pat his arm in an attempt to offer comfort. He was scared to ask her, she realised. He was scared to talk to Erica. Their next conversation could end what they had. Overcome with the urge to go home to her family, Jess turned Bubbles around.

'I'll tell her. Are we safe in my house?' Jess asked as she started walking home. Alfie and Bubbles followed her.

'For now,' he said.

Ruby

Marshall and Ruby arrived home at the same time that Bubbles and Jess returned from a walk with the strange man that Erica had brought to the birthday party. Ruby knew his name was Alfie, she'd spoken to him but he was still strange. He smelled of the woods and summer meadows and wet grass, whether he was at a birthday party in her home or returning from a walk with the dog. His eyes, despite softening when he looked at her, seemed too intense to meet, and there was something unnervingly soothing about his voice. It made Ruby want to sleep, or follow him some-where.

But Erica really liked him. She'd spent the whole of the birthday party with him, hand in his hand and stroking his arm and kissing him. Ruby pulled a face at the memory as Alfie said goodbye and waved to her. She waved back, but was happy to run ahead of her mother and Marshall, racing Bubbles into the house.

'Go wash up, Rubes, and I'll make you a sandwich,' her mother told her before following Marshall into the kitchen. They probably had to talk about grown up stuff. That was what they did, ever since they'd met, they'd have to be just the two of them 'to talk'.

Ruby ran up the stairs and into her bedroom, throwing her bag on the floor and sitting on her bed. It had been a difficult day, and this was what her mother did on difficult days. She sat on her bed, stared into space, maybe sighed, and changed her clothes. Ruby couldn't be bothered to put her pyjamas on, she still wanted to play with Bubbles in the garden. So, instead she sat on the edge of her bed and stared into space, relaxing her eyes and thinking through her day.

Now that she was home, the day didn't seem so bad. Sure, she had gotten questions wrong and her art hadn't gone the way she'd liked, but it was over now. She was home and safe, and tomorrow was a new day.

Something pinched her hard and sharp on the back of her right calf.

With a squeal, Ruby jumped up and looked down at her leg. There was nothing there. Leaping to the floor, she looked under her bed. There were toys and books, but nothing that could have pinched her. Maybe she'd leaned on the corner of something? Although she was sure she hadn't moved.

Frowning, Ruby looked around the room and as she turned, something cold gripped around her arm. It felt like Marshall's hand but it was tighter, too tight, and so cold that it sent a chill through her whole body, setting her teeth chattering. She turned to face whatever it was but there was nothing there.

Ruby screamed.

The sensation of frozen fingers dissipated as thuds sounded on the stairs.

Bubbles arrived first, four legs being faster than two, bounding through the doorway and heading full speed straight for her. Ruby latched onto the dog as Bubbles skidded to a halt, cuddling up to the puppy's warmth as Bubbles snuffled her, checking her over.

Her mother arrived seconds later, breathing hard at the door, looking around before scooping Ruby up and away from the dog.

'What's wrong? What's going on?'

Marshall arrived next, his eyes hard as he searched for an attacker. One hand trailed over Jess's back as Ruby told them what she'd felt, and then Marshall went in search of the intruder.

Jess removed Ruby from the room, which she was glad of. She buried her head into her mother, breathing her in, as Jess sat her on the large bed she shared with Marshall, running her warm hand over where the cold fingers had gripped.

It was getting dark when Erica arrived. She'd driven there as fast as she could without breaking any laws. Esther had offered to join her, to help with Ruby, but Erica had assured her that Marshall would be there, that it would be fine, and that Rick had to leave.

Rick, looking downtrodden, had understood there was no arguing and had left, with the promise that Erica would call him.

She needed some space, and hearing that Ruby had been attacked by something that couldn't be seen wasn't exactly the right space, but it would do. She'd considered calling her grandmother, but decided to wait. Not just yet. This might all be nothing to worry about.

A shiver ran through Erica's whole body as Marshall opened the door.

'Shit,' she murmured and Marshall frowned at her.

'What?'

'There's something here,' she told him. Her hands trembling, Erica pushed past him. 'Jess?' she called into the house. 'Where's Jess?'

'She's in the kitchen, with Ruby. What's here? What do you mean? A ghost?' Marshall, his face paler than Erica had ever seen, shut the front door and guided her into the kitchen. Jess sat with Ruby at the table, paper and colouring pencils sitting untouched in front of them. Jess, her eyes red-rimmed, looked up at Erica.

'There's something in my house, Ric.' Her voice trembled. Those were the words she'd uttered when Erica had picked up the phone. There's something in the house and it's attacked Ruby.

Erica nodded.

'I can feel it.'

Jess's eyes widened.

'What do we do?' she whispered.

'Where did the attack happen?' Erica asked, fighting to keep her voice strong. Both Jess and Marshall were teetering on the edge, that much was obvious. Marshall had gone into full protective mode, standing over the girls in his life, his chest thrust out, while Jess wrapped her arms around Ruby, pulling her close, biting her lips to hold back the tears.

'In her bedroom,' Marshall told her when Jess

couldn't. Erica nodded, looking Ruby over as best she could as the child cuddled up to her mother.

'What did it do?'

'It pinched her leg and grabbed her arm.'

'Can I see?'

Jess nodded, prising Ruby from her.

'Where did it touch you, Rubes?' Erica asked, crouching down so she was lower than Ruby, and softening her voice.

Ruby pointed to the back of her calf and then her upper arm.

'Can I have a look?'

Ruby nodded, holding out her arm for Erica to inspect.

Erica ran her fingers over Ruby's soft skin. There was a faint bruise coming up, light blue against the soft cream, patched with red.

'Does it hurt still?'

Ruby shrugged and then turned so Erica could see her leg. It was obvious where she had been pinched. The skin was red, turning purple.

Erica swallowed bile and tried to push the anger that was building back down. She had to keep a level head. Ruby had no use for three emotional adults right now.

Erica straightened and looked to Marshall.

'Let's see what's in her room,' she told him. 'You see anything, hear anything, feel anything, you shout. Okay?' she said to Jess and Ruby. Ruby buried her head in her mother's shoulder but Jess nodded, grabbing hold of Bubbles' collar to keep the dog with them.

Erica followed Marshall upstairs.

'How did this happen?' Marshall asked her quietly. 'Did something follow her home? What if it's that demon thing?'

'It's not the demon,' Erica assured him. 'It feels different. It's a spirit but it's a strong one.'

'So, it could have followed her home?' Marshall looked back to Erica. 'From that hotel or something?'

Erica sucked on her lower lip. It was a possibility but not one she felt comfortable with.

'There is a small chance, I suppose. But it's very unlikely,' she said.

Marshall opened the door to Ruby's bedroom and Erica walked inside. She stood in the centre for a moment. It was hard to tell the difference between this room and the rest of the house at first, but gradually the feeling of being watched made the tiny hairs on the back of Erica's neck stand on end. Goosebumps rose along her arms and she gave a small shiver.

'Is this because of me?' came Marshall's voice from behind her. She turned and they both watched as Marshall's exhale came out in a mist.

Erica rubbed her bare arms against the falling temperature.

'Why would it be because of you?'

Marshall shrugged.

'Maybe it doesn't like me being here. Now that I've moved in.'

'I'd say that's a coincidence,' Erica murmured. 'The majority of spirits aren't malevolent. Just because it hurt Ruby doesn't mean that it wanted to hurt her. I think sometimes spirits can put so much energy into trying to make contact that they overdo it.' She met Marshall's eyes, hoping that this was one of those cases.

'Alfie was walking with Jess when I came home,' Marshall told her in a low voice. 'Apparently he sensed something but he told Jess she was safe for now.'

Erica's brow creased.

'What was he doing with Jess?'

Marshall shrugged. Apparently, that part hadn't bothered him.

'He helped her go back to the woods. She won't go near there since the demon. She's not been sleeping, Ric.'

'I know. The nightmares. That's good of Alfie, to have helped.'

'Yeah, well, I'm sure he had his reasons too.'

'Hmm.' Erica looked around Ruby's room again. It was a small and sweet square room, with a small bed covered in a soft pink duvet and littered with cuddly toys. Beside it was a white bedside table piled high with colourful books and a small bookcase filled with colourful spines . Opposite was the tiny wardrobe and a chest of drawers, with a chest sat between them, no doubt full of toys. Erica stood on a pink rug which had plasticine pressed into it in more than one spot.

'Does it bother you?' Erica murmured.

'What? About Alfie? No. Why? Does it bother you?'

Erica flashed Marshall a small smile.

'It surprises me, I guess.'

Marshall shrugged and folded his thick arms against his chest.

'I think it would bother me, if I didn't know how much Alfie is into you. He wants you as much as I want Jess. So, there's nothing to be bothered about.'

Erica sighed. Maybe for you, she thought.

She turned around the room again and sighed through her nose.

'Okay,' she murmured. 'Let's get this sorted. Hello?' Erica called out into the room. If the spirit had the strength to touch Ruby, then it should have the strength to make contact with her. Nothing moved, nothing happened.

'Okay, I'm going to make this as easy for you as I can,' Erica told the spirit. She didn't have the motion detector box that they used with Lizzie, but she did have a Dictaphone app on her phone, which she pulled out and set up. 'If you talk, this machine will hear you and let us hear you,' she continued before hitting record and holding the phone up. 'Who are you?' She left a pause. 'What do you want?'

After a moment, she stopped the recording and played it from the beginning with the touch of a finger. Her voice sounded in the room.

'Who are you?'

Static followed.

'What do you want?'

More static.

Erica sighed.

'Come on,' she said. 'You've made yourself known. Make yourself known again. Knock something over. Touch me. Talk to me.' She pressed record and held her phone up again. 'What do you want?'

She played it back but there was still only static.

'What do we do now?' asked Marshall, still watching from the doorway.

Erica closed the app and her phone. As she went to return it to her pocket, the screen flashed back on and the assistant that came with the phone started talking.

Frowning, Erica held her phone out so they could both see it.

The word 'Filthy' was at the top of the screen and the phone assistant had brought up results from a search of the word.

'Filthy? What the fuck?' Marshall peered over Erica's phone and then stood back until she met his eyes. 'What the fuck?' he repeated.

'No idea.' Erica cleared her phone and brought

up an app that Jess had recommended. 'Okay,' she called out to the room. 'This is a word generator. It has loads of words so you can talk to us. Use this machine to find and say the words you want to. What do you mean by "Filthy?"' She held out the phone.

The app remained silent while the screen flicked through words at random.

Just as Erica went to lower her arm, the app spoke.

'Devil.'

Marshall jumped back and Erica froze.

'I'm getting Jess and Rubes and we're leaving,' said Marshall.

'Wait!' Erica shouted and Marshall stopped.

'Are you the Devil?' Erica asked the room.

'You,' said the app.

'Me? I—'

'Witch.'

Erica stared at her phone.

'Witch. Witch. Witch,' the app repeated, until Erica closed it down. She looked around the little girl's room.

'I am a witch,' she growled. 'And if you're going to talk like that, then you're going to leave.'

'Witch. Witch. Witch,' said Erica's phone assistant as the screen lit up in her hand.

'Ruby isn't a witch,' Marshall told the room as he backed away.

'Witch. Filthy. Devil,' said Erica's phone.

'Enough!' she shouted, closing her phone again and storming out of the room, pushing Marshall away and slamming the door behind her.

They stopped in the hallway, both breathing hard, Marshall watching Erica.

'I'm getting them out of here,' he told her.

She nodded.

'Do it. Now. I'm calling Gran.'

Marshall ran down the stairs, Erica close behind.

'We're leaving,' he shouted as he entered the kitchen. Jess stood, holding Ruby in her arms.

'What happened?' she asked them both as Erica placed her phone to her ear.

'Nothing good,' Marshall grumbled, reaching out for Jess. 'Come on.'

'Where will we go?'

'My parents,' Erica said. 'Go to mine. We'll figure it out from there. Gran? I need you at Jess's. Where are you?' She hung up. 'Answerphone. I'll try again once we're out.'

'What happened?' Jess asked Marshall.

'It kept saying "witch",' Marshall murmured, looking to Ruby and putting his arms around them both.

Jess paled and turned to Erica.

'This is because of me,' she said.

'No. It's because of me. Get out, go to my parents, now.' Erica pointed to the door and as she did, the lights went out.

Jess

No one moved. In the shadows, Jess's grip on Ruby tightened. The house filled with the buzzing silence of apprehension and heavy breath.

'Marsh?' Jess murmured as Ruby whimpered, burying her head into her mother's shoulder. Marshall's strong grasp found Jess, his thick arm wrapping around her waist, a hand on Ruby's back. Just like that, he had encompassed them, creating a protective cocoon.

They all jumped as Bubbles started barking.

It wasn't her usual there's-someone-at-the-door bark. The noise came in short, sharp sounds, too high-pitched. The noise squeezed Jess. Bubbles was doing her best to be protective, she was defending her family but the fear in her bark was unmistakeable. Jess felt the puppy's fur and warmth against her leg as Bubbles backed up. She needed to touch them, to know they were there while her back was turned, barking into the house.

'Ric? What do we do?'

Jess wanted to reach out to grab her friend, to pull her into their family huddle, but her arms were full of Ruby.

'I'll go check the fuse box,' Marshall rumbled. His lips found Jess's head, kissing her hair as his grip on her fell away. Jess staggered a moment and then she found Erica, standing close to Bubbles, staring up the stairs.

'What the hell is going on?' Jess hissed.

'I don't know how and I don't know why but there's a spirit here,' Erica told her in a low voice.

In the shadows, they both glanced at Ruby who watched them back with large eyes. 'Go to my parents. Right now,' Erica finished, giving Jess a meaningful look.

'Should we take things?' Jess asked and then stopped. What a stupid thing to ask. There wasn't any way she was going back upstairs, where their clothes and bags were.

'The fuse box has completely tripped. I could get it all back on, but it'll take time,' said Marshall, walking back into the kitchen and taking Ruby out of Jess's arms. He held her comfortably in one arm, picking up Jess's car keys and his own keys with his free hand. 'I'll come back in the morning. Come on.'

Jess grabbed Bubbles by the collar and found her lead, clipping it on. As an afterthought, she pulled out a bag and filled it with Bubbles' food, chucking in a tennis ball, and then grabbed her box of tarot cards and the silver knife Emily had given her. Bubbles, who would normally have been fighting Jess to get into the bag, hardly noticed.

The puppy was slow to move, staring up the stairs and growling.

'Bubs, come on. We're leaving.' Jess tried to drag her. Eventually, Bubbles turned and pulled Jess towards Marshall, following him out of the front door, leaping over the door step and towards the car.

Erica was the last to leave the house, waiting just inside, her eyes fixed on the stairs.

Once Bubbles was safely in the boot of the car and Marshall was putting Ruby in her child seat, Jess ran back to her house.

'Ric? Come on.'

'Witch.'

They both looked down at the phone in Erica's hand.

'Witch. Witch. Witch.'

Erica looked back up the stairs.

'You do not belong here,' she murmured, her voice somehow strong and full of the anger that was roiling in Jess's gut. 'You do not belong here. This is your chance to leave. If you're still here when I come back, you will discover the true meaning of the word "witch".'

Erica stepped out of the house, closed the door and caught the key that Jess threw to her. Locking the door, with the spirit inside, Erica strode down the driveway. Jess trotted to keep up with her, determined not to be left behind. Jess climbed into the front passenger seat, beside Marshall, and watched Erica get into her Mini.

As soon as their doors were closed, Marshall reversed out and drove away from the house.

Part of Jess wanted to look back. This was her home, her refuge for herself and her daughter. It wasn't just a safe place for them, it was proof from Jess to the world and her parents that she could make it as a single mother. That she could provide for her child without the need for Ruby's father. That she could make a success of her life despite her relationships falling apart and finding herself pregnant at the same time as discovering she didn't love the man she was with. That house was Jess's badge of honour, the mortgage she got almost on her own, the roof she bought and gave to her daughter, the setting for her romance with Marshall and the centrepiece of her new family. And now it was tarnished. The shadows that had once been safe now held terror.

There was a spirit in her home, a spirit that sat in her daughter's bedroom and pinched and twisted and spat vitriol.

Jess twisted her fingers together, holding her hands in her lap, as the anger that had landed in her gut grew and morphed, evolving into something primal. It was a rage that warranted a cry of war, a physical urge to stand her ground and fight.

This spirit would not claim her home, this spirit would not win.

Jess would reclaim her badge of honour. That house she had fought so hard to buy would become their safe place once again.

This spirit would not take the memories, would not muddy the love.

Jess gritted her teeth.

Erica was right. This spirit would learn the true meaning of 'witch', but more than that, it would learn what a mother was capable of.

14

Rick

'Good morning!' said the receptionist as Rick walked past her. He mumbled a reply, his mind too busy to really register her smile and chirpy customer service demeanour. He walked through to the breakfast area of the hotel, aware that he should eat something. Taking a seat, he ordered a coffee and, after a moment of listening to his stomach rumble, a bacon roll. Then he took out the phone he'd bought on his first day back in this time and checked it. The time on the screen told him only seven minutes had passed since he'd last checked it and that no, there were no new notifications. He hadn't somehow missed a call from Erica, she hadn't messaged him.

It had been a quiet and long evening and then a long and frustrating night, devoid of sleep, as he'd waited for her. She was busy, he knew. Jess was in trouble and he had to be patient.

He'd spent a good hour or so trying to remember what was going on. What was happening with Jess right now?

He wasn't due to come into Erica's life as a fixture for another few years. Maybe he had come back too far. He shouldn't have asked Erica to find him. Perhaps, if he'd just left well alone, they would find each other the way they originally had.

But no, it was too late for that. It hadn't worked. He'd ruined it. And now he had to fix it.

He thanked the waitress who brought over his breakfast, and then filled his mouth with coffee. When he had first realised that he'd lost everything, going back to find Erica and ask for her help had seemed the right thing to do. Maybe the only thing to do. He may not have known how to fix his life, but he had been certain the answer would come to him. He just needed to see her, to talk to her, or perhaps stepping back in time would have made him see the answer.

Rick hesitated and took a bite from his bacon roll.

He'd seen the answer, the reason that he'd never met Erica in his time, and it was because of Alfie. He knew Alfie had been around when they'd met, he knew Erica's mother had warned her away, he had assumed she'd listen to that warning.

His Erica had.

This Erica hadn't.

At some point, the timeline had shifted and Alfie

had broken through. Could that really have happened because Rick went back in time when he shouldn't have and presented himself to her?

He rubbed his head as he chewed.

Time travel was complicated at the best of times. By coming back yet again, all he was doing was tying further knots to unravel.

The real issue he had was that despite travelling back in time again, despite breaking the law and the rules yet again, he still didn't have a solution to getting his life back.

He went over his memories yet again, replaying them, working hard to keep them vivid. If he didn't, if he stopped, there was a chance that the timeline would catch up with him and he would lose those memories forever.

He would lose Erica forever.

Finishing his coffee and roll, he headed out to the car park and sat in his driver's seat, staring at the wheel. Erica still hadn't called him, or messaged.

What if he truly had lost her.

Rick drove out of the car park, onto the main road and towards the Victorian cemetery that Erica loved so much. She might not go back there, considering she was busy with Jess, but it wasn't Erica he wanted to see at that moment.

Despite the early hour, there were cars parked in the cemetery. Staff, perhaps, and volunteers. A few dog walkers strolled past as Rick parked the car and stepped out. He didn't venture to the café or hang around near the chapel. Head down, he marched towards the back of the cemetery, to the recent plots.

Finding the gravestone, he smiled knowingly at the name.

George Warner
1920 – 2009
Loving husband, father and grandfather
Who loved this cemetery
Who protected the trees
Who sang with the birds

This was where Erica sat, drinking a coffee and eating a brownie, talking to her grandfather. Rick had always respected Erica's need to visit the cemetery, rarely accompanying her, giving her the space she needed to visit her family.

'I wish I could speak to you,' Rick murmured, barely audible. 'Maybe you would have the answers. I can cope with losing my job. I can just about stand being punished for breaking the law. But I can't lose her. I can't. Everything changed the day that I met her,' he told the gravestone. 'She showed me a whole other world. Not the spirits or witches, but a world of family and love and laughter. Your family. The women of your family are truly magical.' Rick sighed. 'What am I going to do if I lose her?'

Rick hugged himself as the air around him chilled but there was no breeze lifting his hair or rustling the leaves of the trees around him. He narrowed his eyes, looking down to his arm as goosebumps rose. 'I wish I could speak to you,' he repeated, his breath coming out in a cloud of mist for just a moment before the summer morning sun warmed it.

15

Erica

No one in Erica's family home slept well that night. Come morning, Erica ventured downstairs to find Marshall asleep at the dining table, his head resting on his crossed arms. Ruby was in the living room, watching cartoons, and Jess lay with her, sleeping sprawled across the sofa.

Erica watched them for a moment until Ruby took notice of her.

'Wanna watch cartoons?' she asked.

Jess woke, blinking up at Erica.

'What time is it?' She stretched.

'It's early. Go back to sleep,' Erica whispered.

'Where's Marshall?'

'Asleep at the table. For some reason.'

Jess nodded, as if it made complete sense, and swung herself into a sitting position.

'Is it breakfast time?' Ruby murmured.

'Yup. Come on.' Erica gestured to Ruby who

sprang up and followed Erica into the kitchen.

Marshall woke as Ruby scraped a chair back to sit next to him. Rubbing at his eyes, he glanced at Erica and then at Jess as she followed them in.

'What's happening? What time is it?'

'Seven,' Jess told him, placing a kiss on his head. 'Why don't you go back to bed? Get some more sleep?'

Marshall shook his head.

'I'll have a shower, though. If that's okay?' He looked at Erica who nodded.

'I'll show you where the towels are,' said Jess, taking his hand and leading him away, out of the kitchen and up the stairs.

Ruby watched them go as Erica turned to the cupboards.

'Cereal?' she asked.

Ruby nodded.

'Please,' she added, after a moment.

Erica poured the cereal and milk into a bowl and placed it in front of Ruby.

'Would you like some juice?'

Ruby nodded again, shoving her spoon into the cereal with a satisfying crunch.

'Is there a monster in my bedroom?' Ruby asked after a pause.

Erica hesitated, wondering how to answer that one. She glanced at the door, hoping Jess would appear or that she'd at least hear her footsteps on the stairs.

'No, sweetie, there isn't,' said Erica, her heart pounding. Lying to Ruby was like a test of strength.

'Something in my room hurt me.'

'I know. But it won't be there when you go back. Next time you're in your bedroom, you'll be completely safe.' Erica took her own bowl of cereal and sat next to Ruby. The girl smiled at her but it was a weak forced smile. Erica spooned crunchy cereal into her mouth and Ruby copied her.

'What's in there? What hurt me?' said Ruby after she'd chewed and swallowed.

'I'm not sure. But what I do know is that we'll figure it out and make it go away. Okay? And we'll be here with you until then, so nothing can hurt you.'

'Mummy'll be here?'

'And Marshall.'

Ruby nodded and gave a genuine smile this time.

'Marshall makes things better,' she murmured.

Erica cocked her head at the child and then grinned.

'Oh yeah? How so?'

'He makes Mummy happy,' said Ruby, putting down her spoon so she could count on her fingers. 'And he makes me happy.' She lifted another small, podgy finger. 'And he makes Bubbles happy.' She seemed content with three fingers and so went back to her cereal.

Erica watched her, her chest aching.

'That's the most important thing,' she whispered,

mostly to herself although Ruby nodded in agreement.

They both jumped as music started blaring from Erica's phone. She checked the name flashing up, heart pounding, expecting it to be Rick.

'Oh,' she exhaled in a rush, answering it as fast as she could. 'Hi.'

'Ric, love, what's going on? I just got your message,' came her grandmother's voice.

'Erm.' Erica looked down at Ruby and again, listened for the sound of Jess's feet on the stairs. 'I can't really talk right now but it's big and I think I need you here. We need you here. Everyone's okay,' she added quickly. 'No one's hurt.'

'I am,' said Ruby.

Erica watched her, wondering if she'd shout and repeat it. Ruby stared back, perhaps wondering the same thing, and then went back to her breakfast.

'Okay. I'll grab a lift off someone. Unless someone can come get me?'

'Oh, right, yeah. You're not with Eolande?'

'No. The home get suspicious if I spend too many nights away, apparently. I think they're cottoning on that I'm not always staying over at your house.'

Erica laughed despite herself.

'You're not as covert as you think.'

'Old age will do that for you. So, shall I find a lift?'

'No, I'll come get you. Hang on. Be there in a bit.'

Erica hung up and then went to call for Jess up

the stairs. She appeared immediately, thankfully. Erica had been worried Jess had followed Marshall into the shower, although now was certainly not the time and the family bathroom was definitely not the place.

'I'm going to get Gran. Ruby's just finishing breakfast. Help yourself. Mum and Dad will be up soon, I imagine.'

Jess nodded, hugging herself.

'I just met your mum on the landing. They're up. Your dad's going to take all the dogs out, which is brave of him. You go. We'll be okay.'

Erica grabbed her keys and left the house.

Minerva Warner, eighty-nine years old with the spirit and mind of a twenty-year-old, lived in a residential home twenty minutes' drive away. With full use of her faculties and still mobile, although lacking in speed, Minerva had put herself in the home after deciding she required more company, that is, she required more living company. Esther had offered her a room in the family house but Minerva liked her privacy and independence. She was enjoying the latter years of her life in ways that her daughter didn't approve of and, in her words, was far too old to give a crap.

Erica had hated the home when she'd first visited her grandmother there. It had seemed sickly and like a waiting room for whatever came next. Then she'd heard her grandmother's loud voice as she'd organised those able into a waltz around the communal living room, and all of her tensions had eased.

Minerva might be nearing ninety and be living in a home, but nothing was going to stop her doing exactly what she had done her entire life. Which was make friends, influence people and generally be a nuisance to those who barred her way, which often included the friendly staff and carers who worked at the home.

Erica had prepared herself for running into the home to find her grandmother but instead Minerva was waiting for her outside with a bag packed. She tapped on the passenger window as Erica pulled up.

'Do I need anything?' she asked.

'I don't know.'

'You said it was big.'

'It's a spirit, Gran.'

'Pfft.' Minerva straightened, wincing at pain in her back.

'No, Gran. It's a nasty one.'

'No such thing.'

'It pinched Ruby and called her or me or us, whatever, "filthy devil witch".'

Minerva stared at her for a moment and then opened the car door and plonked into the passenger seat.

'I can come back for anything I might need. Let's go. Now. Go.'

Erica turned the car around and headed for

home.

'Are we sure it's a spirit?' Minerva asked. 'It's not a demon?'

'Can you imagine what Jess would be like if it was another demon? She'd move away! No, it's definitely a spirit. I could feel it, as soon as I walked into the house, I could feel it. And it wasn't friendly. I don't think I've ever met a spirit like that. Angry, yes, but not so...I don't know, horrible. Mean. I guess maybe this spirit is angry but it's directed at us, or at Ruby. What if it's directed at Ruby? Why would anyone be angry with a little girl?'

'Not a little girl,' Minerva corrected. 'You said the spirit called her or you or Jess a witch.'

'A filthy devil witch.'

'Hmm. First inclination would be it's a spirit with a thing against witches.'

Erica looked at her grandmother out of the corner of her eye.

'Well, yeah. How did it end up in Ruby's bedroom?'

Minerva shrugged.

'Come to that when we come to it. First things first, I'd like to meet this spirit.'

There was a long pause as Erica drove in silence and Minerva stared out of the window. 'I blame myself, of course,' Minerva said quietly.

'What? Why?'

'I should have cleansed the house. The moment she moved in I should have cleansed it, but things just kept getting in the way. Excuses kept being made. But it's not like I never had the opportunity. It's not like I didn't have the time.' Minerva sighed. 'This is my fault. With the right cleansing and protection charms in place, a malevolent spirit couldn't have gained access.'

They arrived back at Erica's family home to find everyone up, dressed and fed. The three dogs were out on a walk with Erica's father and Esther was watching cartoons with Ruby in one room while Marshall held Jess in another as they whispered to one another. Esther, Marshall and Jess sprang up as Minerva strode in, entered the kitchen and sat at the table.

'Esther, tea please, my darling. Jess, my love, how is Ruby?'

Esther gave her mother a kiss on the cheek.

'Morning, Mum.' She walked past to make the tea.

Jess took Minerva's outstretched hand and Minerva squeezed it.

'She's okay. A little scared.'

'And you?' Minerva asked, glancing behind her to Marshall. 'Put mine in a flask, will you love?' she called over her shoulder to Esther.

Esther exchanged a look with Erica and rolled her eyes.

'We're okay,' Jess murmured.

'I'm not,' said Marshall. 'That thing, whatever it

is, hurt Ruby. Jess is scared. I'm scared. I want it out of our house. Now. How the hell did this happen?'

Minerva took his tone in her stride.

'Give me your key, child,' she said to Jess. 'Erica and I will go there as soon as the tea is ready. I'd like to meet this spirit who doesn't seem to like witches and pinches small children. And we'll find out the answers to your questions.'

Jess found her bag and pulled out her keys, taking off the house key. She went to give it to Minerva but she gestured to give it to Erica instead.

'I was just saying to Erica that this is my fault,' Minerva said gently to Jess. 'I should have cleansed your house properly the moment you moved in. Did you put the charms up that I gave you?'

Jess cleared her throat.

'Erm, well, not at first.'

Minerva sighed.

'It's okay. It's not your fault. Those charms were too little too late, I imagine. And they were to ward off demonic entities, not spirits. Plus, we don't know when this spirit entered your home. I doubt it was within the last twenty-four hours.'

'Unless it was attached to a birthday present.'

They all turned and looked at Esther who finished screwing the lid on the flask for Minerva.

'Shit,' murmured Erica.

Jess looked from Esther to Erica, wide-eyed.

'The knife that Emily gave me?' she whispered.

'Do you think it could have been that? We don't know where she got it from.'

'I doubt it,' Minerva told her. 'Emily may have been rough around the edges, but she knew what she was doing. She'd know a knife with a spirit anchored to it if she met one. What else did you get?'

Jess hugged herself and shrugged. From behind her, Marshall wrapped an arm around her, pulling her close.

'The usual. A bottle of wine, some flowers, some socks. Mum sent me some money and a book for Ruby. Ruby also got a book from an aunt who got me a scarf I'll never wear. I think I'd have preferred Ruby's book. Oh, and a pretty bag from a friend. The tarot cards from you. I think that was it.' Jess glanced up to Marshall for confirmation.

'What were the books?' Erica asked.

'Oh, a new one from my mum, in a series Ruby loves. And my aunt sent a really sweet book. Old. I thought it was a first edition to begin with, but of course it's not. She told me to not let Ruby touch it until she's older, in case she gets it sticky or tears the pages. Way I see it, the book should be enjoyed and anyway, Ruby insisted on having it on her shelf with the rest of her books. I reckon she got it from a charity shop. It's definitely secondhand but it's in good nick. There's a sweet inscription inside to a boy called Eddie. She likes old things, my aunt. The scarf is probably from a charity shop too. It's a story about witches and wizards...' Jess trailed off and looked at Erica. 'You don't think...'

Minerva stood up and took the flask of tea from Esther.

'Let's go find out, shall we?'

16

Jess

The house was quiet without Minerva and Erica, or the three dogs for that matter. Just the sound of cartoons coming from the living room and Marshall's occasional sigh. Jess had told him to go to work, to take his mind off things, but he refused. He didn't want to leave them, despite not being able to do anything. The relief when he refused to go to work had been immense. Of course, Jess would cope without him at this stage. She was in the family home of witches with more adults than necessary, but there was something inside her that needed everyone together. If she was being honest with herself, she wasn't happy that Minerva and Erica had left, or that Erica's father was still out with the dogs.

She'd be happy once everyone was back and under one roof again. No, she'd be happy if she could have her own home back.

Jess sat at the dining table staring at her closed laptop. Her mind was spinning, throwing back the same questions and worse case scenarios at her, over and over.

'We can move house,' Marshall had offered last night. 'Sell up and move on. We don't have to stay there.'

That wasn't the point, though. Of course they could sell up and move, but Jess had bought that house mostly by herself. She'd worked hard for that house. She'd cried tears of joy the day she'd picked up the keys and videoed a tour to send to her parents to show them what their part of the investment had bought her.

'I don't want to move,' she'd told Marshall, snuggling into his chest in Erica's parents' spare bed and trying to not wake Ruby asleep on a blow up mattress on the floor. 'I want to go home.'

Now, Jess opened her laptop and tapped in her password. Across the table, Marshall watched.

'I have to do something,' she told him. 'I'm going to go crazy just waiting for them to get back.'

He nodded and scraped his chair back.

'I'll make some coffee. Shall I?'

'Yes. Please. Check if Esther would like one. And maybe Ruby wants some juice or something.'

Marshall left the kitchen a little too eagerly, glad to have something to do.

He was back before Jess had a chance to finish her password.

'Three coffees, one juice coming up,' he murmured, moving to stand over the coffee machine and stare at the buttons. Jess watched him, distracted.

'Want a hand?'

'No, no. You get on with some work. You have your distraction, let me have mine.'

'I think you're mine,' Jess mumbled and then smiled, turning back to him. 'You've been my distraction for a couple of months now.'

Marshall softened, grinning. He moved to stand behind her, wrapping his arms around her and kissing her neck. She held onto him tight.

'Any idea how to find out who once lived in a house that's now a hotel?' she murmured, placing a soft kiss on his arm.

'Not a clue,' he whispered, his lips beside her ear. His proximity sent a shiver through her and for a moment she considered sneaking past Esther and Ruby and dragging Marshall upstairs. To the spare room in a house that wasn't theirs, that they shared with her nearly five-year-old daughter.

That wasn't going to happen.

'Oh god.' Jess tightened her grip on Marshall. 'Ruby's birthday party. What if this isn't over by then? What are we going to do?'

Marshall sighed.

'Have it here?'

Jess allowed herself a second to consider that before they both laughed. Marshall kissed the top of her head and went back to staring at the coffee machine, tentatively pressing a button.

'Seriously, though,' Jess said, typing in her password again and waking up her laptop, which had gone to sleep due to inactivity. Jess knew the feeling. 'What are we going to do?'

'We'll cross that bridge when we come to it,' said Marshall, finding the coffee capsules. 'For all you know, Ric's going to come back and tell us it's all sorted and we can go home.'

'True.' Jess tapped her fingers on the table. She opened a search window, her fingers hovering over the keyboard. 'I don't even know what to search for to figure out how to search for this. Why did I agree to do the research?'

Marshall chuckled and then jumped as the coffee machine began whirring.

'See.' He sniffed. 'It's not that hard.'

'You're a trained engineer. What do you mean it's not that hard?'

Marshall gave Jess a look and once again she considered pulling him up the stairs. No. She looked back to her laptop. She had to stop using sex to avoid doing work.

She sighed and typed in the name of the hotel along with the word 'residents'. Nothing relevant came up. She typed in the hotel's address and 'history'.

That brought better results.

As she flicked through the various pages,

Marshall disappeared to deliver a cup of coffee and a glass of juice to Esther and Ruby. Then he stood behind Jess, watching the screen over her shoulder.

'That's only a bit annoying,' she murmured.

He kissed her head again in response and went back to the coffee machine.

An hour later and Jess had found a mention of an Elizabeth who shared the same address as the hotel, but there wasn't much else. There was nothing about a girl who had died or what had become of the family this Elizabeth belonged to. She'd need to get into some official records but that required more organisation and energy than she was capable of at that point.

With a sigh, Jess closed the laptop and rubbed her eyes. She lifted her coffee cup to drink the last of it but found she'd already finished it.

She was alone in the kitchen, Marshall having gotten bored and gone to see what Ruby was up to. After checking over her shoulder and finding the Murray's old golden Labrador asleep in her bed, Jess rummaged through her handbag and pulled out her box of tarot cards. Placing them on the table, she went to get herself a new cup of coffee. She should have offered the others drinks, but she didn't.

While she waited for the coffee machine to do its thing, she took out the deck and placed them carefully on the table, followed by the booklet that explained each card. A few minutes later, she sat with a cup of coffee and began shuffling the cards.

She wasn't sure at this point what she should ask and even as she picked up the deck, a sense of dread overcame her. What if she picked up a bad card again?

'I never quite got the hang of tarot.'

Jess's head snapped to the door and she relaxed to see just Esther standing in the doorframe, her arms folded and a weak smile on her lips.

'I'm trying to distract myself,' Jess murmured. 'Researching dead people isn't quite doing it for me. Shouldn't they be back by now?'

'They've hardly been gone according to my watch but time moves differently when something like this is happening.' Esther noted Jess's coffee and moved into the kitchen to make her own.

'Sorry...'

'Don't be ridiculous. I understand. I can leave you to it, just give me a moment.'

There was a pause as Jess looked back down at her cards.

'Why couldn't you get the hang of tarot? Minerva told me her and Erica are rubbish at it. I don't understand how you can be.'

Esther smiled.

'Then obviously it's something you can do.'

'Why?'

'Because you find it easy. Haven't you noticed that the things we find easiest in the world are the things that we don't understand how anyone else can find hard? Could be you're a natural.'

Jess ran her fingers over the cards, wondering how much she wanted that to be true.

'I keep picking up bad cards.'

Esther sat at the table with her coffee.

'There's no such thing as bad cards. Each card is neutral, but they each have a message and that message is subjective. That's part of reading them. It's why Mum and Ric are so bad at it. They have trouble reading between the lines, between the messages, and seeing the truth. I struggle with it but sometimes I get it right. The part I don't like about tarot is that when you don't have that instinct, you never really know how right you are until the thing has happened. You only get the answer in hindsight, which seems pretty pointless to me. But I know of some who can read the cards so well that hindsight isn't required. So, don't think of the cards as bad. They're the messenger.'

'Okay, I keep getting bad messages.'

Esther watched Jess and took a sip of her scalding coffee.

'Probably because there was a bad message to deliver.'

Jess blinked.

'Were the cards warning me about the spirit in my house?'

Again, Esther smiled.

'You were warning you, Jess. The cards may feel real and some may say that angels or spirits guide us in choosing them, but I believe it's the energy around the cards that chooses them. You ask them a question and you put all of your focus and feeling into that question, it creates an energy which finds the appropriate card.'

Jess frowned.

'Sounds like something Minerva and Erica would be good at. Sounds like something you'd be amazing at,' she admitted.

'And yet we're not. Maybe tarot is your calling. Or rather, tarot is calling to you.' Esther glanced down at the cards. 'Try it. Do a reading.'

Jess shook her head.

'I can't...'

'Okay. Do a reading for me, then.'

Jess met Esther's eyes.

'Really?'

The woman nodded and reached out her hand to Jess.

'Just pull one card. Let's make it simple. I'll ask a question. What should we have for dinner?'

Jess stared blankly at Esther for a moment until Esther gestured to her. Jess began to shuffle the cards. She closed her eyes and repeated silently to herself, *Esther would like to know, what should we have for dinner? Esther wants to know, what should we have for dinner?*

Her hands stopped of their own accord and she pulled a card, turning it around and placing it on the table.

'The Three of Cups,' said Esther.

Jess reached for her booklet and found the page. 'So?' Esther asked. 'What's my reading?'

Jess read the whole page and then gave it some consideration.

'Friendship and collaboration,' she told Esther. 'And celebration.' She glanced up. 'That sounds good. Your friends and family are here to support you. Okay, so you'll have a full house for dinner.'

'The whole family is here.' Esther grinned.

'And collaboration. So, perhaps a sharing meal.'

'Fajitas?' Esther offered.

'Yes, please!' Ruby ran into the room, waking up Daisy asleep in her bed. Bubbles followed, bounding after Ruby, and Bramley sniffed at Marshall's heels as he walked into the kitchen.

Esther laughed.

'It's for the whole family, a full house, so we have to wait for Erica and Mum,' Esther told Ruby as the girl threw herself into Esther's waiting arms. 'But we can start the preparation now.' She glanced at her husband who had followed Marshall in.

'Oh. I know that look. I'm going to the shops, aren't I?' he asked.

'Yes please, John.' Esther blew him a kiss.

'We can go,' Jess offered, collecting up her cards before Ruby could take an interest. 'The three of us will go, give you some peace.'

'I'll go with Marshall,' said John. 'Give you girls a chance to chat.'

Marshall, looking a little too grateful for the chance of an escape, agreed and gave Jess a smile before going to find his shoes.

21
Ruby

Ruby wasn't happy about Marshall leaving the house. Erica and her grandmother had already left and weren't back yet. Ruby didn't know why, but she felt a strong need for everyone to stay together. Her mummy was being too quiet and Marshall seemed distant. Ruby had no memory of her parents splitting up, but something seemed heavy in her tummy.

It was her fault. She'd heard them talking that night, whispering to one another when they thought she was asleep. They'd been whispering about selling the house.

Her house. Her home.

All because of whatever was in her bedroom.

That had been ages ago. Ruby was sure the thing would have left by now, if she hadn't dreamt it. She enjoyed being with Erica's family, but there's nothing quite like home. Sitting on the sofa, cradled in Marshall's arm, or sitting at the kitchen table drawing while Mummy and Marshall cooked and laughed together.

'Can we go home soon?' she asked and then watched as Jess and Esther exchanged a look.

Things were going unspoken and Ruby didn't like that. Why did adults always have to hide things?

'Not yet, sweetheart. But hopefully soon.' Jess lifted her up to sit on her lap and squeezed her tight. The heavy feeling in Ruby's tummy lifted. She wrapped her arms around Jess's neck. 'Marshall isn't leaving us, is he?'

'What? Of course not. What makes you think that?'

'He isn't happy.'

Jess sighed and kissed Ruby's head.

'He's just worried.'

'Because of what's in my bedroom?'

'Yeah. We all are. And that's why Auntie Erica and Minerva have gone to check it out. They're going to get rid of whatever's there. Make it all nice and safe again. Then we can go home.'

'I'm sorry I messed up,' Ruby murmured, burying her head into her mother's neck. Jess stroked her hair.

'Oh, baby. You haven't done anything wrong. Nothing at all.'

'This could have happened to anyone,' Esther told her.

But it happened to me, Ruby thought.

'I've got an idea,' Esther said gently, touching Ruby's arm. 'How about we make some fairy cakes for pudding?'

Ruby lifted her head and wiped her nose on her hand, nodding.

'Okay.' She grinned and looked up at her mother. 'We're going to make some fae cakes.'

Jess's eyes widened and she looked up at Esther who giggled.

'Did you just call them fae cakes instead of fairy cakes?' Jess asked.

Ruby nodded. Jess kissed her daughter.

'Don't let the fae hear you call them that,' she whispered.

'Oh, I don't know. I think Alfie would get a kick out of that,' Esther said, and for some reason that Ruby couldn't understand, Jess stared at Esther open mouthed.

18

Erica

Erica unlocked the front door to Jess's house and stopped. Minerva took a sharp inhale but both women remained on the doorstep.

'Really hits you, doesn't it,' Erica murmured. Minerva nodded.

'It's strong, whoever it is.'

Erica entered the house first, Minerva staying close behind. Erica considered leaving the door open but on second thoughts, closed it behind them. They stayed in the hallway and listened to the sounds of the apparently empty house.

'Do you want to go straight to Ruby's room?' Erica whispered.

Minerva nodded.

'Might as well.'

Erica wasn't sure why they were keeping their voices so low. Perhaps so that the spirit wouldn't hear them, and there was definitely a spirit. It had apparently consumed the whole house since the family had left, a dark presence filling each room. The hair on Erica's arms and the back of her neck stood on end, and the primitive voice in her head was screaming that she was being watched. By whom, she asked, and from where? But the voice didn't know. *Everywhere*, it said. *It's everywhere.*

Erica led the way, up the stairs and to the left, pushing open Ruby's bedroom door.

Nothing happened.

Tentatively, they entered.

'Oof,' said Minerva. 'It's definitely in here.'

The pressure in the room had increased, leaving a weight on them both.

'Hello?' Erica called softly, her voice cracking. She cleared her throat. 'Hello?'

They both turned around at the sound of someone moving. 'Was that you?' Erica asked her grandmother.

'I don't think so,' said Minerva. 'Hello? Can you talk to us?' she called out, her voice stronger than Erica's.

The curtains shifted.

'It's definitely strong,' Erica murmured. 'The spirit we've been talking to at the hotel can hardly move anything. Why is it so strong?'

Minerva shrugged.

'Who knows. An age thing or a rage thing, perhaps.'

'A rage thing?'

'I have noticed that the more emotional spirits tend to be stronger. The happier ones are weaker. You said yourself your spirit at the hotel is happy where she is. She only came out of hiding because she was warning us of the demon. This one, on the other hand, I get the feeling is quite angry. Given what happened last time you were here, I would hazard a guess that it's angry at being brought into the house of a witch.'

Erica watched her grandmother.

'Jess isn't a witch.'

Minerva gave her a look.

'Is that what you think?'

'You giving her tarot cards doesn't make her a witch.'

'No, but her being able to read them easily and with such clarity does. Her being able to sense that demon does. I wonder what else she can do that we haven't noticed yet.'

Erica stared at Minerva. She opened her mouth and then closed it as those comments were processed.

'Did I do that, make her a witch? Did you do that?'

Minerva cocked her head at her granddaughter.

'You don't make a witch, Ric. You're born a witch.' She shrugged, looking around the room. 'Maybe it's why you and Jess were attracted to each other. Something inside you both drew you in.'

Erica frowned, looking down at the pieces of

plasticine stuck and meshed into the rug under her feet.

'You've never mentioned that before.'

Again, Minerva shrugged.

'It hardly seemed appropriate. Or necessary, for that matter. Until now, that is. Or, until you went into business together.'

'That's why you gave her the tarot cards?'

Minerva smiled.

'I think it's time we found out where her strengths lie.'

'Well, it's not in spirits. Or demons. She's still having nightmares.'

'We all do. That doesn't mean anything.' Minerva walked over to the little desk under the window and studied the drawings Ruby had left on there. 'I wonder if her daughter has the gift too.'

Erica moved to stand beside her.

'Do you think that's why this spirit is focusing on Ruby?'

'I think this spirit is focusing on a little girl because it's a coward,' said Minerva a little too loudly. She turned, narrowed eyes studying the room. 'A coward who preys on the innocent and vulnerable. You wouldn't dare touch an actual witch.'

'Gran!' Erica hissed.

Minerva opened her arms.

'If you can pinch a small child then I dare you to pinch me. Pinch me and find out what hap— Ouch!'

Minerva flinched away from her right and grabbed her arm. She pulled up her sleeve to reveal a red blotch. 'The bastard pinched me.'

Erica, eyes wide, searched the room but there was no sign of anyone else there.

'I think we should go,' she said. 'I think we've got enough for now.'

'No.' Minerva dropped her sleeve and stood square, reaching up to her full height of five foot two. 'You dare pinch me!' she growled into the room. 'You dare threaten our little girl. Tell me your name, spirit, or face the consequences.'

'You always told me not to threaten spirits,' Erica whispered.

'It's self-defence,' Minerva hissed back. Erica shot her a look.

The spirit, however, remained silent and the room still. 'Just as I thought. Coward,' spat Minerva. 'Come on, it's time we left.'

Erica followed Minerva through the cold, dark house. It was darker than it should have been. The curtains were all open, the light streaming in, but there seemed to be a shadow permanently hanging over the place. Not just in the corners, not just where you would expect them, but out in the open, where the sunlight should have hit. Erica picked up the pace.

They stopped on the front door step, Minerva rubbing her arm as Erica locked the door behind them.

'Well, that was new.'

Minerva made a soft noise in agreement, her eyes distant.

'Gran?'

'Hmm? Oh, yes. It's been a long time since I met a spirit that angry.'

'We didn't even talk to it. We have nothing to go on.'

Minerva lifted her sleeve again and showed Erica her skin turning blue and purple.

'I think we have something.'

'What? That it likes to pinch vulnerable people? Like you said, it's a coward.' There was a pause as Erica looked into the ferocity of Minerva's glare. 'I didn't mean that you're vulnerable, Gran, I just mean that...this thing pinches small children and...you know...'

'Old women?'

'Who also happens to be a powerful witch.'

'Damn straight.' Minerva sniffed, dropping her sleeve.

'So, what do we do? Find the book or whatever this thing rode in on and destroy it? I don't think we can reason with it or ask it kindly to move on, although, you know, we didn't try that yet.'

'You want to go back in there and ask it to kindly move on?'

Erica considered this, staring at the door.

'Maybe we should try.'

Minerva shrugged, crossing her arms.

'Be my guest.'

Erica took a deep breath and unlocked the door once more. Stepping into the shadows, her chest tightened as the oppressive presence fell over her again. She didn't go far, just into the middle of the hallway, glancing into the kitchen and then the living room. Finally, she faced the stairs.

'You do not belong here,' she said in a loud, clear voice. 'And you are not welcome. Please leave. Please go somewhere else. Maybe where you might be happier,' she added under her breath. 'Where there aren't any witches.'

The silence that followed stretched out and Erica was about to rejoin her grandmother on the doorstep when a foul breeze came rushing down the stairs. Erica listened to it in horror and then began coughing uncontrollably as the wind hit her, engulfing her and filling her lungs. Minerva reached in and pulled her out, slamming the door behind them and taking the key from Erica's hand.

'I think we have our answer on that one. Good of you to try though, love. Can't say this thing hasn't been given enough chances or had enough warnings.'

'What the hell was that?' Erica asked between coughs, her voice breaking.

'Another show of strength.'

'Smelt like death.'

Minerva hesitated and looked her grand-daughter over.

'Anything else?'

Erica smacked her tongue, trying to dislodge the taste.

'Yeah. Burning. And...I don't know.' She hugged herself, her heart pounding against her ribs, her stomach tingling. She placed a hand over her belly and Minerva watched.

'Fear,' her grandmother murmured, looking up to catch Erica's eye.

'Fear,' Erica agreed. 'Burning and death and fear. Like I can't breathe.' Tears pricked at her eyes.

'Come on. We're going.' Minerva grabbed Erica's sleeve and dragged her down the driveway.

They sat in the Mini Cooper, Erica staring at the steering wheel while Minerva watched Jess's house out of the passenger window.

'What do we do, Gran?' Erica asked, her voice coarse. 'Should we get Eolande and Alfie in?'

'No. No, we don't need them. Not this time.'

'You think we can handle this one ourselves?'

Minerva turned to her.

'I was battling angry spirits before I met the fae. Long before I met Eolande. We don't need the fae with this. We need witches.'

'But...that's you.'

'Yup. We need more than me, though.'

'So....Mum and me, too?'

Minerva shook her head, staring back to the house.

'No. More.'

'More than the three of us? Who else is there?'

Minerva sighed and turned away from the house.

'I'll have a word with my coven and you have a word with Jess, see if she wants to be a part of this. It would be good if she's willing. It being her house will make us stronger if she's there, but it'll also be good for her. She can learn from it and we can see what she's capable of.'

Erica had been staring wide-eyed at her grandmother as she'd spoken.

'Sorry, you lost me there after "coven".'

Minerva smiled.

'I've been meaning to introduce you.'

'Since when do you have a coven?'

Minerva tutted.

'You don't think I stay at that home for the joy of it, do you? I mean, the company is nice but my freedom is restricted, and I certainly don't need a man or a woman as a lover. Which, by the way, is all these retirement homes are good for. That and the talk. And, in my case, access to other witches.'

Erica blinked.

'You moved into a retirement home because there's a coven there?'

'Of course not. I moved into the home because your mother gave me a choice. Move in with her or move into the home and I didn't want to burden her or you.' Erica raised an eyebrow, as if the home had really made any difference. 'It was a nice surprise to find other witches there.'

'Okay. Okay. You talk to your...coven...'

'And you talk to Jess. Get her involved.'

'Right. Marshall'll love that.'

'What's it got to do with him?'

Erica rubbed a hand over her face and started the engine.

'He won't want her going into a dangerous situation again. Not only days after the demon.'

Minerva shrugged, fastening her seatbelt.

'He's a protector. Of course he won't. But he'll understand. He's a good boy.'

That made Erica smile. The idea of anyone calling big, wide, tall Marshall a boy.

'All right. I'll talk to Jess. She'll talk to Marshall. And you can talk to your coven.' Erica pulled away from Jess's house, shaking her head in disbelief.

19

Jess

Erica and Minerva still weren't home but Esther had made a start on dinner anyway. Ruby stood on a stool, reaching up to help grate cheese while Esther sliced up peppers, keeping a watchful eye on the little girl.

Jess watched from the dining table feeling a little useless. She'd already offered to help whenever she had the urge to move and Esther had told her no so many times now that Ruby had started joining in.

'No, Mummy. You stay there. We've got this.'

Esther and Jess had exchanged a look, both smothering grins as Jess had sat back down and accepted that she would just watch her little girl helping to prepare a big family dinner.

'Do you regret going into business with Erica?' Esther asked after a moment.

'What? No! Absolutely not. I love it.'

Esther glanced at Jess over her shoulder.

'Do you enjoy talking to the spirits?'

'I... Okay, fine. Yes, it scared me at first but I do find it fascinating. I love watching Ric work. And yes, this is new territory for me, but I enjoy talking to Lizzie. I'm not sure about this new spirit.'

'Well, no. But angry spirits are rare. Although, I admit, a spirit doesn't need to be angry to give you a pinch. Sometimes they're just a bit naughty.'

Ruby looked up at Esther then and Esther winked at her.

'It's the timing of it. Why did this have to happen so soon after...' Jess trailed off, looking at her daughter.

'Well, yes, the timing could have been better if this had to happen. But maybe it's happened this way for a reason. Mum always said everything happens for a reason,' said Esther, finishing one pepper and starting on another.

'Maybe,' Jess murmured, unsure of what to make of that. Thankfully, she didn't have to think on it too long as Bramley and Bubbles leapt to their feet in a fury of barks. The front door opened and Bubbles leapt onto Marshall carrying bags of food, followed by John.

'Hey, Bubs. Hang on, back up.'

Jess went to Marshall's rescue, grabbing Bubbles while John tousled with Bramley.

'Everything okay?'

Marshall nodded, placing the bag on the dining table and looking to Ruby.

'Having fun, Rubes?'

'I'm grating cheese!'

'Brilliant. Watch your fingers.'

Ruby looked at Marshall and then stared down at her fingers. Jess resisted the urge to hug her man, instead she started unpacking the bag.

'They're not home yet?' John asked.

'Not yet.' Esther checked her watch. 'They'll be home soon, I'm sure. But we can't start cooking until they're here.' She glanced at Ruby. 'I think that's enough cheese. Well done, Ruby. You've done a great job. Shall we go wash our hands?'

Ruby held out her hands and nodded. 'Let's use the bathroom, give your mum and Marshall some space. Come on.'

She lifted Ruby off the stool and led her out of the kitchen. John whisked all three dogs away with the promise of a tennis ball.

Jess watched them go, a smile on her lips, and then she turned to Marshall and opened her arms. He held her tight.

'You okay?' he asked.

'I'm not crazy, am I? For wanting to run this business with Erica?' Jess asked, her voice muffled as her lips pressed against him. 'Am I just putting us all in danger?'

Marshall sighed and let Jess go, bending to make her look him in the eye.

'Do you enjoy running this business?'

'Yes.'

'Have any of Erica's family ever mentioned terrifying demons or ghosts before now?'

'No.'

'So, chances are these things don't happen often and at least you're learning how to deal with them. So, we can deal with them. If we actually want to deal with them. Right?'

'Right.' Jess didn't sound convinced.

'Look. It's like my clients. Some of them don't pay me. I know, I know, it's bad business, I shouldn't help them out. I shouldn't do anything for them. But, you know what? They're usually the ones without any family. So, I do it anyway. Our neighbour, Mr Horton?'

'Mr Horrible,' Jess murmured, sounding like Ruby. Marshall laughed.

'Right. He moans about every single thing I do.'

'He does?'

'Yup. I can't do anything right. You know why I keep him as a client?'

'Because you want to sleep with his neighbour?'

Marshall grinned.

'Well, yeah, there's that.'

'And the commute is good now.'

Marshall laughed.

'It's because his son never visits, Jess. The man's lonely and because he's mean, no one really talks to him. And I don't blame you for not wanting to talk to him but it's part of my job.'

'He does pay you though, right?'

'Oh, yeah. He does. But my point is that, especially when we're running our own businesses, we get to pick and choose this stuff. In theory, on paper, I shouldn't be working with those clients, the non-paying or mean ones, but I do because I want to. And it's the same with your business. If you want to do this, then you'll do it. We'll make it work.'

Jess put her hands around Marshall's neck and pulled him down for a deep, long kiss.

'You're amazing,' she murmured.

'I know. It's all part of my plan.'

Jess grinned and kissed his lips gently.

'Go on then. What's the plan?'

'I make you fall madly in love with me so that when I propose, you say yes.' Something pleasurable turned over in Jess's stomach. 'Then we have a beautiful wedding and two honeymoons.'

'Two?'

'Yup. One just the two of us and one with Ruby and maybe Bubbles. We'll see.'

'Okay.' Jess kept her arms looped around his neck, her fingers stroking his warm skin.

'And we live a lovely family life together. An extended family life. You know, with Ruby's dad and Erica's family, but at the centre of it all will be you and me, growing old together. We'll have a baby and maybe, eventually, move to a bigger house. And when the kids leave home, we'll do something big that's just for us. I don't know, put the businesses on hold or sell them and retire early or something, and we'll go see the world. Or move to live by the sea. Whatever we want.'

Jess, unable to keep the grin from her lips or the tears from her eyes, nodded.

'That sounds like a perfect plan.'

'You like it?'

'I love it. So, erm, we're going to have a baby?' she whispered, in case anyone overheard.

Marshall kissed the tip of her nose.

'I'd like to. Wouldn't you?'

Jess took a moment to imagine being pregnant again, carrying Marshall's child, seeing him with their baby.

'You know what, I really would.'

Marshall grinned and they kissed again, harder this time.

'How do you think Ruby would take it?'

'Are you kidding? A baby brother or sister to boss around? She'd love it.'

'I know, but, her baby brother or sister being... you know...mine.'

Jess shrugged.

'She's already telling people that she has two dads, Marsh. She'll just lord that over the baby.'

Marshall laughed again and let her go.

'So, all we need to do is get rid of this pesky ghost, then, huh?'

Jess nodded, clenching her fists as if she could go fight it right now.

'Let's go kick its arse out of our house.'

Marshall beamed.

'And in the meantime, I'll go see what Ruby's up to, shall I? Make sure she's not terrorising Esther.'

'Probably for the best. I'll be there in a moment.'

Jess watched Marshall leave and then sat back at the table, taking a deep, shuddering breath. Still, the smile stayed on her lips.

Of course there was an angry spirit in her house, she thought. Of course there was a demon in the woods. Everything else was falling into place. Her career, her place in Erica's family, Ruby growing up happy and loved, Marshall filling Jess's heart and future plans. There was so much happiness to be had, it made sense that something had to test her, that something had to come along and try to ruin it.

It wouldn't win. The demon wouldn't stop her sleeping or enjoying the woods again, and this spirit wouldn't hurt her family or take her home from them.

Jess reached for her tarot cards and began shuffling them as she thought it through. Whatever Erica and Minerva suggested when they came home, she wanted to be a part of it. She wanted to embrace this business and she wanted to defend her home. Unless, of course, they came back and said they'd already sorted it.

Jess sighed. She really hoped they came back and said the spirit was gone.

Smiling, she looked down at her cards, closed her eyes as they moved between her fingers and put the idea of spirits and demons from her head.

What does the future hold for me and Marshall? she asked, immediately regretting it. What if she didn't like the answer? *What does the future hold?* she repeated, before stopping and turning the card in her hand.

The card showed two people entwined and Jess's heart pounded. She flicked through her booklet and found the card.

The Lovers.

Love, Jess read, harmony and alignment in values. She sat back and pressed the card to her chest before returning the card to the deck, and placing everything back into its box. That was enough for today. She scraped her chair back and stood just as the Labradors started barking and the front door opened.

20

Rick

Rick was just getting back into his car when he saw him. The tall, stocky man with brown hair that curled around his ears. Rick narrowed his eyes and stopped, standing by his open car door.

Alfie approached slowly, unreadable.

'Hello, Rick Cavanagh,' he said in a low, deep voice. Rick looked him up and down but didn't respond. 'You're a long way from home.' Alfie gave him a slow and sickening look. Rick swallowed on his dry mouth.

'Yeah. I am,' he mumbled.

'Are you waiting for Erica?'

'No.'

Alfie smiled then, showing his white teeth.

'No. You're here to see me. She never told you how to find me, did she?'

'My Erica had nothing to do with you.'

Alfie's smile dropped and he studied Rick, his

eyes going distant.

'No. She didn't.' He focused on Rick and cocked his head. 'Somewhere along the way, our timelines have been mixed up.'

Rick started.

'Mixed up?'

'Can I buy you a coffee?' Alfie turned and began walking towards the café. After a moment, Rick slammed his car door, locked it with a beep and hastily followed.

They found a table in the corner, relatively out of the way, and Alfie waited until they were both settled with a coffee in front of them.

'What do you mean, mixed up?' Rick hissed. 'I haven't come back to the wrong timeline.'

'No. But somewhere along the way, our Erica made a different decision. It's changed your time, right?'

Rick nodded.

'But I'm in the right timeline?'

Alfie gave a sad smile.

'Unfortunately. You realise, in other timelines, in other variants of this universe, I'm the one who gets the girl.'

Rick's stomach turned. The smell of his coffee was making him nauseous.

'So...I get Erica in this one?'

Alfie shrugged.

'Perhaps. She's a strong one, isn't she. Erica Murray has the power to change her own timeline.'

Alfie chuckled to himself. 'But then, of course, so do we all. At some point, my Erica made a decision differently to your Erica.'

Rick's hope fell away and he found himself glaring at the man sitting opposite, his hands involuntarily curling into fists.

'She chose you.'

Alfie watched him, bemused.

'As much as it pains me to say, Erica's heart is not yet entirely mine. I see the way she longs for you. I see the way she desires you. To be honest, it's like a knife in me, but what can I do? It's her heart to give to who she wants. Your problem,' said Alfie, leaning forward across the table, 'is that she is in love with the you of her future. She doesn't want the you that is of this time.' That annoying smile was back on his face. 'A shame, really.'

'Because she hasn't given me of this time a proper chance yet,' Rick told himself as much as Alfie. 'When we meet properly, she'll see it then. She'll feel it.'

'And if she doesn't?'

Rick stared at the fae. He wished he could be more like Alfie, willing to let Erica choose and simply wait for her answer, but every part of him was screaming to fight for her.

'She will.'

Alfie sat back and sipped at his coffee.

'We'll see, then, shall we?'

'Erica used to talk about the fae. My Erica, I

mean, my wife.' Rick put the emphasis on that last word and took some pleasure in watching Alfie's expression darken. 'She told me that you were a helpful lot. So, how about you help me now?'

'Help you to win Erica over so that I lose her?' Alfie raised an eyebrow.

'Help me out of this situation. And help me to help Erica make a final decision.' Rick leaned back and crossed his arms. 'Unless you're scared you'll lose?'

'I already know the outcome.' Alfie shrugged and Rick faltered.

'And?'

Alfie grinned.

'That would be telling.'

'You said Erica had the strength to change everything.'

'So she does. And if she does, I'll know the outcome of that.'

Rick sighed, a small growl emerging from it.

'Just help me,' he told Alfie. 'Tell me how to fix this. She can be with you now, if that's how it has to be, but how do I end up with her? How can I go back to my time and find my wife and child there? How do I fix this?'

'It's not up to the fae to fix the mistakes of humans,' Alfie told him. 'You either need to leave and try to rebuild your life—'

'I can't. If I leave, I'll forget her and if I forget her, I'll never get her back, will I.'

'—Or, as much as it pains me to say this, you can stay.'

The men stared at one another.

'Stay and what?'

'Talk to the woman you want as your wife,' Alfie told him. 'Stay and talk to her.'

Erica

The Murrays decided to leave the fajitas until Minerva and Erica had told them what they'd discovered. They wouldn't be able to eat until decisions had been made. There was a small argument over whether Ruby should be present but when the men declared that they wanted to be involved in the conversation, Ruby was placed at the table with the adults and had paper and crayons put in front of her. Erica wondered if Ruby would zone out once the adults started talking but of course they were talking about her home and her bedroom. She drew and coloured slowly, Marshall helping her along when she seemed too distracted.

'Well?' Esther gave a glance to Ruby in warning and then looked to Minerva.

Minerva sighed.

'There is indeed a presence in the house and Ruby isn't the only one it pinched.'

Ruby looked up and then back down to her drawing as Marshall got her attention. Minerva pulled up her sleeve to reveal her new bruise. Esther gasped. 'I'm okay,' her mother told her, pushing her sleeve back down. 'But as you can tell, it's not a happy spirit, that's for sure. As Jess and Marshall probably already know, this one is angry rather than mischievous. It doesn't want you there.'

'Even though we were there first,' Jess mumbled.

'Indeed. I didn't see the point in testing whether the thing came in on that book of Ruby's. Taking the book from the house would likely mean bringing the spirit with us.'

'So...we could just get rid of the book and problem solved?' asked Marshall.

Minerva screwed up her face.

'Well, maybe, maybe. Although there is potential for the spirit to attach to something else. It really does depend on its strength and this one is a strong one. No, getting rid of the book either means passing the spirit onto someone else or the spirit reattaching. The best course of action is to detach the spirit from the book and remove it entirely.'

Erica and Esther stared at her.

'You're talking about an exorcism,' said Esther.

'Like the one we did with the...in the woods?' Jess asked, glancing at Ruby.

'Sort of. A little bit different,' Minerva told her.

'Isn't that dangerous?' Esther murmured.

'No more than anything else. And we're going to

play it safe.' They all stared blankly at Minerva except for Erica who closed her eyes in anticipation. 'I'm going to get my coven involved on this one.'

Erica opened her eyes.

'Coven!' Esther sat back and then looked to Ruby, aware of how loud she'd spoken. Ruby stayed focused on her drawing. 'I didn't know you had a coven. Since when do you have a coven?' Esther hissed.

Minerva shrugged.

'You don't know everything about me, my love.'

'They're all in the home,' Erica told her mother. 'It's why Gran likes it there.' She smiled as Minerva glared at her.

'You created a coven in the home? Of course you created a coven in the home.'

'What's that supposed to mean?' Minerva asked.

Esther rolled her eyes.

'So, you're going to get a load of old women from the home into Jess's house to get rid of this spirit?'

'Old women, indeed! I'm going to ask my fellow witches, Esther, as well as you and Erica. You know, it would do you both good to do some work with a coven.'

'I'd like to see a coven at work,' said Erica, enjoying the look her mother gave her. Jess cleared her throat.

'Erm, me too.'

Marshall looked up at Jess and she gave him a smile.

'Oh yes, I want Jess there too. Naturally. It's your home. You need to be there to defend it,' Minerva declared.

'Does she?' Marshall asked. 'Is this going to be dangerous?'

'Of course not,' Minerva told him. 'We'll keep her safe. Don't you worry.'

Erica studied Marshall, as he blinked and looked back to Ruby. Jess was studying him too with a frown etched into her forehead.

'Plus, of course, I think it's time that Jess exercised the gifts she was born with.'

The whole table, apart from Ruby, stared at Minerva.

'You what?' asked Jess.

'You, my dear, are a witch, and I think it's time you were brought into the fold. As it were.'

'A witch?' Jess scoffed but Minerva nodded. 'I'm not a witch, Minerva. I'm not like you or Ric or Esther.'

'Why not? You can read tarot, can you not? How's that going?'

'She can,' said Esther. 'You seem to have picked it up remarkably quickly,' she added to Jess.

'You sensed that...thing...in the woods before Ric did,' Minerva continued. 'You might not have known what it was but you knew there was something.'

'But I couldn't hear the trees talk,' Jess breathed.

Erica wanted to speak up but she couldn't find

the right words. Jess looked like a rabbit caught in headlights and Erica was aware that the more Minerva spoke about Jess being a witch, the darker Marshall's expression became.

'Gran,' she murmured, furious at herself for not being able to say more. Minerva either ignored her or didn't hear. She pressed on.

'We are each born with our own gifts, Jess. Erica has an uncanny gift for communication, Esther with plants. We just don't know what yours is. Given your natural knack for tarot, I would be inclined to suggest you might perhaps be someone who can see something of the future. The gift of foretelling, or of sight.'

Jess caught Erica's eye and this time Erica frowned.

'What's your gift?' Jess asked.

Minerva shrugged.

'Erica takes after me. I've been able to speak with spirits since I was Ruby's age.'

They all looked to Ruby who, feeling the attention of the table shift to her, glanced around, her gaze landing on her mother. Marshall wrapped an arm around her and Ruby visibly relaxed a little.

'Maybe I should take Ruby to another room,' he murmured. 'While you talk about witches.' He flashed Jess a look and went to stand. Jess flinched and stood, ready to follow him.

'You said you were okay with this,' she told him as he gathered Ruby's papers and crayons. Ruby stayed put on her chair at the table, watching them.

'I am. I was.' Marshall sighed. 'I am. If you're happy.' He gave Minerva a pointed look. 'Come on, Ruby. You come with me.'

Ruby slipped off her chair and went to follow Marshall out of the kitchen. Jess caught up with him before he made it to the door.

'What's that supposed to mean? You said we'd work it out. Less than an hour ago, you said that.'

Marshall glanced beyond Jess to the others at the table, pretending not to listen.

'I did and I meant it. Go back to your little chat about covens and gifts.'

'Marshall.' Jess followed him as he left the kitchen. 'What's this about?'

He turned on her, just inside the doorway. Erica tried not to watch but it was hard not to strain her ears, listening to their hushed words.

'I know I don't understand this world,' Marshall told Jess as quiet as he could but they could all make out the anger in his words. 'But are you sure about this? Fae are one thing, Jess, but a coven? This thing, whatever it is, is real. It hurt Ruby. And you're going to go back in there with a bunch of women and what? Chant at it with candles until it goes away?'

'And sage,' Minerva muttered under her breath, folding her arms across her chest. Erica hushed her.

'And what if it attacks you?' Marshall continued. 'What if this thing comes after you?'

'What do you want me to do?' Jess asked, her arms open. There was a catch in her voice and, despite her back being turned to Erica, she knew there were tears building in Jess's eyes. 'What should I do, Marsh? Never let Ruby back in her home? Sell up and move elsewhere? We can't just leave all our stuff there, can we?'

'We can just throw out the damn book,' growled Marshall.

'And what if it attaches to something else?'

Marshall rolled his eyes.

'Why aren't the fae involved?' He looked from Jess to Minerva. 'Huh? Why not just ask the fae? Surely they can just go in and zap this thing.'

Minerva shifted in her chair.

'They will see it as beneath them.'

'Well. Fuck them.'

'Marshall!' Jess put her hand on Ruby's head in a vague attempt to cover her ears. Marshall clench-ed his eyes shut for a moment.

'Sorry, Ruby,' he mumbled. He opened his eyes and stared hard at Jess. 'I think I need some air.'

'No, no, Marshall, wait.' Jess followed as Marshall went for the front door and they both went out of sight.

'Ruby, love, come here,' called Esther. Ruby did as she was told, her skin pale, her chin quivering.

'Marshall's mad,' she murmured, letting Esther gather her into her arms and hold her tight.

'He's not mad at you, sweetheart.'

'Mummy's upset.'

'Not with you.'

Ruby went to say more but a sob stopped her.

Chest tight, Erica sucked in air and scraped her chair back, leaving the kitchen to find Jess standing at the open front door, Bubbles waiting beside her. Erica listened to the sound of Marshall's van wheels grinding against the driveway gravel.

Jess's shoulder heaved and Erica moved forward, wrapping her arms around her friend.

'He'll be back,' she murmured. Jess nodded, her cheeks already wet. Jess hugged Erica tight for a moment and then stepped back. 'Where's Ruby?' she murmured, wiping her face.

'With Mum.'

Jess gave a nod, her breath stuttering.

'What was that about, Ric?'

Erica shrugged.

'I don't know. Maybe it's just all a bit much for him.'

'He'd just told me, before you got home, about how he wants to marry me. How he wants us to grow old together and how I have to do what I have to do for this business and then that happens.'

'He's worried, that's all.'

'What changed, though?' Jess sniffed. Erica led her to the downstairs toilet and unravelled some toilet paper for her to blow her nose.

'He just wants you to be safe.'

'I'll be with you. And Minerva. And Esther.'

'Maybe it's because it's his home too, now, and his family too, and he wants to be the one in there protecting it.'

Jess took a moment to consider this.

'Would he be allowed in?'

Erica sighed and then laughed.

'I doubt Gran would allow a man in there. Not when she's bringing in her coven.'

'Maybe I shouldn't go in then.'

Erica didn't reply. It wasn't her place to. Jess had to do what was right for her and her family. Erica left her there to compose herself, returning to the kitchen to tell Ruby that everything was okay and to give Minerva as much of a piece of her mind as she could without actually saying anything.

22

Marshall

Marshall wasn't sure where he was going. Part of him wanted to go back to his old flat, the one he'd just moved out of, but mostly he just wanted to go home. Back to Jess's house that was now also his. Back to their kitchen, full of warmth and laughter and good smells. Back to her arms and her smile. Back to Ruby and Bubbles and everything that was going well in his life.

But he couldn't. Because there was a damn ghost in there.

He considered going to the house anyway and screaming at the ghost to leave, but instead he headed for a pub. It wasn't his local anymore but it was worth the drive. Some friendly faces and gentle chatter and a pint, that would give him some perspective and put his mind at ease.

Even just pulling into the car park helped. His van slid into its usual spot and he took a breath before he jumped out and headed inside. The warmth of the pub hit him immediately, along with the voices and smell of chips and beer. He made his way to the bar.

'Marshall! Been a while. How's it going?'

'All right, Ben. How's it going here?'

'Not bad. We've missed you. Actually, might have some work coming your way if you're up for it.'

'Yeah, sure, why not.'

'Pint?'

'Please. Got any food going?'

'Whatever you want, mate.'

Marshall's stomach growled. All that talking about ghosts and covens, he never would get those fajitas.

'Don't suppose steak's on the menu?'

'One steak and chips, coming up. Go find a table, I'll open a tab for you.'

Marshall thanked Ben, took his pint and found a small table in the corner, out of the way. Somewhere almost in the shadows where he could face the warmth of people talking about normal things and he could mull over what had just happened.

He hadn't meant to get angry. He'd meant it when he told Jess that he would support her, that she had to do what she had to do. It was the talk of covens and gifts and Minerva's unrelenting attitude that had chipped away at him.

What did she mean, Jess had gifts? Of course

Jess had gifts, but foresight? A gift of seeing the future? No one had that. Anyone could interpret a picture on a card.

Whatever was in their house was real. It had hurt Ruby. A load of old women chanting, hopefully fully clothed, wasn't going to help the situation. How could it?

This was a ghost they were dealing with. An actual, bonafide ghost.

Of course Marshall had believed Jess when she'd told him ghosts were real. He'd been there to encourage her and Erica, in fact he was pretty sure the paranormal investigation agency had been his idea. Hadn't it?

So why was this bothering him so much?

Marshall looked up, expecting the shadow that had fallen over him to be the steak and chips he'd ordered. He stared up at Alfie as the man collapsed into the chair opposite Marshall, placing his pint on the table with a sigh. The fae leaned back and gave Marshall an easy-going smile.

Marshall blinked.

'No offence, mate, but I'm having a rough night. Sort of need to be alone for this one,' he said.

Alfie shrugged, that annoying smile still on his face.

'Women trouble? You're not the only one. A lot of the men in this pub right now are having trouble with the woman in their life. Including the one sitting opposite you.'

Marshall narrowed his eyes.

'You and Ric had an argument?'

'Not yet,' sighed Alfie, reaching for his pint. 'Not yet. But we will.'

'Because you can see the future.'

'In a way.' Alfie grinned.

Marshall glanced away in thought.

'Can you tell if other people can see the future?'

Alfie studied him.

'Go on,' he urged.

'Like, if they have a gift.'

Alfie took a long gulp of his beer, set the glass down and smacked his lips.

'You're talking about Jess.'

Marshall, eyes wide, sat forward.

'So...she does have a gift?'

'Of foresight, yes.'

'And what does that mean, exactly?'

Again, Alfie shrugged.

'It means whatever she wants it to mean. If she chooses to see the future, it's there for her to see.'

'And that isn't something anyone can do?'

Alfie scoffed.

'Of course not. Can you do it?'

Marshall sat back, nursing his pint.

'She reads pictures on cards and interprets things. Anyone can do it. It doesn't mean anything.'

'Ah, I didn't figure you for a sceptic.'

Marshall looked up at Alfie.

'I'm not. I believe in the ghosts. I believed in that

demon in the woods. And I support Jess, I do. I'm pretty sure some of this was my idea. It's just... I can't... If there's a ghost in our house and it's a nasty one...' Marshall sighed. 'There has to be a logical way of getting rid of it. Couldn't you get rid of it?'

Alfie watched Marshall talk, his fingers brushing over his pint glass, soaking up a stray drip.

'Minerva can rid you of a strong spirit. So can Erica. You don't need me for that.'

'No, but...' Marshall bit his lip. He had to be careful what he was saying. For a moment there it was as if he was talking to a friend, but Alfie wasn't a friend. Alfie wasn't human. He might care for Erica and, as an extension, be caring towards Jess, but that didn't mean Marshall could trust him.

'But? You think it would be simpler if I walked into your house and rid you of your spirit.'

'Well. Yeah.'

'And why do you think that?' Alfie took a sip of his beer and then held up a finger to silence Marshall. A man approached and placed two plates on the table, two steaks and chips, one in front of Marshall and the other in front of Alfie.

Alfie thanked him and immediately picked up his cutlery to start carving into the meat. Marshall watched, not moving.

'You ordered food too, huh,' he murmured.

'Hope you don't mind,' said Alfie, shoving a large piece of steak into his mouth. 'You were saying.'

Marshall sighed and prodded his steak with his knife.

'Minerva's talking about getting a...coven,' Marshall whispered, 'involved and it all seems a bit...silly.'

Alfie laughed.

'There's nothing silly about a coven. It must be a strong spirit though, for Minerva to go to those lengths.'

'So, couldn't you just come get rid of it?'

Alfie grinned at Marshall as he chewed.

'Absolutely not. This isn't a demon, Marshall. If it were a demon, I'd be there. It's a spirit and the witches in your life can handle this.'

'It's hurt my little girl,' Marshall told him in a quiet voice.

Alfie faltered but regained his composure quickly, piling his fork high.

'I'm sorry,' he murmured, the smile finally gone from his lips. 'That is unfortunate. I can understand your pain.'

'Can you?'

Alfie nodded.

'If a spirit were to come into my home, threaten the woman I loved and hurt my child, I wouldn't stop until that spirit was gone and had suffered for it. No wonder you're here. You're angry, you need to protect your family and instead the witches will be keeping you away.'

Marshall frowned down at his food as his

stomach gurgled.

'That's exactly it,' he said. He felt the anger that Alfie described, feeling the heat coming off his words, deep in his belly. He looked up at the fae. 'Can I do anything to stop this thing and protect them?'

'What do you think?'

Marshall sighed.

'I can't, can I. All I can do is sit back, yet again, while Jess goes into danger. And I have to. One of us has to stay behind with Ruby. And it has to be me, doesn't it?'

Alfie smiled.

'Have you considered that by staying behind with Ruby and supporting Jess with all of your heart, that you're protecting your family in the best way possible?'

Marshall sighed heavy through his nose.

'It's not quite the same, though, is it.'

'We each have our part to play, Marshall,' Alfie told him. 'And you know better than others that often the right thing to do is not only the hardest but the most painful.' Alfie's smile slipped from his lips and he stopped eating, staring down at his plate. Marshall waited and when Alfie didn't speak, he took a gulp of beer.

'Have you got to do the right thing too? Is that what your argument's going to be about with Ric?'

A sad smile flittered across Alfie for all of a second before it was replaced with his usual cocksure expression.

'It would appear the love of her life has returned for her and what sort of a monster would I be if I held her back from happiness?'

Marshall studied Alfie for a moment.

'You what?' he said eventually.

Alfie sighed.

'Rick Cavanagh, Erica's future husband, has returned to this time to win her heart.'

Marshall frowned.

'I thought she had to meet present time him, or whatever.' He rubbed his forehead. 'I hate this time travel shit. It's too confusing.'

'Tell me about it,' Alfie muttered.

Marshall studied the fae and smiled to himself.

'How do you know this Rick guy is the love of her life?'

'Because I've seen it.'

'Foresight.'

'Exactly.'

'I dunno,' said Marshall, spearing some chips. 'Erica seems pretty into you. She was happy at Jess's party. What makes you think she won't change her mind about this love of her life?'

Alfie sat back.

'There is always a possibility. But then again, like you, I have to do the right thing by her and that right thing involves having just told Rick Cavanagh to stay put in this time, talk to Erica and see what they can do to ensure they end up together.'

'Well…that was a stupid thing to do,' Marshall told him.

Alfie's smile was weak this time.

'You wouldn't have done the same for Jess? If it would have meant her happiness?'

Marshall considered that.

'I guess. Maybe.'

'Just as you'll go back to her now, apologise for whatever you said, and support her. Even though it should be you going into your house and protecting your family.'

'Because we're the type of men who do the right thing for the women we love,' muttered Marshall.

'And sometimes the right thing is a bitch,' Alfie agreed.

23

Ruby

Marshall had never left like that before. Each time he had left, it had been with smiles and hugs and a promise to return. Even in the beginning, he had given her a look each time that told her he'd be back.

He'd never left her mummy in tears before.

Jess was trying to hide it but Ruby saw her red eyes, she heard how she breathed. Sometimes adults forgot that Ruby knew what these things meant. Sure, Jess had wiped her eyes and was trying to smile, but Ruby saw through it all.

Her mummy hadn't just been crying, she'd been sobbing. She was in pain, and it was because Marshall had left. More than anything in that moment, Ruby wanted to be alone with her mum, but the others wouldn't leave.

'I'll make some dinner,' Esther offered. 'Do you want to help, Ruby?'

Ruby shook her head, her arms crossed tight over her chest in an attempt to stop herself crying. Her lips were pressed shut as tears filled her eyes.

'What would you like to do, Ruby?' Erica asked. 'We can do some drawing?'

Ruby shook her head again. Drawing was what she did with Marshall. He made it more fun than anyone else. From the first time he'd looked after her, he'd drawn whatever she'd told him to. He'd asked her questions and waited for her guidance in a way that no other adult ever had.

No, she didn't want to draw.

She wanted Marshall back.

'What do you want to do, sweetheart?' Jess asked, holding her arms out, and trying hard to keep her voice strong. Ruby heard the quiver in it, Ruby heard the pain.

She moved into her mother's arms and allowed herself to be wrapped up in Jess's warmth.

Then, she shrugged.

'Come on,' said Jess, standing up. 'Come upstairs with me.'

They left Erica's family in the kitchen, silently cooking, while they went upstairs to the bedroom the three of them had slept in that night. Bubbles followed closely.

Jess sat on the bed and Ruby climbed up beside her. The covers were ruffled and there was a large dent in Marshall's pillow. Ruby sniffed and looked up at her mother.

'Talk to me, Ruby,' Jess said softly, her arm around her daughter. Ruby snuggled closer.

'Have you and Marshall broken up?' she whispered, scared that speaking the words would make them true.

She wanted her mother to laugh, to make her feel silly for even thinking it, but she didn't. Instead, she held Ruby tighter.

'No, sweetheart. We haven't.'

Ruby looked up at her mother and finally Jess looked down at her daughter and then sighed. 'We've had an argument, that's all.'

'Like you and Dad do?'

Jess's eyes filled and Ruby's chest tightened. She wrapped her arms around her mum. 'I'm sorry, Mummy.' She closed her eyes tight.

Jess hugged her back and kissed her head.

'Please don't be sorry. None of this is your fault.' Jess pulled away so she could look Ruby in the eye. 'You know that, don't you? None of this is your fault and Marshall still loves you.'

Ruby nodded.

'Are you going to break up?' she whispered.

Jess drew her daughter in close again.

'I don't think so, sweetheart.'

'But you might?'

'I love Marshall,' Jess told her. 'With all my heart. We're a family, aren't we? He's just gotten a little stressed, that's all. He wants to protect you and he doesn't know how to.'

'I always feel safe with him,' said Ruby, not quite sure what her mother was talking about. She stopped. 'Oh. This is about the ghost that pinched me?'

Jess squeezed her.

'Yeah. He just wants to keep you safe.'

'But you're going to get rid of the mean ghost?'

'We are but Marshall won't be there to help.'

'Why not?'

'Well, I'm hoping he'll be here with you, keeping you safe.'

Ruby nodded.

'He always keeps me safe.'

Jess laughed and hugged her tight again.

'You tell him that next time you see him, yeah?'

Ruby nodded.

'Love you, Mummy. And I love Marshall.'

Jess sniffed and kissed her daughter's forehead hard.

'Love you too, sweetheart.'

'And Bubbles.'

At the sound of Jess crying, Bubbles lifted her head onto Jess's lap, tail wagging slowly as they reached out to stroke her and bring her into the hug.

'Oh yes, we all love Bubbles,' said Jess quietly.

Erica stepped out of her car and stretched her back. The evening was still bright but the cemetery would be closing its gates soon. Locking her Mini, Erica wandered past the closed café and found her way to her grandfather's grave.

He lay on the grass, hands behind his head, eerily just over where his coffin lay. Erica shuddered and shook it off.

'Everything all right?' she asked as she approached.

He lifted his head to look at her and then sat up with the ease that only came to small children and the dearly departed.

'Ric! I'm so glad you're here.'

'Oh? What's wrong?' Erica sat on the grass beside George's spirit, careful not to sit on his grave as he was doing.

'A man came to see me.' A chill washed over Erica. 'He talked to me although he didn't hear me and he couldn't see me, but he told me that he loves you. That you were magical. Of course, I agreed and I asked him who he was, but like I said, he couldn't hear me.'

Erica stared at her grandfather.

'So, a strange man told you he loves me?'

George nodded.

'He had a long brown coat on.'

Something shifted inside Erica.

'And brown hair? Blue eyes?' she murmured.

'That's the one.'

'Rick.'

'Your detective future husband? Oh. Because to me, he looked like that man who was watching you the other day. While you were here talking to me.'

Erica's eyes widened.

'Did he? He did, didn't he.'

'He did.'

Erica sighed.

'Well, now, that was a big sigh. What's wrong?'

'Oh, everything.' Erica threw her hands up. 'Rick's come back from the future because his time is all screwed up and he wants me to help and I don't know how because even though I do want to be with him, actually I'd quite like to be with Alfie right now, thank you very much, and there's a nasty spirit haunting Jess's house, Gran wants to take her coven in to get rid of it and then Marshall flipped out, they had a big fight and he left.'

Erica sighed again, rubbing her hands over her face while her grandfather stared at her in silence.

'Yes. Well. That does sound like everything.'

'I don't know what to do,' said Erica, her voice muffled behind her hands on her face.

'Well, I would recommend taking one thing at a time. I'm guessing there's not a lot you can do for Jess, otherwise you wouldn't be here.'

'No. Ruby's in a state because she thinks Marshall's going to leave them. Turns out this is the first proper big fight Jess and Marshall have had. Ruby's refusing to leave Jess's side.'

George tutted.

'Poor girls. Do you think this Marshall lad will come back?'

'Yeah. He loves them both. There's no way this is the end. It can't be.'

'Right, well, let's focus on you then, shall we?'

Erica pursed her lips and blew out a raspberry.

'Please don't ask me what I want.'

'I don't have to, you've already said it. You want Alfie but you don't want to ruin any chance of a relationship with Rick in the future.'

'Did I say that?'

'Pretty much. Isn't it true?'

Erica gave a small smile.

'It is true.' She laughed. 'It's really that simple, huh? Except it isn't, is it. Because Rick's here and he's going to make me choose.'

Erica looked up at her grandfather when he didn't answer and frowned. He was staring past her, over her shoulder. She turned to follow his gaze and saw Alfie approaching them, hands dug deep into his pockets, his charming smile playing on his lips as his eyes met hers.

'Just because someone loves you,' her grandfather whispered. 'Doesn't mean you owe them anything.'

Erica turned back to him and he gave her a meaningful look.

She smiled back, wondering if he meant Alfie or Rick. That was probably up to her to decide. Standing and brushing herself down, she said goodbye to her grandfather and went to meet Alfie. His grin broadened as she approached and he immediately slipped an arm around her waist and kissed her lips. In that moment, all Erica wanted was Alfie. He smelt of soil and freshly mown grass and he tasted sweet and warm, and, strangely, of beer.

The scar the demon in the woods had left him with was a silver reminder on his cheek of how he had protected her. Her fingers trailed over it as he kissed her.

'I've missed you,' Alfie murmured as the kiss broke. He kept his forehead against hers, his hands on her hips, swaying as if they were dancing. She wrapped her arms around his neck, closing her eyes. 'Stay with me tonight,' he said under his breath.

Erica nodded.

Alfie took her hand and led her away from her

grandfather's grave, towards the Secret Garden. A small, enclosed area seemingly cut off from the rest of the cemetery, hidden behind a door where the public thought they weren't allowed. They were allowed, but this was where the fae had made their home, and they'd rather stay undisturbed.

Beyond the gate and enclosed by the walls was a stretch of grass with a bench at one end, resting against the brick. The rest of the garden was given over to trees, self-planted closely together and between which the fae came and went.

Erica wondered what they would see if they were to cut the trees back. A door, perhaps, or a portal to the world of the fae.

Alfie led her to the bench and they sat in silence for a while as Erica listened to the birds singing, her body relaxing.

'Marshall and Jess had a fight,' she said carefully into the silence. 'Marshall walked out.'

'I know. He was at the pub. I've just come from him.'

Erica looked at Alfie.

'You went to the pub with Marshall? I didn't know you were friends?'

Alfie shrugged.

'His love is best friends with my love, why wouldn't we be friends?'

Erica smiled, leaning into him. He sat back and put an arm around her.

'He's going back to Jess, though, right?'

'He is.'

'Did he tell you what the fight was about?'

'He did.'

Erica said no more. It wasn't her business, and Jess would tell her later. Instead, she enjoyed the heat of Alfie's eyes on her. 'Before I saw Marshall, I had a chat with Rick.'

Erica's stomach turned. She pulled away from Alfie, staring at him.

'What do you mean, you had a chat with Rick?'

'Exactly that. Rick Cavanagh, the man who wishes to make you his, the detective from the future. He came to the cemetery, I saw him talking to your grandfather.'

Erica stared down at her hands in her lap.

'And?'

'I'm not going to ask you to choose, Ric,' Alfie said gently. 'I know you'll make the right decision for you.'

'Because you've seen it?' She looked up into his eyes and caught her breath at their sadness. 'Oh god, I choose him, don't I?'

Alfie smiled, running his fingers down her arm.

'Maybe. But not just yet. Right now, here, you're with me.'

'Yes. I am.' Erica leaned back into him, snuggling against him as his arm tightened around her. 'I don't want to choose,' she whispered, concentrating on the feel of his chest rising and falling against her. 'I don't want to hurt anyone.'

'You don't want to hurt me,' Alfie whispered, his lips against her hair. 'You won't hurt me.'

'Don't lie.'

'Okay, you will hurt me, but I'll be fine. I'm older than you and I've still got a long way to go yet. You only have this chance. Don't worry about hurting me.'

'Because you'll get over it?' Erica asked, unsure of how she felt about that.

'Because no one falls in love just once, especially when you live as long as the fae.'

Erica frowned and turned to look at Alfie.

'Yeah, I'm not sure how I feel about that.'

He laughed and pulled her back into place.

'Take your grandmother as an example. She fell in love with your grandfather and she was happy. Then, she lost him and she fell in love with Eolande. Do you think she doesn't love your grandfather anymore?'

'Of course not. She loves him just as much.'

'There you go. I will always love you Erica Murray, even though there may be others. There will always be you.'

There was a pause.

'So...there have been others before me?'

Alfie shifted his position, moving Erica with him.

'There may have been.'

'Hmm. Still not sure how I feel about that. I don't want to know,' Erica told him. 'Which is selfish of me, isn't it. Because what if we don't stay together?'

'That doesn't matter. All that matters is the here and now.'

Erica pressed her cheek against his chest.

'If we did stay together, what would that be like? Would there be a house and a marriage and a baby?'

Alfie left a long enough pause that Erica moved to look at him, finding him staring across the garden in thought.

'A baby,' he murmured, before gazing into Erica's eyes.

'It isn't the fae way?' Erica offered him a small smile and he grinned back.

'Of course it is. How do you think fae are born?'

Erica frowned.

'So was your mother a human?'

'No. My father was.'

Erica lifted a hand to run her fingers over Alfie's curly brown hair.

'Somehow that makes a lot of sense.'

He caught her hand and pressed his lips against it.

'Let's stay in the here and now,' he reminded her. 'The future is undecided. Let's leave it there.' He kissed her lips, and then again, harder.

A voice in the back of Erica's head was tutting. He doesn't want to discuss the future, it was saying. Because he doesn't think we have one, she told it. He would talk about it if I chose him.

As if hearing her thoughts, Alfie pulled away and

searched her eyes.

'You don't have to make any decisions yet,' he told her gently. 'And you don't owe me anything.'

Erica stopped, her grandfather's voice sounding in her head. This time she was the one who leaned in and kissed Alfie.

'My Gran once told me she came here to have sex.' She accidentally pulled a face as she spoke. 'Would that be in this garden?'

That charming smile was back on Alfie's lips, his eyes brightening.

'Not here. There are too many eyes on us.'

Erica looked into the trees and shivered. Alfie stood and took her hand. 'Come with me.'

Heart racing, Erica followed him to the tree line. They were going in, she realised. He was taking her into his own world. She kept close, her skin tingling and then a song sang from her pocket.

Alfie stopped and looked down at her jeans. Swearing under her breath, Erica pulled out her phone. It was her grandmother.

'Hi,' she answered, her eyes on Alfie.

'We're going to Jess's in an hour. The coven are ready. I need you there. Okay?'

'An hour,' said Erica, and Alfie visibly relaxed, squeezing her hand. 'I'll be there.' She hung up. 'You have less than an hour,' she told him.

'That's enough.' Alfie pulled her between the trees and out of view.

Jess sat at the dining table with Ruby on her lap and Bubbles by her side, the puppy's head resting on Ruby's knees as the girl stroked the dog's ears. Jess checked her phone again, but there was nothing. No messages, no missed calls, no notifications.

She sighed and drained the last of the tea Esther had made her. Minerva had left soon after eating to gather her coven and after that Erica's parents had taken the Labradors and left Jess and Ruby alone.

At first, Jess had suggested drawing or playing a game but Ruby wouldn't be pulled from her misery. She clung to her mother and they sat in silence. Jess checked her phone again.

Bubbles shifted, looking towards the front door. Tail wagging, she pulled away from Ruby and trotted to the door giving one sharp bark. From the depths of the house, the Murray's Labradors started barking.

Heart pounding, stomach churning, Jess lifted Ruby from her and approached the door. Opening it a fraction, holding Bubbles back, she took a sharp intake of breath and opened it fully. Marshall looked down at her with reddening eyes.

He opened his arms, a little unsure, and Jess threw herself into them.

'I'm sorry,' he murmured into her hair, holding her tight. 'I'm so sorry. I won't do that again. Ever. I promise.'

'You scared me,' Jess told him, her tears staining his top. 'You scared us.' She pulled away and looked up at him. 'I'm glad you came back.'

Shock washed over Marshall's face.

'Of course I did. I was never going to leave you. I never want to leave you.' He took a deep breath. 'I meant what I said, about supporting you, I just…It was just…Erica's gran is a little full on,' he whispered, glancing behind her.

Jess laughed.

'Minerva's gone. It's okay.'

Marshall smiled but the smile soon fell as his gaze lingered beyond Jess. Jess stiffened.

'Oh, Ruby,' Marshall murmured. 'I'm so sorry.'

Jess turned to her daughter to find the four-year-old standing behind her, eyes red, chin quivering, hands clenched into little fists. Jess moved out of the way, allowing Marshall in and he immediately went to his knees in front of the girl. 'I'm so sorry, Rubes. Forgive me, please. I didn't mean to scare you.'

'You left,' Ruby said, barely audible.

'Only for a little while and with every intention of coming back. But you're right. I didn't do it very well, did I? I screwed up. I'm sorry, Rubes. I never, ever want to hurt you, I promise. I'll never do it again. Ever.'

Marshall and Jess both waited. Jess caught herself holding her breath.

Eventually, Ruby nodded and stepped into Marshall, letting him wrap his arms around her and hold her tight. He picked her up and bounced her, giving Ruby no choice but to laugh. They turned back to Jess and Marshall held her gaze.

'Can we talk?' he asked.

Jess nodded, closing the front door and taking Ruby from him.

'Bubbles. Come here,' she called, although the puppy didn't need telling. Having sniffed Marshall's jeans and ascertained that he had indeed been somewhere interesting but no longer had food on him, she bounded after Jess and Ruby.

Jess knocked on the living room door and Esther opened it, looking over Jess's shoulder to Marshall.

'He came back,' Jess said with a smile. 'Would you mind having Ruby and Bubbles? Just for a little while.'

'Of course, love, of course.'

Jess placed Ruby on the floor and she stepped into the living room with Esther. 'Let's watch something, shall we? What shall we watch?' Esther asked, herding Bubbles inside with her. She flashed Jess a warm smile, gave her a supportive nod and closed the door.

Jess took a deep breath before she turned back to Marshall, beckoning for him to go into the kitchen.

'Did you eat?' she asked, putting on the kettle.

'I did.' Marshall sat at the table. 'Don't worry about the tea. Come here. Sit down with me.'

Jess did as she was told and they hesitated for a moment as she awkwardly looked down at her hands, aware of Marshall's gaze on her.

'What happened, Marsh?' she asked, scared of the answer.

Marshall took a moment to reply and when he did, he took her hands in his.

'I got frustrated,' he told her. 'You see, you're mine. And Ruby's mine. And that's my home now. And now there's something nasty and horrible inside it and it's hurt Ruby, and all I want to do is go in and rip the fucking thing out, and I can't. I want to protect you, Jess, all of you and I can't, and I feel useless. What's the point of me if I can't protect you?'

Jess softened, stroking his coarse hand with her thumb.

'You protect us all the time,' she told him in a soft voice. 'You look after us. You fix things and you cheer us up and you cook for us and you make us happy. And I know you feel helpless when it comes to the supernatural stuff, but I still need you. Ruby still needs you. She needs you with her to keep her safe and I need you with her so I know she's safe. And I need you because when all of this is done we've got a bloody birthday party full of five-year-olds and I'm going to fall apart, Marsh.' Jess's voice broke. 'I can't do this alone. I've tried so hard for four years and I just...can't anymore.'

Marshall wiped a tear from her cheek.

'And then I went and ran out on you.'

'And why? Because Minerva talked about a coven? It's the same as the fae stepping in to help, that's all.'

'No, it's not. It's not like that at all. It's a load of women going into our house and dragging you with them and doing whatever the hell witches do. How do we even know it'll work?'

Jess shrugged.

'I think I'm one of them, you know. They won't be dragging me.'

Marshall sighed.

'I know.'

'And I know Minerva can be a lot. You get used to it, though. You need to sort of...cut through what she's saying to how you're feeling and concentrate on staying with your own thoughts. You know?'

Marshall smiled at her.

'I'll remember that.'

There was a pause.

'Where did you go?' Jess asked.

'The pub. I needed to think. And eat. Guess who I saw there.'

'Who?'

'Alfie.' Marshall chuckled at Jess's wide eyes.

'Don't tell me you had a pint with a fae.'

'A pint, steak and chips and a surprisingly interesting chat.'

'Oh?' Jess leaned closer. 'What did he have to say?'

'All the right things,' Marshall murmured, bringing Jess's hands up to kiss them. 'He made me realise I don't need to think because at the end of the day, I've found you and I don't want to let you go.' He searched her eyes and something about his expression made Jess hold her breath. 'You took me into your home and family pretty much the moment we met, Jess, and I don't think you really know how much that means to me. I've always wanted my own family. A beautiful woman who knows her own mind, children, a dog, our own home. I've spent all these years wondering if I'd ever meet you and then all of a sudden, there you were. I didn't know I would ever love another man's child as my own until Ruby, but I do. With all my heart. And I love you with all my heart. And I just want to make you all happy and keep you safe, even if that just means hiding out here with Ruby while I worry about you. I guess the thing I want to say, the thing I'm trying to say is... You see, the thing is, I've been saving my money since the day I met you,

Jess, but I haven't got round to actually buying it yet. So, I'll do this again, later, with more romance, to do it officially.'

Jess tried to concentrate on her breathing, biting her lower lip to stop any words spilling out. She couldn't help emitting a squeak as Marshall slipped from his chair, her hands in his as he lowered to one knee.

'I want to be there for you and Ruby, for as long as you'll have me, and I want us to be a family. I want you, Jess. To wake up with you every morning and go to sleep next to you every night. For the rest of my life.' Marshall took a shuddering breath. 'Will you marry me?'

Jess exhaled in a rush, tears dropping from her eyes.

'Of course I will,' she told him.

Grinning, Marshall scooped her up. He kissed her lips and the tears from her cheeks, running a hand over her hair, slipping an arm around her waist.

'There'll be a ring next time,' he whispered, kissing her cheek. Laughing, she threw her arms around his neck and held him close. 'Should we tell Ruby?'

Jess shook her head.

'Not yet. I want you to myself a little bit longer.' She kissed him hard. 'God, I wish we were home.'

'We will be soon.' Marshall pressed his lips to Jess's forehead. 'What's going on with that? What did Minerva say?'

Jess searched his eyes.

'She left soon after you. I'm waiting to hear back from her.' They sat back down at the table. 'Look, I don't have to go if you don't want me to. I can stay here with you and Ruby, if you prefer. Minerva and Ric can do this without me.'

Marshall considered this and then shook his head.

'No. It's our home. It's your home. I think Minerva's right, you need to be there. One of us should be there.' His gaze found Jess's box of tarot cards, still on the table. 'I just have to get used to being with a witch.' He smiled at her. 'And then I'll have to get used to being married to a witch.'

Jess couldn't hold it in. She squealed and clapped her hands excitedly, glancing down at her left hand.

'You're buying me a ring, though,' she told him. Marshall laughed.

'Definitely. Do you want to tell Ruby tonight?'

'No. Not yet. Let's keep this as ours. I want this to just be ours for a little while, at least. And I love that you love Ruby, of course I do, but sometimes I just want you to be mine.'

Marshall gave her his lopsided smile.

'Honey, I'm all yours.'

Jess ran her fingers down his chest and then reached forward for another kiss. It threatened to be deeper than the others, something more passionate and inappropriate for the kitchen of her best friend's parents, but then her phone started ringing.

They jumped apart and Jess checked who was calling.

'It's Minerva,' she murmured, glancing up at Marshall. He gestured for her to answer it. 'Hi,' Jess started, holding the phone to her ear while keeping her eyes on her fiancé.

'Jess. It's happening, dear. Tonight. Do you want to be there? It would be for the best if you are. Meet us at your house in an hour. Okay?'

Jess swallowed, her mouth suddenly dry.

'An hour. Got it. I'll be there.'

26

Rick

The sun was going down as Rick sat in the driver's seat of his rented car, tapping the top of the steering wheel. He was watching the front door of a terraced Victorian house a little way down the road from him. People were walking past, some with their dogs, one with a pushchair, a few students passed laughing with one another. No one came through that front door. Rick sighed. He probably had time. While he waited, he ran through his conversation with Alfie, ignoring the fact that he'd quite like to hit the man. Was man the right word? He wouldn't dare touch Alfie, of course. His Erica may not have had a relationship with Alfie but she'd told Rick enough of the fae for him to be cautious.

Still, the fae spoke wise words. Rick couldn't deny that Alfie had gotten him thinking, and what he'd said rang true. Of course it was Erica's choice who she decided to be with, but what was life for

Rick without her?

He had thought about it, usually at night as he lay in bed, terrified that if he allowed sleep to come he would wake without any memory of her. Time was a fickle thing. This had been covered in their basic training when time travel had been given to the UK police force and rolled out wide. If you did anything, anything, to mess up the timeline, then the repercussions could be not just world-changing, but they would always affect the memory of those involved. Sometimes memories were altered immediately but often the person who had enacted the change was the last to forget. Rick knew he'd lose his memory of Erica and their child eventually, and he had no idea when.

He couldn't risk sleep and he couldn't risk wasting time.

Rick sat up straight as the front door opened and a man stepped out, closing and locking the door behind him. He turned to walk down the path towards his car and Rick took a good look at him.

The man was the spitting image of Rick, although younger. Rick started his engine and waited until the blue VW Polo in front pulled away. He followed at a distance, keeping his eye on the car even when others managed to get between them.

They drove into the city, parking in a multi-storey car park where Rick managed to secure a parking spot close to his target. He got out of the car and followed him down the stairs, along the road and towards the police station.

Unsure of what he was looking for, Rick hesitated outside the doors. He couldn't follow him in, how would that look? Questions would definitely get asked. If he were starting an evening shift then Rick would have a long time to wait. He sighed again, running his hand through his hair and looking around in case the answer would just present itself.

Then, strangely, it did.

His target came back out of the building carrying a bag and Rick ducked behind an old woman walking past. She gave him a strange look but he quickly moved away, following his target back down the road. After a long walk, they ended up at a gym and Rick held back.

'Really?' he muttered. The memories came back to him now. He was a police officer, eager to pass his detective exams, and single, so he often spent his evenings at the gym. Rick smiled. There had been a vague hope that he would meet a woman there, although he never did. He'd even taken a yoga class in the hope but none of the women there had caught his eye.

'What's wrong with me?' he murmured. Why wasn't Erica interested? He didn't have Alfie's charm, he guessed, but Erica hadn't given him a chance. All Rick needed was for her to talk to him, to give him the time he needed to prove himself to her.

Perhaps he was being too eager. If he hadn't messed with the timeline, he wouldn't have met Erica yet. Not for another few years. He should have come back then, but he hadn't thought. He'd travelled back in a panic and ended up here.

Again, Rick shoved his hand through his hair, turning on the spot, wondering what to do next.

27

Erica

Erica unlocked her car and tried hard to wipe the grin off her face. Her body still tingling, she needed to get into the mindset of going to her best friend's house to get rid of a nasty entity. She hesitated as a familiar car rushed into the car park, her smile replaced with a frown. She turned, following the car and waited for it to stop. The moment the engine was off, Rick climbed out and slammed his door shut, facing her.

For a moment, they just stared at each other.

'You can't just come zooming in like that. What if there were children running around? Or dogs? Or a funeral going on? Or someone just stood in the road admiring the trees?' Erica approached him.

'I need to talk to you,' he said. She stopped. That was his response?

'I don't have time for this.' She turned back to her car. 'I need to be somewhere.'

'No, wait, hang on. Please.' Rick rushed after her, stopping beside her as she opened her car door. 'Please.'

Erica risked looking into his eyes.

'Fine. Get in.'

Rick rushed to the passenger door and climbed in, closing the door behind him. Erica sat the driver's seat, watching him warily.

'This isn't great timing,' she told him.

'No. I don't want to know, trust me.'

They caught each other's eye and exchanged a small smile.

'I really do have to go,' Erica urged.

'Right, yeah. It's just that, I can't fix this,' said Rick, throwing up his arms. 'I don't know what to do. I've been over and over it, trying to remember every bit of my training, trying to work out the logic which is hell when it comes to time travel because there is no logic, and I even asked Alfie.' Rick looked to Erica. 'I even asked Alfie,' he repeated in a quiet voice. 'Ric, I'm desperate.'

Erica laughed gently.

'Yeah. You must be.' She took a breath. 'What can I do?'

'Nothing. That's the problem. I've been over and over it and that's it. There's nothing we can do. It is what it is. I've lost you.'

Erica's gut turned and she fought the urge to vomit.

'No,' she murmured. 'You haven't.'

Rick studied her and then shrugged.

'I guess, if we still meet the way we were supposed to. But it won't be a surprise to you anymore, will it. You'll see me coming, and now you have expectations. Which is all my fault. I should never have come back. It's my fault,' he repeated. 'And I have to suffer the consequences.' After a moment, he looked back up into Erica's eyes. 'You need to do what makes you happy and I...I need to let you go, if that's what you want.'

Erica caught herself shaking her head and stopped. Rick gave a soft smile.

'You want Alfie, Ricci.'

'I want you,' she whispered. 'I asked for you to come back and you did. But I can't have you, can I.'

'You can. Go find me.'

Erica sighed.

'I've found you, Rick. You're right here, right in front of me.'

'No. No, you have to go find the me of this time. Present me. Not...not me.' Rick gestured to himself. 'It can't be me.'

Erica pressed her lips together.

'I saw that Rick and there was nothing there,' she murmured.

'But there will be something there,' he urged. 'I promise you.'

'Really? What happened when we met? What do you remember?'

Rick opened his mouth to speak and then closed

it.

'I remember,' he said after a moment's thought. 'A beautiful woman and just as she was about to leave, the words just spilled out of my mouth. From nowhere. And she said yes. And I was in a daze from that moment until our first date, where I basically spent three hours not believing my luck.'

Erica bit her lip.

'You said you remembered seeing me in the car park, by the woods.'

Rick nodded.

'I did, but only in hindsight. Only after you told me about that...demon thing. I didn't recognise you when we first met.'

'But you said you noticed me then.'

'I did. A beautiful woman with her friends being questioned by my boss while the car park was in chaos and it was only an hour or so after I'd seen that...thing. That's why I didn't fight it when you told me about what you do, about the spirits and supernatural things. Because I'd already seen it with my own eyes. It was only when you were telling me about that time that we realised we'd seen each other before. We laughed about it then. We probably won't now, will we. Not after all this.'

Erica wasn't sure what to say to that. He was right, it wouldn't be the same, but that didn't mean everything had to be different.

'That's why you're with Alfie,' Rick continued quietly. 'Because you saw me and you didn't feel anything.'

Erica struggled, thinking it through.

'I think so. I was determined not to be with him, but I thought that was because I wanted you. I didn't know if I'd ever see you again. This you, not now you.' Erica sighed again. 'Why does this have to be so confusing?'

Rick gave her a gentle smile that made something inside her twist pleasurably.

'I love you so much, Ricci,' he told her. 'It's always been you. It broke my heart to go home and find you were gone, that you'd never been mine, that our child never existed. I don't know where to go from here, I don't know what to do without you. But that's my problem, not yours. I just wish...' Rick took a deep breath. 'I wish I could show you what we had.'

Erica's eyes stung.

'I feel it,' she told him, her voice barely audible, on the verge of cracking. She sniffed and took a deep, shuddering breath. 'And I want that. What we had. I've always wanted that. I don't know what to do. Tell me what to do.' She rubbed her fingers over her eyes and sniffed again. 'God, Rick. I can't do this. I've just spent an hour in Alfie's world with him and now I have to go get a nasty spirit out of Jess's house and I don't know what to do about this. I don't know what to do about us. What can I do?'

Rick had visibly swallowed at the mention of Alfie.

'Come with me,' he said.

'What?'

'Come with me.'

'Where? To the future?'

'I don't know. Wherever you like. Let's go to the past. Let's go to the future. We can visit whatever time you want. Let's just go, you and me, together.'

Erica studied him and then laughed.

'You're crazy. Isn't that illegal? And dangerous? And I can't just leave my family. I'm not leaving Jess or my parents or Gran.' Rick's smile fell. 'Look,' Erica continued. 'I don't know what to do about this but it's going to have to wait. Okay? Just give me tonight. Let me help Jess, and then we'll talk about this. All right?'

'You won't leave them and I get that. Will you leave Alfie?'

Erica put both hands on the steering wheel.

'You want me to meet present day you and fall in love, right?'

'Well, yeah.'

'Right. Well. I don't. I don't think. I wanted you, Rick. This you. You, you. And if I can't have you, then, yeah, I want Alfie. And I can't have you, can I, so...' She drifted off, trying not to notice Rick's eyes reddening as he fought to stay calm. 'I'm sorry,' she murmured. 'You know what, I also can't have just spent that last hour with Alfie and then talk about leaving him right outside his home. He's a good person, Rick. He loves me. He nearly got himself killed protecting me. And I know I don't owe him anything but, I think I love him too.' Erica hadn't meant to say that last bit but the words just slipped out. Rick's features crumpled. 'But I'm pretty sure I'm in love with you as well,' she murmured. His eyes flicked up to hers. 'And I don't want to hurt either of you. So I'm going to ask you to get out and I'm going to drive to Jess's house and do my job and not think about it for at least a few hours. Okay?'

Rick nodded, his jaw tense.

'Be careful,' he told her, climbing out of the car frustratingly slowly.

She kept her eyes on him as she started the engine. Finally, she looked away as she drove the car out. Without thinking, she glanced back in the rear view mirror and saw Rick watching her go.

Her body still ached from Alfie's touch but right then, in that moment, she wanted Rick's lips on hers.

How had this happened? She'd waited years to meet a man she felt this way about. After years of horrible first dates and weak chat up lines, how on earth had she come across two good men at the same time?

'The universe sure has a shit sense of humour,' she muttered to herself, allowing the tears to come as she entered the city's traffic.

28

Jess

When Jess pulled up outside her own home, she found a minibus in her driveway. What were the neighbours going to think? That was her first thought. Mr Horton's curtains were twitching and for a moment, Jess wondered if he'd be at all interested to discover just how many women around his age were on that minibus. He'd probably be fascinated until he found out they were all witches.

Minerva climbed out of the minibus as Jess stepped out of her old car, slamming the door shut.

'I'm glad you came,' Minerva called to her, waiting for Jess to wander over. She did so, slowly, looking up at her home. Nausea swirled in her stomach, threatening to bring up the little fajitas she'd forced down. Now, she regretted eating at all. It would have been better to do this on an empty stomach, even if it took a few hours. If it wasn't for her home, looking dark and cold, she would have turned back, run into Marshall's arms and told him they'd start fresh. Leave everything behind and start again.

But she'd worked too hard for this house. She'd worked too many hours in jobs she hated to save the money, to convince the bank. She'd spent too much of her parents hard-earned savings. She'd only owned the house for three months and already it was filled with the memories of meeting Marshall and welcoming Bubbles and making it a *home*.

She wasn't going anywhere.

'I don't think I have much choice,' she told Minerva, not taking her eyes from the house. She dared a curtain to twitch or a shadow to pass over a window.

Show yourself, she willed. Because I'm going to take you down.

'We'll be stronger with you here,' Minerva said, turning to stand beside her, looking at the house with hands on her hips. 'This is your home, so your anger and love will be the strongest. We'll need that. Whatever's in there is strong, my dear, and I need you to be just as strong if not stronger.'

Jess nodded.

'That thing hurt my baby girl.'

Minerva patted Jess's shoulder.

'Keep hold of that.'

They both turned as another car pulled up. Esther climbed out of Erica's sky blue Mini Cooper, but Erica stayed put, staring at nothing, fingers tapping the steering wheel. Esther gave them an apologetic look.

'We're here but I don't know how here Erica is,' she said in a low voice as she reached them. 'Something's happened with that Rick bloke.'

'What?' Jess asked, her attention momentarily drawn from the house.

'I don't know. She won't tell me. She just says she needs to figure it out but she's having to choose, I think.'

Minerva sucked noisily on her teeth.

'Choosing between a man and a fae. It's a difficult one. I don't envy her.'

Esther glared at her mother.

'You're the reason she's having to make this decision. If you hadn't introduced her to Alfie, none of this would have happened.'

Minerva turned calmly to her daughter.

'In one timeline, you kept Erica from Alfie. In another timeline, I introduced her to Alfie. In one timeline, she chose Rick. Now it's time for us to see who she chooses in the other timeline.'

Erica got out of her car and locked it, taking a deep breath, straightening herself, throwing her shoulders back before she approached them.

'Are we doing this?'

Minerva stared hard at her granddaughter.

'Are you with us?'

'I am.'

'We can't have distractions in there. I need focus.'

'I'm focused.'

Minerva raised an eyebrow but was interrupted by a peeling laugh as the women began to disembark from the minibus.

'Gran. How many women are in your coven?' Erica breathed as they watched.

'Enough. These are only the ones who can manage stairs,' said Minerva, stepping forward to breach the gap between them and the women. 'Ladies! I would like to introduce you to my family. My daughter, Esther, granddaughter, Erica, and my beloved Jess, whose house this is. My darlings, this is my coven.'

'This is all of the women from the home, isn't it?' Erica whispered.

'Looks like,' Jess agreed.

'And suddenly it all makes sense,' said Esther. 'Why she's so determined to stay in that damn home even though she keeps escaping and running off.'

'To be with Eolande,' Erica pointed out.

'Crafty old witch,' Esther muttered, leading them forward towards the coven.

There were around fifteen women in all, although Jess didn't have the brain capacity to count them. Minerva gathered them around.

'As I explained, what we're going up against is strong and, truth be told, we haven't done the proper research to understand what or who it is. But, we don't need to. Whatever it is, whoever it is, it's nasty. It's pinched Jess's little girl, hard. It's pinched me, hard. This thing doesn't like witches, ladies, and it's strong. Very strong. I'm going to need all of you on top form. Think about Jess's little four-year-old, scared to go into her bedroom, bruised and crying. Think about this spirit, taking over a home, bullying Jess and her family out. Take that anger, take that rage, and let's use it. Are you ready?'

The women all gave varying degrees of agreement, from punching the air to murmurs to one scream of 'Yes!'

'Stay strong, ladies, and stay together. This is but one spirit, no matter how strong. We are the wise women of this town and we shall not let this evil in.'

Another round of agreement, this time stronger.

Minerva gave them a fierce nod and together they approached the house.

'How are we going to do this, Mum?' Esther asked, trotting to catch up. Erica and Jess stayed behind, exchanging a look.

'There is a ritual. The ladies know it. I'll need you to join in as best you can,' Minerva told them in a low voice, glancing back to Erica and Jess. 'Just like with the demon, okay?'

Jess nodded. Minerva's eyes stayed on Erica.

'And what you did back then, in the woods with the demon, Ric, I'm going to need that again. Do you think you can do that? Harness that rage inside you. Remember? When the demon lashed out at Alfie. All that blood. Poor Alfie's face.'

Erica blinked at her grandmother and then seemed to shake herself.

'I don't know,' she murmured.

Esther elbowed her grandmother.

'It's been, what? A week,' said Minerva. 'A week since your love for Alfie helped to get rid of that demon. Has so much really changed so quickly?'

Erica and Minerva stared at one another, one waiting for an answer, the other desperately searching for one.

'I'm fine,' Erica told her. 'I'm fine. Let's do this.'

Minerva hesitated but then shrugged and turned to her coven.

The women made room for Jess, gathering on either side to make an aisle for her to walk down leading to her front door.

Jess steadied herself, found her key and unlocked the door to her house.

The silence that followed was palpable. The only sound was Jess's own breath as she looked into the hallway of her home. It was darker than it should have been, as if a large storm cloud had placed itself directly over her house and only her house.

She should have taken a step back, allowed the witches in first, but instead Jess took a deep breath and stepped inside. The air around her wobbled, shimmering, and goosebumps reached up painfully from her arms. She rubbed them, finding static on the ends of her fingers. Minerva stepped in behind her and sniffed the air.

'It's gotten stronger,' she murmured. 'No time to waste, ladies!' she called over her shoulder as she stepped past Jess. The coven, Esther and Erica entered the house, following Minerva through to the living room. Jess stayed where she was, turning slowly to look up the stairs.

She blinked.

There, at the top, on the landing, was something watching her.

'You okay?' Erica hissed, placing her hand on Jess's arm. Jess didn't take her eyes from the stairs as she nodded.

'You see that?'

Erica followed her gaze and frowned. Jess relented, rocking back on her heels. The thing, whatever it had been, was gone.

'What if this doesn't work?' she asked Erica, wrenching her gaze to her friend. Erica gave a tight smile.

'It will work. You've got a house full of witches, Jess. It's going to work.'

'Have you ever felt a spirit like this before?' Jess asked as Erica went to join the coven in the living room. Erica stopped and seemed to be feeling the room, holding out an arm as she glanced up to the ceiling. 'It's like the demon, isn't it,' Jess whispered, scared that if she said the words too loud then they'd come true.

Erica dropped her arm to her side and gave a subtle nod.

'Demons are a type of spirit, in a way,' she said. 'I guess that's why.' She looked over her shoulder, catching Jess's eye. 'But this isn't a demon, Jess. It's a spirit. For demons, we needed the fae but for spirits? We've got this. You and me, and Mum and Gran and her coven. We've got this.' She held her hand out to Jess who took it. Jess allowed Erica to lead her into her own living room, risking one last glance up the stairs. The landing was empty, save for the heavy shadow that filled the house.

Inside the living room, the women chattered amongst themselves. Many had their arms crossed, offering what protection they could, hugging themselves. One, standing close to Jess, gave a shiver.

'I've never felt anything this strong,' she murmured. She caught Jess's eye and looked away, her cheeks growing pink. Jess's stomach turned. Just how much experience did these women have?

She pushed her way to the front, to where Minerva was facing her coven, watching over them. Erica followed.

'Erm, Minerva?' Jess stepped forward, keeping her voice low.

'Yes, dear?'

'These women were witches before you found them, right? You didn't just go into the home and convince them all they should be witches. Right?'

Minerva's gaze faltered and she turned back to the coven. Jess studied her and then turned away. 'Shit.'

Before she could say another word, Minerva clapped her hands and caught the attention of the room.

'Ladies! My daughter will be handing out the things we need. We'll be starting down here before moving upstairs. The spirit is based, as far as I'm aware, in the girl's room so we'll be gathering there. Any questions?'

One woman raised a hand and Minerva gestured for her to speak.

'Should we take our clothes off?'

Jess closed her eyes and clenched them hard. This had been a mistake. How could she get these women out of her house? When she opened her eyes, nothing had changed so she turned to Erica and raised an eyebrow that said, *they're going to get themselves hurt.*

Worse, said Erica's expression.

Jess, chewing on her lip, surveyed the women as Minerva responded.

'No. No. Everyone keeps their clothes on. We don't need to be naked for this.'

Erica sighed and Jess almost smiled.

'That suggests that there are times when witches do need to be naked,' Jess whispered.

'There are,' Minerva replied. 'But usually just when you're alone with someone.' She gave Jess a wink before she and Esther began handing things out to the women. Jess watched, catching glimpses of the objects. Candles, which were lit as they were handed over, sage which was held to the candle flames, and scraps of paper with writing on them.

'Now, everyone got something? Are we ready?' Minerva asked.

As the women went to answer, a foul breeze travelled through the room from the stairs and snuffed each and every candle out at once.

The women's voices raised as they all looked to Minerva. The old witch set her jaw, looking towards the door.

'Oh, no,' she murmured. 'You're not getting out of this that easy.'

Ruby

Sitting on her makeshift bed, a blow-up mattress on the floor covered in sheets and blankets, Ruby curled up and watched as Marshall carefully lowered himself to the floor to sit beside her. He held up the covers so she could wiggle underneath and then he tucked her in, so tight that she couldn't move as she giggled.

'Right. Well, you're not going anywhere,' he told her as he settled back and opened a book. 'Are we reading this one?'

Still giggling, Ruby shook her head.

'No. Not that one. That one.'

'Which one? Point to it.'

Ruby laughed, unable to move her arm from under the blanket. 'Why aren't you pointing?' asked Marshall. Ruby laughed harder. Grinning, Marshall untucked her so she could sit up and reach for the book she wanted.

Marshall held out his arm and Ruby nestled up to him as he opened the book and began to read to her. Ruby knew the words by heart but this time she wasn't listening.

The sound of Marshall turning a page broke her thoughts.

'Marshall?'

'Hmm?'

'Will Mummy be okay?'

Marshall glanced down at her and gave her the lightest of squeezes.

'Of course she will be. We'll finish reading this, you'll go to sleep and have lovely dreams and by the time you wake up, she'll be back. We'll have breakfast and then we'll go home and this will all be over. Okay?'

Ruby nodded, her brow furrowed as the thoughts still whirred through her mind.

'You promise?'

Marshall kissed her head, as if that was an answer. It wasn't good enough for Ruby.

'This book is boring,' she said as Marshall continued reading.

'Oh. Well, do you want to read something else?' He closed the book and began leafing through the few others Esther had found stashed away.

'No,' said Ruby. 'Why can't you tell me what Mummy's doing?'

'We've told you, Rubes. She's gone to tell the bad thing that's in our home to get out.'

'With Erica.'

'Yup. And Erica's mum and her grandmother and a bunch of other women.'

'Why?'

Marshall sighed and Ruby wondered what she'd asked wrong. She could tell he was unhappy, something about his body had changed although he still held her gently. 'I'm sorry,' she murmured, shaking her head, trying to dispel the question. 'Sorry.'

'Don't be sorry.' Marshall gave her another squeeze.

'But you might leave again.'

There was a pause and when Ruby looked up Marshall's eyes seemed redder than before.

'I don't want to ever leave you ever again,' he told her, putting the book down. 'Do you like me, Rubes?'

Ruby nodded without thinking. Of course she did. That was a stupid question.

'And how would you feel about having two daddies? Officially. One mummy and two daddies.'

Ruby frowned, sticking her bottom lip out.

'I told you. I already have two daddies. Daddy and you.'

Marshall's face softened, his eyes growing watery as he smiled.

'You really do think of me as one of your daddies already.'

Ruby nodded, wondering again if she'd said

something wrong. Why was he upset?

'Am I not supposed to?' she asked carefully.

'No. No, it's lovely Ruby. It makes me happy. These are happy tears,' said Marshall, using his thumb to wipe his eyes. He sniffed loudly and wiped his hand on his trousers.

'Oh. Good.' Ruby wrapped her arms around the bulk of Marshall's torso and hugged him hard.

'But what if it became something more official?' Marshall asked.

'Official?' Ruby let go and craned her neck back to look up at him again.

'Yeah. Like...if me and your mum...I don't know, got married or something.'

Ruby's eyes widened.

'There'd be a wedding,' she murmured.

Marshall chuckled.

'There would be, yes. And then we'd be a proper family.'

Ruby pouted as she thought.

'I thought we were a proper family now. Because you've moved your stuff in with us and you live with us now.'

'We are. But what if me and your mum stood up in front of people and told them all how much we love each other and how much we want to be together. And there'd be dancing and music and food. There'd be cake.' Ruby snapped up to look at him again. 'And pretty dresses,' Marshall added. 'To show everyone we're a family. Because I never

ever want to leave you again. Either of you. Because I love you both so much.'

Ruby gave this some thought and then, just as Marshall started to shift position, she nodded.

'Yes. Yes, that would be okay.'

Marshall grinned and kissed her forehead.

'Good. Thank you.'

They settled back together.

'You're going to stay with me tonight, aren't you Marshall?'

'Of course.'

'Until Mummy comes home.'

'I'll be right here. Whenever you need me.'

Ruby nodded, pressing her cheek against Marshall's chest, her eyes slowly closing.

'Because you keep me safe,' she murmured as she drifted off to sleep.

'Always.' Marshall squeezed her and then there was only darkness and his warmth.

'Spread out, ladies,' Minerva told her coven.

With murmured whispers and some nervous giggles, the women in Jess's living room spread out into the hallway. Esther and Erica walked between them, relighting the candles. Esther stayed near the back, protecting the rear while Erica found Minerva at the front, standing at the bottom of the stairs and staring up.

Jess hovered behind her, wringing her hands.

'It's okay,' Erica murmured, touching her friend's arm. Jess gave her a weak smile, completely unconvinced.

Erica turned to her grandmother. 'Should we try making contact first?' she whispered.

Minerva, without taking her hard gaze from the stairs, nodded.

'You do it,' Minerva said in a low voice. 'This is your part to play.'

Erica stepped up beside her and cleared her throat. The landing above them was darker than it should have been given that the curtains were open and outside was bright.

'We know you're here,' Erica said and almost tutted at herself. Of course they knew, how could anyone miss the dark presence sitting over the house? Not to mention, houses didn't usually have a wind blowing through them. 'Would you like to talk to us?'

The coven waited but nothing happened. There came no response, no foul breeze to snuff their candles, no sign at all that the spirit had heard her. Erica took a slow deliberate breath, then she reached into her pocket and pulled out her phone. She unlocked it, pulled up the assistant and stretched as far as she could to place the phone on the stairs.

'Use this to speak to us,' Erica said.

They waited and when Erica thought the time had come for her phone to switch itself into sleep mode, it didn't. The screen remained bright and slowly Erica became aware of the darkness on the landing thickening and drifting down the stairs towards the coven. Erica stood her ground, sensing Minerva stiffen beside her. Jess's breath sounded behind them but she refrained from looking back, keeping her eyes on the moving shadow.

'Can you tell us who you are?' Erica asked.

Behind them, the women from Minerva's residential home stretched up, nudged with elbows and peered between shoulders to get a better view.

'Witch,' said Erica's phone in a female robotic voice.

A hush fell over the coven.

'Who are you?' Erica asked again.

'Witch,' replied her phone.

Erica glanced sideways at her grandmother but Minerva was glaring at the deepening shadow, her hands curled into tight fists, her lip twitching each time the phone spoke.

'I know what I am,' Erica told the shadow. 'I want to know who you are.'

'Thou shalt,' said the phone. 'Not suffer.'

Behind them, the coven began to murmur.

'It wants to protect us?' one asked quietly.

'It doesn't want us to suffer?'

'Maybe this is a mistake.'

'Finish it,' growled Minerva. 'Finish it!'

Erica frowned at her and then turned back to the phone as it continued to talk.

'A witch to live.'

An icy wave washed over Erica, leaving her skin prickling and the feeling of something crawling up her back. Was it just the words doing that or had the spirit done something?

The coven were talking again and as Erica snuck a glance behind her, she caught sight of a few drawing their cardigans and jackets around them.

'I understand,' said Erica, turning back to the

shadow on the stairs. As they watched, the darkness turned and twisted until it had grouped itself into a cloud on the landing. 'You don't like witches. Do you not want to tell us who you are?'

There was a long stretch of silence as they stared at the shadow above them. As Minerva turned to Erica, her mouth open to speak, the phone spoke first.

'Death.'

One woman at the back laughed, another declared the whole thing ridiculous and made for the front door. No one stopped her and no one joined her.

'You're death?' Erica asked.

Minerva barked a laugh.

'I've met death,' she declared. 'And you are not he.'

Erica studied the shadow. It was almost pulsating, as if deep inside was a heart, beating and thinking and reaching out towards them.

'What year is it?' Erica asked.

Minerva gave her a strange look but then turned back to the spirit, eager to hear the answer.

'Ha ha ha,' said the phone and Erica's bowels loosened.

'It's laughing at me,' she murmured, and in that moment she wasn't sure if the notion terrified or angered her.

Minerva had no such dilemma.

'How dare you!' she boomed. For a petite elderly

woman, her voice could be as strong as a strict, angry headmistress at the end of her tether. 'How dare you laugh at us. How dare you come into this home and threaten the child that lives here. How dare you think you have any power over us.'

The phone screen went dark and Erica wondered if she should unlock it again. She flinched as the screen brightened, just as it did when she pressed a button, and then she watched as something unlocked it.

'A spirit can unlock my phone. Who knew,' she mumbled.

'Thou shalt not suffer—'

'Yes, yes, we heard you,' Minerva interrupted the phone.

'—a witch to live. You…tried before God…cast into fiery lake.'

Erica glanced at her grandmother.

'Fiery lake?' she whispered.

'Revelations,' Minerva hissed back. 'You're not from this century, are you?' she asked the shadow. 'I think I know what you are even if you won't tell us who you are.'

Erica looked between her grandmother and the spirit, waiting.

'Witch,' said the phone in a monotone voice.

'Witchfinder,' Minerva hissed.

The coven seemed to gasp as one and the murmurs started again. Erica glanced back to Jess to find her friend's skin ashen but her eyes distant and hard, deep in thought, which Erica guessed was better than wide with fear.

'There's no reasoning with this one,' Minerva told Erica. 'We need to banish it. Right now.'

A flutter of a breeze rolled down the stairs, making the candles flicker. Erica put her sleeve over her mouth.

'Not yet,' she told Minerva. 'We don't know it's a witchfinder. I thought they were few and far between?'

Minerva shrugged.

'I thought witchfinders were mostly in the South East,' came Esther's voice, making all three jump. Erica's mother had wound her way to the front and now stood beside Jess. 'Why would the spirit of one be in the South West?'

'There were witchfinders here too. Witch trials were held all over the country,' said Minerva.

'By scared and stupid individuals, not witch-finders,' said Esther.

'Same thing. Sort of.' Minerva sniffed and glanced back up at the shadow. Erica wondered if it was listening. She would be, if she were a witch hunting spirit with a house full of witches staring up at her.

'How do you tell the difference between someone who is scared and stupid of the old woman down the road and a witchfinder?' Erica mused.

'Their strength,' Minerva said. 'And I think we can all agree that this bastard is strong.'

In reply, the light in the house dimmed further and the candles held by every woman sent flicking shadows up their faces.

'What did a witch do to you?' Erica asked the shadow as Esther and Minerva began hissing at each other in argument. Jess stepped closer to Erica, a hand reaching out and finding hers.

The phone lit up.

'Devil work.'

Erica frowned.

'Bit of a crap answer,' she murmured.

'Ric. The book my aunt sent Ruby was from London. She lives in London,' Jess whispered.

Erica, Minerva and Esther all turned to look at her.

'The book was from London?' Minerva asked.

Jess nodded.

'An old secondhand bookshop she likes going in. I asked my mum. The book is from the seventies.'

'The nineteen seventies,' Esther told Minerva. 'Not the seventeenth century.'

Minerva gave her daughter a withering look.

'So, it's not the book?' Jess asked.

Minerva's eyes softened.

'A spirit can attach itself to anything, my dear. I wonder where else that book has been.' She turned back to the twisting shadow on the landing.

'What do we do?' asked one of the women behind them. 'What happens next?'

'It hasn't attacked us yet,' Esther pointed out.

'I have bruises that say otherwise,' Minerva said. 'As does Ruby.'

They all glanced at Jess but she wasn't listening, she was staring hard up the stairs to the spirit.

'It's all very exciting, isn't it,' said a woman behind them in a tone that suggested that this was anything but exciting.

'I find it strange that a witchfinder has found its way into the home of a witch like this,' Minerva murmured, following Jess's gaze.

'Are you from Essex?' she asked the spirit. 'The witchfinder general was an Essex lad,' she told the others by way of explanation.

'I don't think they called them Essex lads in the seventeenth century,' Erica murmured as they watched the shadow twist.

Her phone lit up and the monotone voice said one word.

'Enough.'

The phone screen went dark.

'Enough what?' Erica asked. 'Enough talking? You haven't told us who you are. If we're to be put on trial, we at least deserve to know who is putting us on trial.'

They waited but there came no response from the shadow or the phone. 'Okay,' Erica tried again. 'In that case, what are our crimes?'

Witch.

It didn't use the phone to talk that time. It used its own voice, a hushed whisper in each of their ears and given the chatter that rose from the women behind them, Erica guessed the word had been spoken to each and every one of them.

'You're outnumbered,' Erica told the spirit. 'There're too many witches here for just the one witchfinder.'

The shadow gave what she interpreted as an angry twist.

'Such rage in this one.' Minerva tutted.

'We can help you to move on,' Erica offered. 'Help you to be at peace.'

On the stairs, her phone flickered and then lit up.

'Thou shalt not—'

'We know!' Both Erica and Minerva screamed up at the stairs.

'I told you, no reasoning,' said Minerva, turning to her family and coven. 'Which means it's time for action.'

'Wait, wait, wait,' said Erica, glancing back at the women watching them eagerly. 'Mum's right, it hasn't attacked us yet. Where's the pinching? Maybe it does just need some help.'

Esther raised an eyebrow of defiance at her mother and Minerva pursed her lips.

'What do you think, Jess?' Minerva asked. 'This is your house. Your home. Your child. Your power, my dear. What do you want to do?'

'Jess?' Erica said gently, placing a hand on Jess's arm.

Jess blinked, breaking from her thoughts, and

looked at each of them in turn.

'I don't know,' she murmured. 'You're the experts.'

Minerva cocked her head at Jess thoughtfully.

'He came into your home and declared you a witch, Jess Tidswell,' she said. 'He didn't come to me or Esther or Erica. He came to you and your daughter. A witch and daughter of a witch, whether you believe that yet or not. You have the power to do this, Jess. What do you want to do?'

Jess, trembling and hugging herself tight, turned to meet Minerva's gaze, her eyes filled with unspent tears.

'I want it out of my house.'

That was all Minerva needed. She spun on the spirit and shouted, 'You heard her! You do not belong here. Leave, now. Go. Or we shall force you from this place.'

The women watched the shadow on the stairs as it pulsed and grew larger, spreading over the landing and down the stairs.

'Cover the flames!' Erica shouted seconds before another foul wind rolled down and over them, blowing their hair back and sending ice cold tendrils over their arms, up their legs and down their necks.

The majority of the coven had managed to shield their candle flames and helped the others to relight as some complained of the smell.

'We shouldn't goad it,' Erica told her grandmother, exchanging a worried glance with her mother. 'This thing is strong.'

'Together we're stronger,' Minerva told them, squaring herself to the spirit. The twisting shadow pulsed and began to take on the shape of something that resembled a human. There was the head and shoulders, what could be described as arms, a thick trunk instead of legs, and from the head branched darkness into a hat.

The witchfinder stared down at the witches, raising an arm, and the screen on Erica's phone cracked.

'Son of a bitch,' Erica muttered under her breath, turning to face the spirit.

31

Jess

'You didn't have to break it,' Erica told the shadow man. With a quick swipe, she reached forward and retrieved her phone. The spirit on the landing watched her, although it had no eyes from what Jess could tell. She studied the figure, made up of thick black smoke, it was obviously a man in a hat and his head cocked to the side as he looked down at them. A shiver ran over her and she knew as a certainty in her gut that he was looking at her.

This spirit who had come into her home uninvited, had hurt her daughter, scared her family, driven them from their house. Had he watched Ruby sleep? Had she dreamt about him?

The idea of him lurking in Ruby's bedroom made Jess want to vomit but the bile didn't rise in her throat. Instead, it was anger that rose. It flowed through her, from her core and down her legs and arms, making her jaw clench and her fingers tingle until she closed her hands into tight fists.

'You could have just said you were done talking,' Erica mumbled, shoving her phone into her pocket.

'I think it did,' Esther murmured. 'It said "enough", remember?'

Erica didn't reply. With a glance back to Jess, she turned to Minerva. Erica kept giving Jess those glances. Jess pretended she didn't see them but she knew what they were. Erica was checking she was okay. Was she okay? No, she wasn't, but Minerva had been right. Jess had to be here. She had to protect her home, she had to be here to take her home back.

'I'll say it one more time,' Minerva shouted up to the spirit. The shadow man turned to her. 'You do not belong here. Leave this place, now.'

There was a long pause as the spirit considered them.

'*I belong here.*' The voice was deeper than before and no longer a whisper. It sounded around them rather than tickling their ears.

'You absolutely do not and if you won't leave of your own accord then you will be removed from this house,' Minerva told the spirit.

The spirit flickered in response but didn't move.

Minerva sidled up to Jess.

'Maybe if you try,' she murmured. 'You have the power to dispel this spirit, Jess. This is your home. When he says "witch", he's talking to you. You have the power to get rid of him. You just need to feel it in your gut. Know it in your heart. See yourself as you truly are. Take back what's yours.'

Jess blinked, feeling the words settle in her stomach. Taking a step forward so that she was level with Erica, Jess attempted to stare down the spirit.

'You do not belong here,' she told it in a voice too quiet. She cleared her throat. 'This is my home. That's my daughter's room. And you do not belong here.'

The shadow man watched her, his darkness pulsating in such a subtle way that at first Jess wasn't sure what was making her skin crawl.

'You feel that?' Minerva whispered. 'You're powerful, Jess. Use it.'

Jess drew in a breath and it caught on the doubt. Then Erica was beside her. Strong, good Erica, who took her hand and squeezed it. The women behind her stepped forward as one, candle flames flickering with the movement, and Jess looked up as the shadowy spirit seemed uncertain for the first time and diminished, fading a little.

Minerva retrieved her sage and lit it using a candle from a woman behind her. Waving it in front of her and letting the smoke fill the hallway, she looked up at the shadow figure.

'You had your chance,' she started. 'I call upon the Mother Goddess to assist me in what I must do,' she said, loud and clear, so the whole house could hear every word. 'You, witchfinder spirit, do not belong in this home. Leave now. I call upon the Goddess to help you from this place.'

The sage smoke drifted up the stairs and the shadow man moved backwards, away from it. A low rumbling growl echoed through the room and Jess swallowed, blinking hard as the smoke went into her eyes.

'*Witches,*' said the spirit, the word following the growl from room to room. '*All die.*'

Somehow, although Jess would never be able to find a logical explanation, water dropped from the ceiling above them, crashing over the coven with a splashing thud. The flames went out, the soaked sage stopped smoking and Jess gasped for breath. Holding her hands out in front of her, she watched water dripping from her fingers, feeling droplets travel down her neck under her clothing, from her hair into her eyes as she looked from Erica to Minerva. Angry rumblings came from behind them as the coven scraped back wet hair and wrung water from their tops.

Minerva blew out drops of water from her lips and with more dignity than Jess felt, dragged the wet hair from her face.

'I don't think sage is going to work,' said Erica, scraping the water from her eyes.

Jess's thigh buzzed, harder and harder. Taking another deep breath and blowing the water droplets from the end of her nose, she pulled her phone from her pocket.

How could it possibly still be working? She wiped the water from the screen as the assistant sprung to life in her hand.

'Trial. Water,' came the monotone female voice.

Jess's eyes widened.

'Was that it?' she asked Erica. 'Was that the trial?'

Erica turned to her grandmother.

'Trial by water was drowning. He can't mean—'

Minerva spun to face the spirit.

'Don't!' she called, moving to go up the steps.

Jess's feet were wetter than they had been a moment ago. She looked down to find water around her ankles. It was clear with an overpowering scent of rain and the level was rising fast. For a strange and slow moment, Jess looked up to her ceiling and was relieved to find no signs of damage. The spirit was trying to drown them but it might not affect her home insurance.

'Mum!' Esther pulled Minerva back. 'What are you hoping to achieve if you go up there?'

Minerva's eyes moved left and right as she thought and landed on Jess. Jess met her gaze.

'Can you do this?' Minerva asked her. 'Are you ready?'

'What do you want me to do?'

'What you must. What's inside you. You know how to do this, Jess. Remember back in the woods? With the demon?'

Jess shook her head.

'That was Erica. Erica helped you do that, not me.'

'You stood in the circle, Jess. It was your power that helped us.'

'No. No. There was Erica and the fae. It was them. It wasn't me or Emily, or those teenagers. They weren't witches.'

'No. But you are, Jess. It was me and Erica and Eolande and Alfie and you. It was you, Jess. And I know you feel it. I know you know it. And I wanted to give you the time to accept it but we just don't have that time. This is your home, Jess, and look at it.' The water was up to their knees. Minerva held out a hand to her. 'That spirit bruised your little girl. That spirit is going to kill us. It's going to take you away from Ruby and Marshall and Bubbles. And you have the power to stop it.'

Jess didn't realise she was crying until she blinked. The tears that fell were warm against the wet chill of her cheeks. She nodded, pressing her lips together.

'This is my home,' she said. Minerva smiled. Jess turned to the shadow man standing on her landing. 'And you are not welcome here.'

'Atta girl. Now, we go,' said Minerva, gesturing to the women behind them. She advanced on the stairs, stepping out of the water, her family and the coven following closely as they approached the witchfinder spirit.

32
Rick

Waiting outside the terrace house in his car, Rick was loathe to move. He remembered how hard it was to park outside his old home, the house he'd had before he met Erica. He smiled, stroking his steering wheel as the memories came back to him. They hadn't faded yet, which was a surprise. According to his training, he should have forgotten Erica by now, especially as he was no closer to convincing her to talk to present day Rick. Yet, the memories remained, unchanged, clear and crisp. He remembered their first meeting, he remembered how bright her eyes had been and how her hair had smelt. He remembered their first soft, warm kiss. He remembered the feel of her skin under his, the taste of her, the sound of her voice, whether she was whispering in his ear or arguing with him in the kitchen. He remembered their child, as well. Their son, who had his mother's hair and his father's blue eyes. Their son who laughed and giggled and cried until snot bubbles burst from his nose.

Rick couldn't breathe. He wound the window down and took in gulps of air, blinking away the memories until his chest loosened.

How was this possible? How could he remember so much? Perhaps there was still hope. Perhaps Erica would meet his present day self as they had met before. Perhaps she would choose him after all.

Rick gave a short laugh and ran his hand over his face. He stared at his old front door, urging something to happen, anything to take his mind off his thoughts.

Present day Rick left the house a few moments later, smartly dressed in clean jeans and a shirt, and jogged down the road to his car.

'Finally,' Rick muttered, starting his car and signalling to pull out once his younger self had done the same. Then, he frowned. Where was he going and why was he dressed so smart? A night out with friends perhaps, there was no reason for Rick to remember something like that.

Rick followed the car into the city and a multi-storey car park. He parked his own car a few spaces down and watched himself leave the car park, trotting down the steps. He followed hurriedly, worried he'd lose him as they stepped out onto the street. There was a bar close by that Rick used to frequent with his friends from the force, so he went to go left and nearly tripped when present day Rick turned right. Where was he going?

The summer evening was still bright and the air muggy. The city was bustling with people, couples and stag and hen parties starting their evening. The smell of perfume followed Rick as he dodged people and watched his younger self go into a restaurant.

Rick stopped and someone swore, nearly crashing into him.

What was going on?

Rick walked up to the restaurant. He remembered the name. He'd brought Erica here on their second date to have burgers. It had been messy and full of laughter and greasy fingers. His stomach twisting, Rick looked in through the window and saw himself kissing the cheek of a woman. She had blonde hair and long legs, her curved figure hugged by a tight blue dress that pushed up her breasts and she looked nothing like Erica.

A hand over his mouth, Rick watched as the couple were seated at a table and given menus.

He's on a date. I don't remember this, Rick frowned.

He rubbed at his eyes and looked around. He knew this road, he remembered this restaurant, but he didn't remember that woman. Who was she?

'This isn't possible,' he murmured, pressing his back to the wall beside the restaurant. 'How is this possible?'

Everything he'd been taught in training

contradicted this. How could present day Rick be on a date with a woman that his future self didn't remember?

His chest tightened. Rick gasped for breath. He needed to get away from here but what if he missed something? He looked back to himself and the blonde woman as she laughed at something he'd said. What if this wasn't a first date? What if he developed a relationship with this woman? Would he dismiss Erica when he finally met her? Rick chewed on his lip. Would he still meet Erica?

It didn't bare thinking about.

He turned away from the restaurant window, having seen enough. Something that Alfie had said niggled at him as he wandered back to his car. Something about different timelines. Could he have changed the timeline?

Whatever had happened, there was a possibility that Erica was truly no longer his future. His chest ached, his head beginning to throb, and then an idea occurred to him.

If Erica was no longer his future, if his future was now unknown, then what would he do? What could he do?

Rick stopped walking and looked up at the clear evening sky as possibilities floated through his mind. He could go anywhere and be anything. Sure, he needed new identification documents and he probably couldn't stay in this city, what with there being two almost identical Rick Cavanaghs.

He looked down at the device on his wrist, the technology that allowed him to travel through time.

He could go anywhere.

Deep in thought, Rick continued towards the car park. Around a corner, past some bins and something made him stop. Was it his imagination or had there been a flash of light?

Rick took a couple of steps back and peered around the large bins. What he saw made him dart back and then hurry towards his car.

Detective Chief Inspector Burns was standing by the bins, twiddling the device on his wrist and if Burns was here then the chances were he was looking for Rick.

'Fuck,' Rick breathed, pulling out his parking ticket and shoving it into the machine, glancing over his shoulder. There was no one there. As far as he knew, DCI Burns hadn't seen him, but that didn't mean he wouldn't come around the corner and into the building at any moment. Pushing coins into the machine, Rick took back his ticket and ran up the stairs two at a time to his car.

Just as he thought he might be free. Why couldn't the universe have just given him this? Rick plonked into the car and started the ignition, slamming the door and yanking on his seat belt. DCI Burns would go to Erica first, he realised in that moment, his body freezing.

'Shit.'

That was, if DCI Burns remembered Erica. His

mind racing, Rick drove out of the car park and headed out of the city.

33
Erica

The shadow man seemed to turn in on himself and then vanished. Minerva didn't hesitate. She marched straight into Ruby's bedroom with Esther and Erica behind her. They made way for Jess and waited for the coven to reach them. The little girl's room wasn't quite big enough for everyone so Minerva arranged the coven into an oval filling the bedroom and landing.

'Just like in the woods. Remember?' Minerva told Jess as she reached for her hand. Jess blinked at her and Erica bit on the inside of her cheek. Bringing up the demon in the woods probably wasn't the best thing to do in this situation.

'With this circle we are strong. Can you feel it, ladies? The energy coming from the women either side of you.' Minerva completed the circle in Ruby's room, Jess on one side and Erica on the other, lifting her face to the ceiling and closing her eyes.

Erica glanced at her mother on her other side who gave her an encouraging smile. The last time they'd formed a circle, the fae had been with them. Sure, it had been Erica and Minerva's chanting that had banished the demon but it had been the strength of the fae who had held it back long enough for the spell to be completed. Who was going to hold back this spirit?

As much as Erica was enjoying the house being filled with witches, she couldn't help but wish that Alfie was there, holding her hand and lending his power, or at least Eolande if it had to be another woman.

The coven took a collective breath and Erica felt it, a sudden surge that warmed her hands. She caught Jess's eye and smiled but her friend barely smiled back.

Not friend, thought Erica, sister. We're a family. All of the women in this house. And you think you can come in here and threaten one of us? You don't know who you're messing with.

Erica stared around the room, daring the spirit to show itself.

'I'm going to give you another chance,' Minerva said. 'But this is your last one. One more chance to leave this place. Move on. You do not belong here, this is not the place for you and so we politely and kindly ask you to move on.'

At first there was silence, then Erica could have sworn she heard a soft, low rumble. The noise grew louder until there was no mistaking the laughter. It echoed through the house, around the empty rooms and seemed to surround them in Ruby's bedroom. Jess hunched up her shoulders, unable to block out the noise with her hands that were still locked in the circle.

A ball of rage fell into the pit of Erica's gut and began to bloom, spreading out, hot and painful, into her legs and arms. It was the same rage that she'd felt when the demon in the woods had attacked Alfie. Her fingers tingled as she gripped the hands of Minerva and Esther, and her grandmother glanced at her, sensing the rage and with it, the power. Minerva gave her a subtle nod and tightened her grip on Erica. Her mother stroked the skin of Erica's hand with her thumb, a comforting gesture that caused Erica to look at her. Was she okay?

Esther gave her a quick smile and then tightened her grip.

'You think this is funny?' Minerva shouted into the house. 'Do you think we're not serious?'

The light in the room dipped and the shadow figure appeared standing on Ruby's bed. Jess flinched, her back to it, her breathing hard as she resisted the urge to break the circle and turn to face it. Erica locked eyes with the figure, staring it down.

The shadow man lifted an arm and reached out to touch Jess but it didn't quite make contact.

'*Devil...child,*' came a low, gravelly voice. Erica

couldn't work out if the missing words were quiet or not being said at all. Perhaps it didn't have the strength or perhaps the words were being skipped somehow.

Jess closed her eyes, her muscles tensing.

'*Shall suffer…punishment…the Lord.*'

'Don't you dare talk to her,' boomed Minerva.

The shadow figure flinched.

'*All…dealings…Devil!*' the low voice shook as it sounded around the room. '*You,*' it lowered to a hiss, '*…tainted…babe. You…taken…soul.*'

Erica frowned and realised she was gritting her teeth. She unclenched and regarded the shadow figure who pulsed as if breathing.

'Where is your evidence?' she called. 'If this is a trial, where is your evidence?'

The shadow man moved to regard Erica and then, horrifically, stepped closer to Jess. Tears squeezed out from Jess's closed eyes as she trembled and Minerva had to clamp her hand around Erica's to stop her from leaping to her friend.

'*Lord's name…vain. She speaks with fairies.*' The words came out slowly, twisted and a little garbled but they heard them nonetheless.

'I wouldn't call them that if I were you,' Minerva told the shadow figure.

'*She communes with spirits.*'

'Yeah, you, you piece of shit,' spat Erica.

'*She has a familiar.*'

There was a pause.

'Bubbles?' Esther asked. 'You mean Bubbles?'

Erica stopped herself from laughing.

'*She whores,*' the voice hissed.

That stole the laughter from Erica and the circle tightened.

'*She has the sight.*'

The circle held their breath at that and Jess's eyes snapped open, red and watery and brimming with unspent rage.

'You have no right to come into this woman's home and judge her,' Minerva told the spirit as she watched Jess. 'You are not welcome here. Leave now. This is your last chance.'

The shadow figure flickered and then vanished. Erica glanced around the walls and up at the ceiling, waiting to see where it would manifest but instead the room fell silent, the light returning.

'Is it gone?' one woman murmured.

'Did it work?' asked another.

Minerva closed her eyes. She was feeling for it, trying to sense where it had gone. Erica did the same, closing her eyes and breathing deep to see what she would feel.

There was nothing there.

She opened her eyes and looked at her grandmother.

'What's going on?' she murmured.

'Jess,' Minerva whispered. 'Where's that book your aunt sent you for Ruby?'

Carefully, Jess let go of Minerva's hand and broke the circle. She stepped quickly over to the small bookcase by Ruby's bed and found the book, offering it to Minerva.

'Place it in the middle of the circle,' Minerva instructed.

Jess did as she was told, her hands still shaking as she placed the book down. She rejoined the circle and the women clasped the hands of those either side of them. Erica took a deep breath through her nose and looked to her grandmother.

'I know you're still here,' Minerva said to the room. 'I feel you. I feel your spite. I see you, Witchfinder. Worming your way into this house by a child's book. We have the book and now I'm going to tell you again. You do not belong here. Leave.'

There was a hushed silence as the coven held their collective breath.

'Ouch!'

Erica looked up to the part of the oval out on the landing, just beyond Ruby's bedroom.

'Ow!'

'What's going on?' Minerva called.

'It's...it's pinching us!'

A woman yelped in pain.

'Don't break the circle!' Minerva roared, gripping Erica's hand. 'Stay strong, ladies.'

Another woman gave a short scream and jumped, and then the laughter returned. That low, rumbling laugh that echoed through the house.

Jess closed her eyes tight against it and Erica glanced around the room, ready to face it.

It moved through the landing, the women hopping and hissing as it pinched and scratched at them, and then the spirit was back in Ruby's room. It worked its way around the outside from the door towards Minerva at the back. The women yelped, lifting their feet, trying to dodge away from the spirit's attacks without breaking the circle.

Then sharp nails dug into Erica's legs. She clenched her jaw shut as a vision of the demon in the woods slashing at Alfie's face flashed before her. Her stomach turned with the rage the memory provoked. There was a pain across the back of her calves and then a wetness against her jeans. Erica frowned. Was the spirit drawing blood?

Another flash, this time of blood dripping down Alfie's face. Erica's chest heaved as she inhaled and she unclenched her jaw with a growl.

'Cut me all you like,' she said quietly to the room. 'We're not going anywhere.'

A hand gripped her ankle and tried to force her forward. Erica stamped her free foot hard onto the floor and the grip vanished. 'We're not going anywhere!' she shouted.

The coven turned to look at her.

'Not until you do,' Minerva added in a low voice.

A soft toy lifted from the bed in invisible hands and flew across the circle, hitting Esther in the stomach. She glanced at Minerva with a raised eyebrow.

The room pitched into darkness as the foul wind rose from a corner of the room, swirling into a black cloud and filling the air with a stench that made it hard to breathe. Some of the women coughed, unable to cover their mouths.

'Ah! It poked me!' shouted a woman from the landing.

Within seconds the women were talking over one another, yelping and shouting.

'Ladies!' shouted Minerva, but no one seemed to hear her. 'This is getting out of control,' she murmured.

'It should have just been us,' Erica told her but Minerva shook her head.

'We need all of us. Close your eyes, witches,' Minerva instructed. 'Grasp the hands in yours, close your eyes and listen for the hum of our strength together. Focus on it. Block out the pain and the smell.'

Something dug into Erica's hip and then her back. She gave a shiver. It wasn't just a prod, it was hands roaming over her clothes, looking for something in her flesh. Erica tried to ignore it. She closed her eyes and listened, beyond the hisses of pain and breathing of those around her. She listened for the hum. It started as a warmth in her hands and a shudder in her feet as the coven became grounded.

'*Witch.*'

Erica screwed up her face, clenching her eyes shut against the whisper in her ear.

'*Whore.*'

There it was. A low hum, just beyond the voices and breathing, beyond the creaks of the house and rustle of leaves in the tree outside the window. Erica centred on that hum, focusing all of her attention on it.

'Listen to it,' came Minerva's voice, only just louder than the hum itself. 'You hear it? That's us, witches. That's our power. Make it louder.'

The hum grew, buzzing around the women.

'*Devil's whore. Sinner. Witch.*'

The voice was still a whisper but now it was agitated. Erica wouldn't let it distract her. She listened to that hum growing louder.

'This is how we will banish the spirit,' came Minerva's voice. 'This is how we will protect our own.'

A scream ripped through the room and something hard smashed into the side of Erica's head. She opened her eyes with a gasp to find the whole of Ruby's small library floating above them. The women murmured, gripping one another's hands harder.

A book flew down, thrown, and hit one woman in the shoulder. She flinched, obviously in pain, but she didn't break the circle. Another book hit Esther in the leg and one flew at Jess's head, although she managed to duck so that it landed with a thud on

Ruby's bed behind her. A thick book remained in the air above them.

'Don't you dare,' Erica murmured.

The book spun slowly then jerked before being thrown at Minerva. Erica side-stepped, pulling her mother and the circle with her, shoving her grandmother out of the way so that the book took a glancing blow off the side of Erica's head.

34
Jess

Esther gave a cry of anguish as Erica blinked through the pain.

Jess watched with wide eyes and then glanced down at the book from her aunt, still on the floor inside the circle.

'Enough!' she shouted.

The women fell silent and for a moment the room was still. Jess looked up and around the room.

'Show yourself,' she demanded. When nothing happened, she sneered. 'Or are you a coward? Scared of a few witches?'

She knew by Erica's change in stance that the shadow figure had appeared behind her.

'I see you,' Jess whispered.

The shadow figure appeared beside her. It lacked detailed features but Jess knew it was looking at her. It leaned forward until the stench it had created with the wind filled her nose. It was daring her. She could feel it. Despite everything inside her wanting to break free and run, her heart pounding, her guts twisting, her bowels loosening, Jess turned her head and looked the spirit in the eye as best she could.

'You do not belong here,' she told it in a quiet voice. 'This is my house, my home and my family, and you do not belong here. Get out. Now.'

The pause that followed seemed to stretch into a minute before the shadow figure disappeared.

Jess closed her eyes again.

'Is it gone?' someone asked.

'No,' said Jess and Minerva simultaneously. Jess opened her eyes to find Erica looking at her with astonishment. 'Lucky guess,' she offered with a shrug.

'Was it?' Minerva asked.

Jess glanced at her but didn't reply.

'We're bleeding,' said a quiet voice from the landing. 'How can we do this? It's ridiculous.'

'You heard the hum, didn't you?' asked Minerva. 'We can do this. We have the strength but only if we stick together.' She turned to Jess. 'But we need more of that from you, Jess, love. You're one of us. You were never a bystander. You've always been stronger than you've given yourself credit for. Single mother, you've raised a strong and fierce girl by yourself while building a career and now a business. You worked hard for this house. You turned it into a home. You created life, Jess, both yours and Ruby's. You are strong. You are a witch.'

Jess blinked back tears.

'I did all of that with help,' she murmured, looking to Erica and Esther. Both gave her warm smiles in return.

'They were only there in case you fell, Jess,' came Minerva's soft voice. 'You did all of the hard work.'

Esther nodded.

'This spirit is strong. We need your strength now more than ever to banish it from the home you made.'

Jess took in a slow, deliberate breath and nodded.

'What should I do?'

'Break the circle,' Minerva told the coven. 'Ready the sage, light the candles, as quickly as you can.'

The coven did as Minerva told them and within five minutes, they were ready. The scent of burning sage filled Ruby's bedroom, tickling at Jess's nose and making her eyes water. There were candles dotted around the room, on Ruby's bookcase, on the floor, on her little desk. Jess took it all in, reminding herself that her daughter was safe with Marshall. The sooner this was over, the sooner she'd be back with them. All she had to do was stay strong, stay adamant and do as Minerva told her.

It should be easy.

Jess swallowed on the lump in her throat. If it

were easy, the spirit would be gone by now.

The women joined hands once more, the circle bent as it spread through the doorway and out onto the landing. Those who hadn't lit the candles had been busy checking their wounds. There was nothing deep, only grazes with some light bleeding. The injuries were soon cleaned up.

During all of this, the spirit had remained quiet. Was he licking his wounds clean too? Or had he been watching them, waiting for his next opportunity.

'Spirit,' Minerva started once a hush had fallen over the room. 'We call upon the strength of the Goddess to help you move on, to help you to leave this place—'

That low rumbling laughter interrupted her, slowly moving around each woman as she shivered.

'What do you want?' Jess asked. 'What's keeping you here?'

Minerva glanced at her but waited silently for a response.

'*You*,' came the whisper in Jess's ear. She blinked, resisting the urge to dodge out of the way and run down the stairs and out the front door.

'You're bound to the book, aren't you,' she whispered back.

The spirit didn't respond but the shadow figure reappeared, this time over Erica's shoulder. Erica stiffened, her eyes on Jess.

'And if we get rid of the book, we get rid of you.'

The spirit growled.

Jess turned to Minerva.

'Let's burn the book.'

There was silence as the women contemplated this. The idea of burning a book was wrong, even if there was a malignant spirit attached to it.

'But it's a children's book,' one woman murmured.

'And it's old,' mentioned another.

Minerva sucked in her lower lip as she studied Jess.

'We burn the book,' she said. 'Yes, I don't think the spirit has left us any other choice.'

Behind Erica, the shadow figure flickered and disappeared. Erica visibly relaxed.

'How do we do this?' Jess asked, staring down at the book on the floor. 'Is there a spell? A chant? A ritual or something?'

Minerva shrugged.

'Nope. Just burn the damn thing.'

Out on the landing, the women murmured to one another, still unhappy about doing such a thing.

'Unless anyone has any other ideas?' Minerva said to them pointedly. No one spoke. 'Well, then.' Minerva sniffed. 'Go into the circle, Jess, take the book and a candle.'

Jess broke the circle but it quickly closed behind her as Minerva took the hand of the woman beside Jess. She stepped inside and picked up the book, reaching over Minerva to take the candle from Ruby's desk.

'*Witch*,' came the spirit's voice. There was a squeal as the shadow figure appeared on the landing, pulsating as if breathing.

'That's me, apparently,' murmured Jess under her breath. After a moment's thought, she pulled Ruby's little bin from the corner of the room, reaching beneath Erica and Esther's clasped hands. Then she held the corner of the book to the flickering flame.

Everyone watched, ignoring the shadow figure by the stairs.

'*Witch*,' the spirit growled and all of the candles went out at once. Jess sighed as tendrils of smoke wrapped around the book.

'Right,' she muttered.

'Get the lighter from my pocket,' said Erica.

Jess pushed her hand into the pocket Erica indicated and pulled out her lighter. Flicking up the flame, she pushed the book into it.

The light bulb above their heads exploded as the flame went out. The coven screamed and Jess, hands over her head, crouched to protect herself from the glass.

'Get out of my house!' she screamed, flicking open the lighter once more and pressing the book to the flame. The lighter was wrenched from her hand and smashed into the opposite wall with a small thud.

Jess looked to Minerva. Now what?

'I have matches,' said a woman on the landing. Jess squeezed through the doorway and found the woman, taking a box of matches from her jacket pocket.

'Thanks,' she murmured as she made her way back to the bin. Dropping the book into the bin, Jess took out a match. The wind picked up, swirling around the room without any warning. Jess's hair lifted, getting in her eyes. She crouched low over the bin, trying to provide some cover as she scraped the match over the box. It didn't catch.

'C'mon,' she muttered, trying again.

The bin wobbled.

As the match caught on the third try, the bin toppled over and rolled away.

'For fuck's sake,' Jess cried.

'*Blaspheme*,' hissed the spirit.

'I'll blaspheme you,' growled Jess, correcting the bin and striking a match. It caught and she immediately dropped it onto the book. The flame fizzled out. Jess looked back to Minerva.

'Try again,' she urged her.

Jess crouched back over the bin as Minerva began murmuring words she couldn't make out. The wind picked up and Jess struck a match. There were three left. She held it inside the bin, against the book and the spirit screamed, making Jess flinch, as one of the pages began to smoulder. Jess held her breath, willing the book to burn.

The bin was ripped from beneath her, scraping against her leg and catching on her arm. The match went out and the bin with book inside tumbled through the circle as if kicked, landing in the doorway.

'I thought the circle protected us? How the hell is it doing this?' Jess asked.

Erica, eyes narrowed against the wind, shouted into the room.

'Either it's too strong or we're weakening.'

'Rubbish!' shouted Minerva over the howl of the wind, whipping round and round the room.

'Ric's right,' Esther told them. 'We need more.'

Jess sighed, wondering how much more she had to give.

'What about the fae?' she offered.

Minerva bared her teeth.

'We don't need the fae for a spirit. They'll laugh us out of the cemetery.'

Jess and Erica exchanged a glance.

'Alfie won't,' said Erica. Minerva ignored her.

Shalt not suffer witch.' The spirit's low whisper sounded in the ear of each woman as the wind whipped faster and harder, picking up toys and books as it went. As the objects swirled above their heads, they were thrown one by one at the witches. The women cried out in pain but still the circle remained intact.

'It's a spirit. A damn strong one, but a spirit, and we're witches. We're more than capable of doing this.'

The spirit roared over the wind it had created.

'Gran—' Erica didn't get to finish her sentence, let alone give Jess a clue of what she might have been about to say. Her legs were swept from beneath her and Erica fell backwards, breaking the circle.

'Ric!'

'Mum!'

Jess turned at Esther's voice to find Minerva on her knees, one hand reaching out, searching for Erica. She bent over, the air escaping from her lungs.

Jess's eyes widened and she stumbled back as Minerva lifted into the air.

'Mum?' Esther screeched. 'Let her go!'

Minerva twisted in the grip of something invisible and then with a speed that made Jess's stomach turn, Minerva shot out of the door, throwing the coven backwards.

35

Rick

Unsure of where to go, Rick sat in his car and listened to the birds singing. He liked to think he would hear his boss' car pulling into the car park and have enough opportunity to duck down and drive out without DCI Burns noticing. Would Burns know to look here? Rick didn't think he'd ever mentioned the cemetery. It had just been a place that his wife had visited often, to see her grandparents. Still, would DCI Burns remember that?

No. Erica was no longer Rick's wife. There might not have been a wife to tell DCI Burns about, never mind any acknowledgement of the cemetery. He was safe here.

Rick stiffened as he watched Alfie amble around the corner, his hands deep in his pockets, before taking the steps two at a time and entering the café.

Glancing out of each window in turn, half expecting to see his boss staring through the glass at him, Rick opened the car door and stepped out. Locking the car behind him, he made his way to the café.

Alfie was ordering a coffee when Rick arrived. The fae glanced back at him and corrected his order to two coffees before gesturing for Rick to take a seat at a table outside.

Rick did so, choosing a seat that gave him a view of the car park.

'Nice weather today, huh? Sun shining, sky is mostly blue, no wind. A perfect summer's evening,' said Alfie, taking the seat opposite Rick and then purposefully moving so that Rick could still see the car park. 'They're closed, otherwise we'd be sitting inside, away from prying eyes. Good thing I know the girl that works here or we wouldn't have any coffee.' His dancing eyes looked up into Rick's frown. 'You're not alone here, are you time traveller?' Alfie whispered, that annoying grin playing on his lips.

Rick couldn't understand what Erica saw in this man. There was something deeply unsettling about him.

'Of course you'd know about that,' Rick mumbled.

Alfie leaned back in his chair and shrugged.

'It's a gift.' He eyed Rick as two coffees were placed on the table. Alfie thanked the woman and began stirring his drink, dropping in some sugar. 'You're not here just to hide, are you?'

'Aren't I?' Rick stared down at his drink. Honestly, he wasn't sure why he was here. Maybe he'd been hoping to find Erica back here, finished with helping Jess. Maybe he'd just needed space to think.

'I just needed some space,' he murmured.

'So you came to the home of your wife's lover?'

Rick looked up into Alfie's eyes.

'Don't say it like that. Like she's cheating. She's not cheating.'

'No. She was never with you.'

Rick pushed his drink away and swallowed in an effort to keep the vomit down.

'I don't know why I came here,' he said quietly, moving to stand.

'Have you decided what you're going to do?' Alfie asked, sipping his coffee.

Rick hesitated.

'About what?' he asked cautiously.

Alfie raised an eyebrow.

'About the loss of your marriage. About the fact that you've broken the law and that you've already been found out.'

Rick swallowed and found his throat painfully dry. He sat back down and sipped at the coffee to wet his tongue.

Alfie watched, his lips twitching into a grin. 'Foresight is something most of my kind are gifted with, you know. I can not only see what is but I can see what will be, or rather, what could be.'

Rick frowned.

'Different versions of the future, depending on the choices you make,' Alfie explained. 'When I first met Erica, she was never going to be mine. She was yours. Completely. Then something changed. She made a decision. Suddenly, she's mine.'

'What decision?' asked Rick in a quiet voice.

Alfie shrugged.

'I don't know.'

'Yes you do. You said you see these things.'

'Some things. I can see some things. The heart of another person is a tricky thing, and her decision was made with her heart.' Alfie looked Rick up and down. 'As was your decision to come back here to find her. But that hasn't worked and now you're trying to fix this problem with your head.'

Rick stared down at the table between them.

'What do you think I should do?'

'I think it's time you made another decision with your heart.'

Rick looked up to find Alfie staring at him with soft and honest eyes, and in that moment Rick caught a glimpse of the man Erica saw.

'Because that worked so well for me last time?' he scoffed, toying with his coffee mug, prodding the hot ceramic with the tip of his finger.

'Some decisions don't work out for a reason,' said Alfie. 'What do you want, Rick?'

Rick stared down at his drink.

'Ricci, our son, I want my family back.'

'What did you used to want? Before you met Erica?'

A hint of a smile grazed Rick's lips.

'Freedom.'

'So, you joined the police?'

Rick looked up at Alfie.

'I needed money and a stable career, but I guess before that I'd always wanted to go travelling. I couldn't, though.'

'Why not?'

'Mum got sick.'

Alfie sat back and tilted his head to the side.

'So, why don't you go travelling now?'

Rick stared at him wide-eyed.

'Because I've just lost my family,' he said slowly, wondering if Alfie had forgotten.

'You lost your family back in your own time, but you're not in your own time now,' Alfie told him. 'You, right here, right now, still have time to build that family in the future.'

'That makes no sense. I'm not getting any younger.'

'No, but Erica isn't getting old fast and you've got a time travel device strapped to your wrist.'

Rick stared dumbfounded at Alfie and then looked down at the device on his left wrist.

'I could go back to before Erica found out about you,' he murmured and then flinched as Alfie shot forward, leaning his elbows on the table.

'Is that what you truly want right now? Erica

back in your arms, tied down to a job with a family to support?'

Rick hesitated.

'Listen to your heart,' Alfie told him, his voice soft and gentle but his eyes now threatening. Rick's chest fluttered.

'Because you want her for yourself.'

'Because I want her for more than five minutes,' Alfie almost growled. 'Go follow your heart, Rick, and when you're ready, when you're sated, come back and see if you can claim her.'

'If you'll let me, you mean.'

'If she'll let you. This has always been her decision. If she turned up now and proclaimed she wanted you, I would step aside. I wouldn't be happy about it, but I'd step aside. Her heart is her own. As is yours. All you have to do is follow it.'

There was a pause as Alfie watched Rick think. The fae drained his coffee and dug into his pocket. 'Think about it,' he said, placing something on the table between them. 'And when you decide, if you decide, then take this with you. It'll help you know when the time is right to return.'

Rick reached out to the pocket watch Alfie had placed in front of him.

'How?'

'You'll know when it happens, and when it does, if you still want Erica's heart, then you're to come back to her as fast as you can. The watch will show you how and when.' Alfie paused to make sure Rick understood and then added, 'Stay safe, Detective.' He stood and walked away from the café without another word.

Rick blindly watched him go and then picked up the pocket watch. It was golden with glittering cogs showing through the glass face, turning slowly as the seconds ticked by. As he turned it over, he ran his thumb over an inscription.

Into The Heart

Listening to the pounding in his chest, Rick eased the watch into his pocket and wrapped his hands around his full coffee cup.

Erica

Esther ran onto the landing, followed closely by Erica, and both women managed to grab hold of Minerva, pulling at her against some invisible force. Erica felt the physical strength of the spirit as it kept its hold on her grandmother. Minerva cursed and swore as she tried to twist away, her expression giving away the pain she was in.

'Let her go!' Erica screamed.

A flash of light flickered across Erica's vision and then Minerva was on the floor, her legs dangling over the top step.

'Fucking thing tried to throw me down the stairs!' said Minerva as Esther knelt over her, holding onto her tight.

'We need to get out of here,' she told Minerva. 'You need to get Eolande in here. We have to go, now.'

'Absolutely not,' said Minerva, pulling on Esther

and Erica to get back to her feet. Erica stared at her.

'Seriously? Because I think this might be a bit beyond us now,' Erica hissed.

Minerva looked her square in the eye.

'What did you see?' she asked.

'What?'

'Just then. You pulled me free, what did you see?'

'See? I— There was a flash of light. The spirit did something that caused a light and then you fell.'

'No, Erica, *you* caused the flash of light. This thing is all shadows and negative energy and rage. It couldn't create light if it used every ounce of its being. That was *you*.'

Erica opened and closed her mouth, then opened it again but no words would come.

'Your strength,' said Minerva, stepping closer to her. 'Your rage. Your power,' she hissed, holding her face close to Erica's. 'And we *can* do this.'

Minerva walked past the women, silently watching, and back into Ruby's bedroom.

'Hold onto that feeling, Erica,' she called over her shoulder.

Erica looked to her mother. Esther's mascara had run and she was close to sobs. There was a slight shake of her head. She was done. She was through.

'I'm not made for this,' she murmured, barely audible.

'Apparently, I am,' Erica told her. She glanced around at the coven, some of whom had followed

Minerva, the rest were watching her and her mother.

Erica followed her grandmother into the girl's room.

'Mum should go home,' she said. Minerva did a double take at her and then glanced behind her to where Esther had presumably followed.

'Do you want to go home?' Minerva asked, her voice now soft. Erica looked back to her mother. Esther struggled for a moment.

'No. I'll only worry about you.' She straightened and walked past Erica to stand by Minerva's side, then turned to hold out a hand to Erica. She took it, holding her free hand out to Jess, standing by Ruby's bed, her skin pale. Jess took Erica's hand and then Minerva's hand, completing the small circle.

'Place the book in the middle,' Minerva told one of the women who grasped the book to her chest. The woman dropped the book like it was hot, and Erica thought it might as well be made of molten metal. If only it were, she sighed, the book would disintegrate and this might all be over. The four women in their circle looked down at the children's book on the pink rug.

The spirit had gone quiet, although who knew how long that would last.

'What do we do?' Erica asked under her breath.

'We try again,' said Minerva.

'There has to be another way,' Esther prompted,

glancing at Jess. Erica's gaze lingered on her friend. Jess hadn't spoken, she'd barely looked up.

'We could take the book out of the house,' Minerva pondered. 'The spirit should go with it. It's how it came to be here, after all. Remove the book and deal with it outside of this home.'

'No.'

All three of them looked up at Jess.

'You said we could deal with this now,' Jess said. 'I want this thing gone. For good. Where it can't hurt anyone else. This thing pinched my daughter. It's drawn blood. It nearly killed you.' She looked up at Minerva. 'And I won't have it. Not in my home, that I worked for and paid for and built.' She looked around the room. 'So, what do you need me to do?'

Minerva's lips twitched.

'The same as Erica,' she told her. 'That rage you feel, that sense of purpose. Harness it. Control it. Use it. And we'll defeat this thing together.'

A throat was cleared behind Erica.

'Erm, what about us?' asked one of the women.

'Ladies!' Minerva cried, dropping her hands and breaking the circle. 'Let's change tact. Everyone downstairs. Living room. Now. Careful on the stairs. Jess, child, bring the book and those matches.'

Erica waited for Jess to pocket the matches and clutch at the book. Esther helped her mother down the stairs while Erica went behind Jess, waiting for the feeling of something watching them from behind. The feeling didn't come.

Where was he?

He was in the living room, standing at the back, waiting for them as Minerva led the coven inside. Erica hesitated when she saw him.

'What?' Jess looked up as Erica stopped her. Minerva and Esther had entered the room without issue and were whispering among themselves. Erica frowned. They couldn't see him. The shadow figure looked directly at her. While she couldn't make out his eyes, she could feel the stare from under the brim of his hat by the way her skin lifted and crawled.

Jess had followed her gaze.

'You can't see him?' Erica murmured as the women filed in behind them. There was enough space in the living room for the whole coven to join hands in a circle. Esther moved the coffee table into the middle to keep it out of the way.

'No. He's here? Why can't I see him?' Jess hissed.

'Listen to them. No one else can see him either. The question is, why can I see him?' Erica didn't take her eyes from the spirit.

'Jess, we need you in the middle of the circle. Erica— Erica?' Minerva spun round to look behind her, where Erica was staring. 'You can see it? It's here?' She squinted into the corner.

'He's here,' said Erica.

The women of the coven murmured among themselves, trying to see into the corner by Minerva. Erica's grandmother turned back to her.

'It appears he wants to deal with you and only you.'

Esther made a strange noise as she held back from protesting.

'Jess and Erica, stay inside the circle,' Minerva told them, pulling Esther back and taking her hand. The circle complete, Erica kept her eyes on the spirit, Jess standing as close as possible to her. The shadow figure hadn't moved. It stayed in the corner, behind Minerva, it's hard gaze still on Erica.

'I call upon the Goddess,' called Minerva, her head bowed, eyes closed. The women around the circle copied her posture, closing their eyes. Jess bowed her head, her fingers finding and gripping the hem of Erica's top. Erica kept her eyes open and on the spirit. 'We call upon the Goddess and those who we love who have moved on. We call upon the spirits who love us. Protect us in this hour of need. Be here with us. Left to right, front to back, bottom to top. We need you now.' Minerva waited a moment and then opened her eyes, lifting her head. 'Spirit, we call on you to leave this place. There will be no judgement. There will be no anger.'

'These witches are weak.'

Erica blinked at the spirit's voice, glancing around at the others, but it appeared only she could hear him. The shadow figure stepped forward until Minerva shivered.

'*This one is old. She will die easily.*'

The breath caught in Erica's throat as her chest tightened.

'Ric?' Jess murmured, watching her friend. 'What is it?'

'*This one will be harder,*' the spirit stepped over to Esther. '*She will cry and scream.*'

Erica clenched her jaw shut to stop any words spilling out.

'*And you.*' The shadow figure stood just behind the clasped hands of Erica's mother and grandmother, unable to move closer. It tilted its head, considering her. '*You will require more.*'

'There will be only forgiveness,' Minerva continued. 'Leave now. Follow a light. Be at peace.'

The spirit laughed. It didn't move, it didn't seem fussed about the idea of forgiveness or finding a light. Minerva still had her eyes closed, listening. If she was aware of the spirit standing beside her, she didn't show any sign of it.

'And what about my friend here?' Erica asked. All of the women looked at her. 'And what about the others here? What will you do to them?'

Minerva sighed.

'Not going into the light, then, huh?'

'I don't think you want forgiveness because I don't think you think you've done anything wrong,' said Erica. 'You think you've been doing God's work, torturing and killing innocent women. If you happen to get a kick out of it, then that's just a bonus, right? So, tell me, spirit, what will you do to my friend here?'

'What are you doing?' Jess hissed.

'*I will make you watch,*' said the spirit.

A smile grew on Erica's face as her stomach turned in rage.

'We will show you, spirit, we will prove to you that all those women you tortured and killed were innocent, because you obviously have never felt the wrath of a true witch. Well, now you're in a house full of them. There will be no forgiveness.'

'Erica,' Esther chastised. 'There will always be forgiveness.'

Erica barely heard her mother's words. In that moment, she was aware of more women, standing behind the coven, encircling them. She was aware of voices and screams and pain and anger and fear.

The shadow figure wavered, flickering a little as it took in the presence of the new spirits.

Erica stepped forward, away from Jess, opening her arms out and circling.

'Spirits!' she called. 'Show yourself. Take what energy you can and manifest before us. Show the coven your presence. Do what you can.'

The air around some of the spirits began to shimmer and the light above their heads, which had definitely been switched on, began to flicker on and off. A lamp in the corner of the room turned on and burned bright before switching off. The television, in another corner, switched on, showing a snowy channel of white noise. Through that white noise, came a voice.

The circle broke as one of the coven screamed, cowering backwards.

'Mend the circle!' Minerva yelled. The women either side of the scared witch grabbed her hands and pulled her forward.

The voice coming through on the static wasn't strong and it wasn't clear, but it was certainly female and, unable to produce words, it began to scream. Soon, the other female voices joined her, the voices of those unable to manifest.

A few of the spirits appeared, gradually, dotted around the circle, behind the women. Many in the coven were breathing hard, sweat appearing on their skin, their knuckles pale as they gripped onto their neighbours.

'Stay strong, ladies!' Minerva shouted. 'They won't hurt you. They are as us. These are the women he tortured, the women he dunked, the women he poked and prodded and humiliated before he killed them. They won't hurt you. It's him they want.'

Erica looked back to the shadow figure to find him missing.

'Now we burn the book,' she whispered to Jess. Jess dug into her pocket and pulled out the matches. She lit one and then dropped it with a yelp as there came a hard knock on the front door.

For a moment, the chaos in the living room stopped as everyone, the spirits included, looked towards the hallway.

Then a spirit pulled a cushion off the sofa and another yanked a magazine, spinning the pages.

There came another knock at the door.

'Miss Tidswell?' came a man's voice. 'What the hell is going on in there? I can hear screaming. I'm going to call the police if you don't answer this door.'

Jess growled.

'Mr Horton,' she muttered. 'Bloody Mr Horton. Of course he would turn up at this moment.' She tried to light another match but the witchfinder sent a breeze through the house, rolling down the stairs, making the letter box on the front door bang, through to the living room, snuffing out the flame.

Jess showed Erica the spent match.

'Now what?'

Jess

Mr Horton banged on the front door with a fist.

'Miss Tidswell!'

As the witchfinder's foul wind filled the house, the screams from the television became louder. Books and toys fell down the stairs, pulled from Ruby's bedroom. A few of the coven broke from the circle, some shouting they couldn't do this. They ran into the hallway and pulled open the front door.

Mr Horton was standing on the door step, mouth open, ready to give Jess a piece of his mind. He wasn't expecting a small group of older women to push him out of the way and make their way down the driveway, shouting and mumbling something about ghosts.

He watched them go and then peered into the house and the open doorway of the living room.

Jess gave him a wave as a giant stuffed elephant landed at the bottom of the stairs.

'Close the circle!' Minerva screeched. A few more

of the women, who had been holding back, looked at one another and shook their heads.

'We can't, Min. Sorry.'

They too walked past Mr Horton on their way out of the house.

The remaining six women of the residential home coven closed the circle, the spirits of the women tight behind them.

'He's back upstairs,' Erica said, turning to Jess. 'Burn the book. Now.'

Jess took the last match and struck it.

'What is this?' Mr Horton boomed, stepping foot into Jess's home. 'This is Satanism. You're Satanists. I should have known. Does Marshall know? That sweet boy doesn't belong here. And neither does that child of yours. I'll have her taken from you.'

Jess blew the flame out as it reached her fingers, and turned to face Mr Horton. The rest of the women followed suit until the old man in the hallway was facing the wrath of a living room full of witches and spirits.

'What did you just say?' asked Jess with an eerily calm voice.

'Jess, the book,' Erica prompted.

Jess hardly heard her. All she could see was Mr Horton, all she could hear, repeated over and over, was his threat to take Ruby from her.

'What the fuck did you just say?' Jess roared.

'Jess. The witchfinder is beside him. We need to

finish this now. We'll deal with this guy later.'

Jess couldn't see the witchfinder so she continued to glare at her neighbour.

Mr Horton faltered and then twitched.

'I said, I'll report you, Miss Tidswell. They'll take your child from you. *Witch.*' He hissed that last word and a voice deep in the back of Jess's mind told her that it wasn't him speaking. Had any of those words been his?

Yes, at the beginning. Erica said the witchfinder had been back in Ruby's room. The initial threat had been his.

'*You will all be judged,*' Mr Horton continued, his voice warping and changing, his eyes bulging.

Just like that, Jess calmed down. She walked towards the edge of the circle, towards Mr Horton and the invisible witchfinder.

'Show yourself,' she said.

Mr Horton frowned at her. He opened his mouth to talk but only a gurgle emerged.

'Show yourself!' Jess screamed.

A shadow gathered beside Mr Horton, building itself, growing taller until the witchfinder was standing before her. Mr Horton tried to scream and his legs twitched but the spirit held him in place.

'We're not Satanists, Mr Horton,' said Jess, her gaze hard on the spirit. A crawling sensation moved up her back. She broke the clasped hands in front of her and stepped outside of the circle.

'Jess!' came Minerva's warning voice.

'We are not Satanists,' she repeated, aware with such certainty that the spirits of the women killed by the witchfinder had gathered right behind her. 'We're witches.'

Mr Horton gave another gurgle.

'And you,' Jess continued, staring at the witchfinder. 'Can kindly get the fuck out of my house.' With that, she moved to the right, feeling the women's spirits behind her surge towards the witchfinder. She didn't need to be Erica to hear his screams and yells, but she didn't falter. She walked into her kitchen, through the patio doors and over to the burner Marshall had bought her. There was already newspaper and wood prepared inside, ready to celebrate Ruby's birthday. Jess grabbed a lighter from the kitchen drawer on her way through and lit the burner. Watching the flames flicker and grow, vaguely aware of the screams and a strange static noise coming from inside the house, Jess placed the book on top of the fire.

She had expected the screaming to intensify.

She had expected the witchfinder to come rushing to find her, to punish her.

She had expected pain or at least some sort of resistance.

Instead, the house fell quiet until the only sound was that of the crackling flames burning through the wood and the sizzle of the blackening pages. Soon, there were footsteps, and Jess glanced back to find Erica and the coven filling her kitchen.

Erica smiled, stepping out onto the patio.

'It is over?' Jess murmured.

'It is. That was incredible.' Erica wrapped her arms around her friend and Jess gave in, letting the tears spill down her cheeks. It was over.

'He didn't try to stop me,' she said into Erica's shoulder.

'He couldn't. The spirits of the women were tearing him apart. Literally. I'm kind of glad you didn't see that. Not sure what Gran's coven are going to make of it all. The ones that are left.'

Jess smiled and they moved apart to watch the flames.

'Where is your gran?'

'Here.'

Jess looked back as Minerva and Esther joined them on the patio.

'I told them to help themselves to tea. I hope you don't mind.'

'Of course not. After everything they did today, they can have whatever they want,' said Jess, watching the women bustle around the kitchen, filling the kettle and searching cupboards for cups. 'That felt too easy,' she added after a moment, looking to Minerva.

'Easy? You call that easy?' Minerva exclaimed.

Esther gave an awkward laugh, pulling up a couple of the patio chairs and sitting in one to watch the book burn.

'I just mean at the end. I came out here, I lit a

fire, I burned the book and it's all over. I was lucky Marshall had this thing all ready to go,' she added quietly, watching the flames.

'Luck had nothing to do with it, child,' said Minerva, sitting down beside Esther. 'Did Marshall prepare it of his own accord or did you ask him to?'

'Well, I asked him to. I wanted it ready for Ruby's birthday but I thought we could use it beforehand. A nice romantic evening after Ruby had gone to bed, maybe.'

'Or to burn a book to banish a malignant spirit from your house.'

Jess stopped and stared at Minerva with a raised eyebrow.

Minerva smiled.

'I told you, Jess. You have a gift.'

Jess's stomach twisted as she looked back to the fire.

'And it certainly wasn't easy,' Minerva continued. 'We needed more power than I'd originally thought. My coven wasn't enough. We weren't strong enough. We needed those other spirits. That was Erica's doing.' Minerva beamed at her granddaughter. 'That was wonderful,' she told her. 'Very powerful.'

Jess glanced at Esther who unwittingly pulled a worried expression as she watched the flames.

'Speaking of which.' Jess turned to Erica. 'Am I now stuck with a load of witch spirits in my house?'

'Oh no. They're sated. They've gone, passed

over.' Minerva stretched her arms above her head. 'Yes, all in all, a very successful day.'

Esther made eye contact with Jess.

'Oh, and we dealt with your neighbour. Horrible man, isn't he,' Minerva added, glancing back into the kitchen. 'He won't be reporting you, otherwise he'll have me to answer to. Turns out, the witch-finder scared him somewhat. Had him by the throat. You released him. I don't think you'll be having too much trouble from him anymore. I think he's just glad it's over. In fact, he's in your kitchen right now, enjoying the company of my coven.' Minerva chuckled to herself as Jess spun round to try and spot him through the windows.

She'd never considered Mr Horton being in her kitchen before and now that he was, sipping from not just one of her mugs but one of her favourites, flirting with a woman who looked a good ten years younger than him, she felt a strange nausea come over her.

'As long as he doesn't stay long, I guess,' she mumbled.

There was a tapping on glass and Jess jumped, her heart pounding. One of the women stepped out onto the patio and passed Minerva and Esther a cup of tea each.

'Thank you, petal,' said Minerva, sipping the scalding drink. 'Calm down,' she told Jess and Erica. 'It's all over. Now, let me tell you what I've gotten little Ruby for her birthday.'

38

Ruby

Unable to sleep, Ruby watched Marshall with fierce concentration. On the other end of the phone, held to his ear, was her mother.

'Okay. Great. And are you okay? Good. And everyone else? Okay.' Marshall looked down at Ruby and gave her a thumbs up. Ruby beamed, clapping her hands. 'Shall we come to you or are you coming back here?' Marshall asked. Ruby waited for the answer. 'Right. We'll see you soon.'

Marshall hung up and Ruby bounced, running to fetch her bag.

'Wait! Rubes,' Marshall called after her.

Ruby stopped, her insides twisting with that horrible sickening feeling of knowing there's bad news coming. She walked back to Marshall, head down, preparing herself.

'The ghost is gone and Mum's okay. They all are,' Marshall added as Erica's dad walked into the kitchen and leaned back against a worktop. 'They'll be back soon,' Marshall told him. 'They just need to tidy up.' He turned to Ruby. 'And once they're ready, you and me are going to go home to Mum. Okay?'

Ruby assessed the words and his tone. Where was the bad news? It sounded like all she had to do was wait a little longer.

'When are we going home?' she checked.

Marshall gave a little shrug.

'When they're done tidying up. Which sounded a little ominous,' he added to John who smiled. Ruby didn't know what 'ominous' meant but she stored it for later.

'I wouldn't worry,' said John. 'There's usually some sort of mess. I doubt it'll be long.' He looked down at Ruby and winked, making her grin again.

It wouldn't be long.

'Tell you what, Rubes, go grab your bag and Bubbles' lead, give them to me and then go use the bathroom. By the time all that's done, it might be time to go.'

'I don't need to go to the bathroom.'

'Have a drink then,' said John, moving to pick up the bottle of squash. 'And you might as well have a biscuit or something to go with it.'

Ruby didn't say anything in case he changed his mind, but after a pointed look from Marshall she said, 'Thank you.'

Settled at the large table, legs swinging, Ruby

sipped at her drink and ate her biscuit in two big bites. Marshall hadn't stopped smiling since her mother's call. He sat beside her, tapping his fingertips on the wood, staring at nothing. Ruby didn't mind. She'd be home soon. Back in her bedroom where no one would scare her or pinch her. Back in her garden with Bubbles. Then it would be her birthday, and no one, not even a ghost, was going to ruin that. The house would be filled with fun instead of scary invisible people. They'd all be there. Her friends, Erica, Erica's mother, father and grandmother, and most importantly, her mum, Marshall and her dad. She could show her dad her latest drawings and how much Bubbles had grown and tell him all about the ghost who pinched her in her bedroom. All on the same day she'd get presents and eat cake.

Grinning, Ruby finished her drink, brushed the biscuit crumbs off the table and declared herself ready to go home.

Erica

The breeze lifted and rustled the thick greenery in the trees and shrubs around the cemetery café. Erica sat outside, sipping at a coffee and staring blankly at an untouched brownie. It had been a while since she'd heard from Rick. Was he still here?

Beside the brownie on the table was her new phone, purchased that morning. She tapped her fingers on the screen, lighting it up and then waiting for it to go dark. It was one way of watching the minutes go by. There were a few other people inside the café and an older couple sitting outside with her, albeit at the other end of the small seating area. Still, it wasn't as busy as it would have been on a weekend. Erica wouldn't have come otherwise. She would have met with Alfie on the other side of the cemetery, or elsewhere. Erica sighed. She wasn't sure where. It was tricky to know where they could go to be alone. She was in her thirties and her only options were to go into another dimension or take Alfie to her parents' home, which was obviously never going to happen.

Erica sipped her coffee. It was time for her to move out.

It wouldn't be the first time. She'd moved out of the family home at nineteen, to go to university, and then again at twenty-five to live with friends. But the friends had met people and moved out, they'd gotten married and mortgages, and Erica had moved back in with her parents in the name of saving money. Money that was slowly being eaten away by a business that hardly made any profit. The less said about the little marketing business she and Jess had started the better.

Erica wasn't going to get a mortgage being a paranormal investigator. How did others do this? She had no doubt others did do this.

Blinking out of her reverie, Erica glanced around. There was no sign of Alfie, so she took a bite from the brownie and let it melt on her tongue as she began a search of paranormal investigators on her phone.

'I heard you brought forth a coven of spirit witches.'

Erica's head snapped up, heart pounding as she looked into the silhouette of Eolande standing over her. The sight hardly calmed her. Erica swallowed her mouthful of brownie and placed her phone down, glancing behind Eolande for Alfie.

'He's not here,' Eolande said, sitting opposite her at the table.

'He's not? Where is he?'

Eolande cocked her head to the side, studying her. Erica tried to maintain the eye contact but it was like looking at the sun. Erica lowered her gaze and took a deep, steadying breath.

'You used to come here to visit your grandfather. Have you visited him lately?'

Erica looked back up at her.

'Of course I have. I just came from him. I always go to see him first.'

A smile touched Eolande's lips although it looked more like a sneer. Erica sat back and crossed her arms.

'Where is Alfie, then?'

Eolande shrugged.

'I'm not his keeper.' She looked Erica up and down. 'Your grandmother was right about you.'

'About what?'

'Your strength. I'm glad you've found it and, I hasten to add, I'm glad you chose Alfie. He needs someone like you. Someone to ground him. Someone for him to focus on. He was lost without you, Erica.'

Erica sighed and leaned forward on the table, breaking off a piece of brownie and popping it into her mouth.

'I don't know if you should be saying that,' she

murmured.

'Because of the time traveller?'

Erica looked up at Eolande.

'You know about him, huh?'

Eolande nodded.

'Alfie didn't tell you that he spoke to the time traveller in this café?'

'Yeah. He told me.'

Erica broke the brownie remains into two, offering one half to Eolande, The fae took it in her slender fingers.

'I don't know what I'm doing,' Erica murmured.

'Do you want Alfie?'

'Yes.'

'Do you want the time traveller?'

'Yes. But—'

'But?'

'But I don't want to leave this time, and present day Rick just isn't...he's not...right. I don't know, I don't understand it. I want future Rick but if I do that, I have to leave this time, don't I? I don't want to do that.'

'Is that what he told you?'

Erica nodded, taking a bite from her half of the brownie.

'Is there a "but" when you think of Alfie?'

'But he's a fae?' Erica smiled to herself. 'No. There isn't. But it isn't that easy, is it. It isn't that straightforward.'

'You'd be surprised. You know, when I met your

grandmother, she was happily married to your grandfather. I admit, I did my best to seduce her, to lead her astray from her marriage vows. But Minerva wouldn't budge.'

Erica watched Eolande carefully.

'You didn't kill my grandfather, did you?'

Eolande laughed.

'Of course not! No. I would never have won Minerva's heart if I'd done that. Her love for him was fierce. As fierce as her grief. I saw his death coming, of course, and I did what I could for her. I didn't expect her to love me back, I didn't expect anything of her. The fact that she fell into my arms was more luck than anything else.'

Erica frowned.

'Or just because you were there for her. You were what she needed.'

'Perhaps, although that suggests that she'll leave me once she no longer needs me.'

This time, Erica studied Eolande. The autumn gold of the fae's eyes, usually so hard and unreadable, were soft and hopeful as she glanced up at Erica.

'She won't leave you,' Erica told her gently. 'She loves you. And what about you? Do you love her?'

'Until my dying breath,' said Eolande. 'As Alfie loves you. He's always tried to do right by you, as I always tried to do right by Minerva. Perhaps I'm not the role model he should have been following. Not if your heart truly does belong to another.'

Erica finished off her brownie and rubbed the crumbs from her fingers.

'I want Alfie. I feel like I could fall in love with him. But I also want that future with Rick, and I'm scared that if I don't grab that now, I'll lose it. Or if I stay with Alfie, then I'll change my mind and want that future to be with him instead.'

'Although, of course, then you wouldn't mind, because you'd want Alfie and not the time traveller.'

'Well, yeah, I guess.' Erica sighed. 'You know though, don't you? You know what I'm going to do and who I'm going to choose at the end of the day, because you can see it all. Can't you?'

This time a genuine smile pulled at the corners of Eolande's mouth.

'I can.'

'And? Can't you just tell me what to do? I'm so sick of people telling me to listen to my heart and asking me what I want. I don't know what I want. My heart wants all of it. I want it all and I obviously can't have it all. So what do I do?'

'You stop planning, Erica,' Eolande told her. 'And you decide for now. Stop worrying about your future. Not everything rests in your hands. Some things come to you without you planning for them.'

Erica wasn't sure that was true. That wasn't what her life experience so far had taught her.

'So, what I want now, ignoring the future?'

Eolande nodded.

Erica sighed.

'That's Alfie,' she muttered, hardly daring to speak the words. 'Isn't it. It has to be. Otherwise I wouldn't be wondering how to have both, I'd be worrying about how to end things with him. But I'm not, because I don't want to end things with him.' She looked up at Eolande. 'And you're telling me that it isn't the wrong decision?'

'Imagine you choose the time traveller now,' the fae said. 'You go with him. You leave behind your family and friends and life, all for him. Every night, you go to bed and who do you wish was there beside you? The time traveller or Alfie? Right now, when you go to bed tonight, who do you want beside you?'

'Alfie.' Erica snapped her mouth shut. 'But Rick is—'

'—That doesn't matter. Just because your heart chooses Alfie now, doesn't mean it won't choose the time traveller later. And anyway, where is this time traveller of yours? Why isn't he here? Filling the gap where Alfie should be?'

She had a point. Erica looked out towards the car park.

'Then why are you here? Did Alfie send you?'

Eolande laughed.

'I saw you sitting here, waiting for a young fae who is somewhere else and realised that we've never spoken, just you and I. That seems like a failure on my part, now that Minerva is open about our relationship. I know that your mother is uncomfortable with me, but I wonder if things might be different with you.'

Erica's eyes widened.

'Do you want to be part of the family?'

Eolande seemed to shrink.

'It isn't how it used to be,' she murmured. 'Fae would once seduce a human, take them into our world, couple with them, perhaps marry, perhaps produce offspring. Maybe the human would come back to this world, changed. Every now and then a fae would seduce a human and stay in this world. It didn't happen often because those stories never ended well. The fae would be discovered, she would be caught and tortured and shared and unable to come home.' Eolande's eyes sparkled as tears built in her eyes. 'It was a risk coming into this world and falling in love,' she breathed.

'Minerva would never let anything bad happen to you,' Erica said gently, moving a hand out to Eolande and resting it near the fae on the table. Eolande nodded and looked up, smiling.

'Because things have changed, Erica. Because the human I have fallen in love with is strong, stronger than any of us will know. And her family are strong. Her family are safe. So yes, yes I would like to become a part of that, as I know Alfie does. Things change, Erica. Alfie doesn't wish to take you into our world to keep. And I believe I can exist in this world and have a happy ending.'

There was a pause as Erica thought back over Eolande's words.

'Why couldn't the fae go back to their own worlds. The ones who were discovered and hurt?'

'Because they'd forgotten the way home.'

This time Erica laughed, making Eolande jump.

'No one ever forgets the way home,' Erica told her. 'Who told you these stories?'

Eolande shifted in her seat.

'The elders, when we were small.'

'To keep you home and safe.' Erica nodded, still smiling. 'Fairy tales for fairies – fae,' she corrected herself. 'You'll never forget the way home,' she told Eolande. 'And if you do, we'll be right here to guide you back.'

Eolande smiled.

'Perhaps we're all told fairy tales. My particular favourite is that humans have such short lives that they must make all of their decisions at once.' Eolande stood and brushed down her long dress. 'Alfie is checking on the woods,' she said. 'He goes there often, to ensure the gateway hasn't reopened and the demon hasn't slunk back in. He'll be back soon, and he'll be glad to see you.'

Eolande walked away, not looking back, not waiting for a response. Erica watched her go and sat back to repeat the conversation in her head.

40

Jess

Any moment now Jess's legs were going to move and she would walk beneath the leafy branches, into the woods and enjoy a peaceful walk with Bubbles through the trees.

She didn't move.

Just the day before, she'd beaten a powerful spirit inside her home. She'd taken back what was hers and everything she'd built and even allowed Mr Horton to drink tea from one of her favourite mugs. But she still couldn't walk into the woods.

The trees moved with the summer breeze and with each sway, Jess swore she could see something black moving. With each rustle of the leaves, she could hear its voice.

'Everything okay?'

Jess yelped and spun round, raising her fist and stopping.

Alfie, hands deep in his pockets and eyebrows

raised, smiled that damn charming smile of his and watched her lower her fist.

'It's you,' she mumbled.

'Were you going to hit me?'

'I thought you were... You shouldn't creep up on people like that.'

'I apologise. I wasn't aware I was creeping.'

'What are you doing here, anyway?' Jess turned back to the woods, glancing down at Bubbles snuffling at some brambles by the side of the path.

'I'm checking on the gateway. Want to join me?'

Jess shuddered.

'Not really.'

'You still haven't been back in the woods?'

'To be fair, it hasn't been that long. You know, some people take months to go back somewhere after something like that.'

'I wasn't aware there were enough demon incidents for you to have that data.'

Jess glared at Alfie.

'There's no rush,' she said, looking back to the trees.

'Indeed there isn't. But there's also no reason to worry. Come on. Loads of people have been in these woods since the demon left and they're all fine. Come help me. It won't take long.' Alfie stepped forward and annoyingly, Bubbles went with him. Even more annoyingly, Bubbles was attached to Jess by a lead, so Jess was pulled forward as Bubbles followed.

'You know, of all the places in the woods I really want to go to, it's that damn gateway,' she muttered, pulling Bubbles back.

Alfie stopped, reaching out a hand to stroke the dog's ears.

'I heard you got rid of a poltergeist.'

'A what?'

'That's one of the strongest types of spirit. Erica didn't tell you?'

Jess shrugged.

'I had a lot of help.'

'What would you have done if you hadn't prepared that burner beforehand, I wonder.'

Jess stared at him.

'Is there anything Erica didn't tell you?'

'Erica didn't tell me. Minerva did.'

'Oh.' Jess fidgeted with Bubbles' lead. 'Why didn't Erica tell you?'

'Because I haven't seen her yet.'

'Oh.' There was an uncomfortable pause. 'How come?'

Alfie sighed.

'Because she's trying to decide whether she wants me or not and I think being there with her might...cloud her decision making.'

'That makes no sense. You being there will help her choose you, won't it?'

Alfie shrugged and looked over his shoulder to the woods.

'You coming or not?' He began striding between

the trees.

Bubbles gave a whine, looking up at Jess with big eyes. Jess knew that look and she was a sucker for it.

'Fine,' she told the puppy. 'But if anything happens in there, just remember, this was your idea.' She took a deep breath and followed Alfie. 'Hang on! Wait up! We're coming.'

Alfie waited, that smile tugging on one corner of his mouth.

'If everything's fine in here, why do you need to check?' Jess asked, faltering as they crossed the tree line into the woods.

'Because, better safe than sorry.'

'Can't argue with that,' Jess muttered.

'Now, wait. Hang on.' Alfie stopped, holding up a hand to Jess. Bubbles gave another whine and pulled her lead longer to go sniff at some ferns. 'Take a moment here, close your eyes, breathe and tell me what you feel.'

'What I feel?'

'Stop thinking. Close your eyes. What do you feel?' Alfie closed his eyes and after a moment Jess copied him. She let her mind go blank, listening to Bubbles sniffing, the birds above them singing, the rustle of leaves in the light wind.

'Peace,' she murmured. 'I feel peace.'

When there came no reply, she opened her eyes to find Alfie smiling down at her.

'Exactly. There's no demon here. Shall we go

check the doorway?'

Jess walked with Alfie along the main path.

'Minerva says I have a gift of foresight,' she murmured when Alfie didn't speak.

'So I heard.'

'I don't know what to do with that.'

Alfie chuckled.

'What is there to do with it other than to hone it, if you choose to. It's a handy gift to have but it can get irritating.'

Jess glanced at him sideways.

'You can do it?'

'Most fae can.'

'Why is it irritating?'

Alfie sighed.

'When I met Esther during her pregnancy, I foresaw Erica and I fell in love. When I met Erica, I foresaw Rick Cavanagh and my heart was broken. When I persisted, I foresaw Erica having a change of heart. And now...'

'Now Rick's back. What do you see?'

'I see a woman and a man both as confused as each other about what their futures hold.'

Jess frowned.

'So, you don't see their futures? Or yours?'

'They need to make their decisions before I can see what my future holds.'

Jess puffed out her cheeks.

'Exactly,' Alfie agreed. 'Irritating.'

'Very. Maybe I should forget about it.'

'And yet, foresight is what made you prepare that burner. Foresight is what made you befriend Erica all those years ago. Foresight is what made you buy your house.'

'Made me buy my house?'

Alfie nodded.

'With its broken fence and elderly, grumpy neighbour.'

Something in Jess's chest fluttered.

'You're saying I foresaw Marshall?'

'You're getting married, aren't you?'

Jess stopped and Alfie turned to face her, grinning.

'How did you know that? We haven't told any-one.'

Alfie shrugged playfully.

'Foresight. Your future with Marshall has always been clear.' He continued down the path.

After a moment, Jess hurried after him.

'But I didn't know I was doing those thing and it all worked out all right, didn't it? So, I could just forget about it and everything will turn out all right?' She smiled to herself. She liked the sound of that.

Beside her, Alfie huffed.

'You could. If you don't want to make use of it. If you knew how to use it properly, you'd have fore-seen what that book was attached to and you wouldn't have placed it in your daughter's bedroom in the first place. You could have avoided the whole thing.'

Jess thought about this as they stepped off the main path, going single file down a rough, overgrown muddy track.

'By that logic, if you're so good at this foresight thing, you wouldn't have pissed off Erica's mum before Erica was born. You'd have met her earlier, she'd have fallen madly in love with you and you wouldn't be in this situation now.'

Alfie stopped and slowly turned to face her. Jess closed her mouth, her gut twisting as she fought the urge to run out of the woods, dragging Bubbles with her.

The puppy sat between Alfie and Jess, pressing into Jess's legs and letting out a small whine. For a moment there, or perhaps for the whole conversation, Jess had forgotten who Alfie was.

His eyes burned and then his shoulders dropped, his gaze softened and he knelt down to Bubbles, rubbing her ears. The dog licked the air around his face, accepting his apology.

'You're right,' he said.

'You what?' Jess was still rigid. She forced herself to relax, filling her lungs and placing her hand on her stomach to calm it.

'I should have foreseen it. Of course I should have. But all I saw was Erica. The words came from my mouth before I could think. It's a miraculous thing, you know, to fall in love. I've never met anyone like Erica and I know I won't again for a long time. I'd been waiting for her and suddenly, there she was. Humans take love for granted.'

All thoughts of fear fled Jess.

'No we don't. We know how important love is. What a ridiculous thing to say. How do you explain how much money is made off finding people love? Of course we know how important it is.' Jess exhaled sharply and looked around them. 'Where are these trees, then?'

Alfie led her further down the track.

'You don't take love for granted because you've found it.'

'You don't think I wanted love before that? Of course I did. I'd just had my heart broken so many times, and then I had Ruby. And for a while, Ruby was enough.'

Alfie nodded and Jess softened.

'If you're that scared of losing Erica, you should talk to her about it.'

'No. I don't want to influence her.' Alfie glanced over his shoulder to flash Jess a grin. 'No more than I already have.'

'Ah. You mean, your work is done?'

Alfie laughed and stopped, pointing.

'There. There's the clearing. You see it?'

See it? Jess's world was tumbling away from her. There was the clearing, the fallen tree trunk, the circular scorch mark on the ground. There was where Minerva had stood, chanting. There was where Alfie had fallen, blood gushing from his face as he protected Erica. There was where Jess had placed herself between the demon and the poor teenagers. There was where Emily had told her to forget this life, to protect her family.

Bubbles barked at the two trees in front of them, joined at the top by ivy that wound its way up the trunks.

'You feel it too, puppy?' Alfie asked, stepping over the scorched earth. He lifted a hand and Jess watched in amazement as something shimmered over his skin as he reached between the trees.

'Is that...?'

'The gateway. It's shut.' Alfie pulled his hand back. 'Still shut and locked. No one can go through, nothing can get in or out.' He turned back to Jess and smiled. 'Job done. Shall we get going or do you want to carry on with your walk? You know, now that you're back in the woods.'

Jess shuddered.

'Don't you feel horrible coming back here? All the memories.'

Alfie looked down at the burned ground. Slowly, his fingers grazed over a tree trunk where the graffitied markings had been removed.

'Of course I do,' he murmured. 'The trees are still healing. There's still pain here. The memories will last more than a generation.' He lifted his fingers to the scar near his eye. 'My memories will last longer.'

There was a pause as he met her eyes.

'For what it's worth,' Jess murmured. 'I like you, Alfie. I'd be happy if Erica chose you.'

Alfie smiled but it wasn't his usual charming grin. If anything, it was sad.

'Thank you, Jess. For what it's worth, I like you too. And your dog.' He knelt and Bubbles pounced on him, falling into his open arms. 'I'd be happy to teach you, if you like. About foresight. About how to hone your gift.'

Jess stared around at the green foliage.

'Maybe,' she murmured. 'Maybe that would be good. I mean, I could see things about clients, right? Maybe I could help Erica when we go to see a spirit?'

Alfie straightened and pushed his hands back into his pockets.

'Maybe,' he said. 'Maybe you could read the cards, tell people their fortune.'

Jess looked at him sideways.

'You're taking the piss now.'

'Am I?' Alfie's charming grin was back. 'Or am I offering you something more? A woman working in the paranormal world with a connection to the fae and the ability to read not just the cards, but the universe. Many think they can do it, Jess. It's known as coincidence. But those with the actual gift are rare. There is such a thing as coincidence, and maybe you buying that house was just that. Or maybe you had a feeling when you saw that broken fence panel. Maybe you had a feeling when you gave

Ruby that book. And maybe you get a feeling when you go with Erica to find a spirit. You just don't realise what that feeling is.'

He didn't wait for a response. He walked back down the track off in search of the main path, Bubbles close on his heels. As the lead came to an end, Bubbles stopped, looking back to Jess and barking to her. Jess broke from her thoughts.

'Coming. I'm coming.'

Had she felt something at those times? That cold dread as she'd put the book into Ruby's bedroom. She'd just thought it was a leftover from her nightmares that night. That fluttering in her stomach when she'd seen the broken fence panel. She'd put it down to the excitement of finding the right house. That odd tingle just before Lizzie the spirit had spoken to them. Jess exhaled slowly. Surely that had been psychological. She'd wanted there to be a spirit so her body had conjured up feelings. But what about the other times? When she'd wanted there to be a spirit and there had been no tingles and no evidence, there'd been no spirit.

Jess jogged to catch up with Alfie, Bubbles bouncing beside her.

'Teach me,' she said as Alfie looked down at her. 'Teach me how to use it.'

41

Ruby

'What are we looking for?' Ruby asked, reaching up on tiptoe to see into the cabinet.

Marshall didn't respond at first and Ruby looked up at him, wondering if she needed to ask again. She opened her mouth, ready to repeat herself but louder this time when Marshall sighed and looked down at her.

'You have to keep this a secret, okay Rubes?'

Ruby, wide-eyed, nodded.

'You can't tell anyone, not even Mummy. Okay?'

Ruby frowned.

'Mummy says I can tell her anything, no matter what people say.'

Marshall smiled and crouched down in front of her so they were almost level.

'And she's absolutely right. You can tell her anything. And I hope you can tell me anything too. No matter what people say. But this secret won't be kept for long and it's a surprise for Mummy. It's going to make her happy. Really happy. I hope. So it's a happy secret, and you can't tell her. Okay?'

Ruby pursed her lips as she gave this due thought.

'It's a happy surprise secret?' she surmised.

Marshall grinned.

'Exactly.'

Ruby cocked her head to the side.

'When do we get to tell her?'

'After your birthday. Your birthday is the most important thing right now, so it'll happen after that. Do you think you can keep it a secret until after your birthday?'

Ruby tried to imagine keeping a secret from her mother for that long but her thoughts were constantly interrupted by the idea of presents and cake.

'Yes,' she said with full certainty.

'Good. And the other thing with this secret is that I want to be the one to tell her. Is that okay?'

Ruby deflated a little.

'Oh.'

'Once I've told Mummy our secret, you can tell her everything. All about today, what we're doing, what happens and this conversation, if you like. All of it. But I need to tell her the secret first. Okay? I'll tell the secret and then you can tell the story. How about that?'

Ruby narrowed her eyes. Was the story better

than the secret? That depended on the secret. The story would be longer though and involve much more moving around the room and talking and finding just the right words.

'Okay.'

'Deal?' Marshall held out his hand.

'Deal.' Ruby placed her tiny hand in his and he gently held and shook it.

'Thank you, Rubes.' Marshall kissed her forehead as he stood up. They both turned back to the counter where a woman was watching them both.

Marshall smiled at her.

'Can I look at that one, please?' he asked, pointing to something in the case in front of them.

'Marshall?' Ruby tugged on Marshall's t-shirt.

'Yeah?'

'What is the secret?'

'Oh, right. I'm going to ask Mummy to marry me.'

Ruby blinked up at Marshall and he stared down at her, the corner of his mouth twitching. He bit his lip.

'Is that okay, Rubes? If I become Mummy's husband? We talked about it, remember? I'll become your stepdad.'

Ruby frowned.

'No. You'll be my other dad. Remember? We talked about it.'

Marshall grinned.

'Okay, I'll be your other dad. Is that okay? If you,

your mum and me become a family?'

'And Bubbles.'

'And Bubbles. One big happy family, yeah? Always there for each other.'

Ruby nodded, wondering why this was in question. It was always going to be this way.

'Of course,' she said with a last defiant nod. 'You have to marry Mummy.'

'Bubbles is the dog,' Marshall explained to the woman who smiled back.

'So, why are we here?' Ruby asked, not liking the woman's smile.

'To buy Mummy a ring,' said Marshall, leaning down to look at the silver ring the woman had taken out of the cabinet. 'What do you think, Rubes? It's traditional for the person proposing to give the love of their life a diamond ring. Do you think Mummy will like this one?' Marshall lowered himself to show Ruby the ring. She studied it carefully. The band was slender and elegant. The diamond glistened and sparkled under the shop lights.

'Hmm,' said Ruby, squinting her eyes to make the diamond sparkle more. 'It's too small.'

Marshall laughed and straightened, passing the ring back to the woman.

'Let's see if we can find something that's just right, then, shall we?'

42

Erica

Erica closed her eyes as three five-year-old girls ran past her screaming. She batted a balloon away as it moved down to attack her and found herself in the kitchen with a group of parents. Wide-eyed, she checked whether she knew any of them. No, all strangers, three of whom were standing in front of the fridge. Erica turned away as two more children ran past her, one knocking into her, and out into the garden.

'Why am I here again?' Erica murmured, glancing up the stairs. A shadowy vision of the witchfinder flashed before her eyes before she blinked it away.

There was a knock at the front door and Erica froze.

'Please be someone I know,' she hissed. 'An adult. Or at least a stranger with alcohol.' She opened the front door. 'Oh thank god.' Her breath came out in a rush.

Alfie's charming grin broadened at the sight of her.

'Everything okay?'

'Please tell me that's a bottle of wine?' Erica nodded at the wrapped present tucked under his arm.

'I didn't realise five-year-olds drank wine.'

Erica sighed and then gave a slow, cruel smile.

'Want to come in?'

Alfie laughed.

'Not really, no.'

'But you bought Ruby a present, so you have to.' Erica grabbed Alfie's sleeve and pulled him into the house. He ended up wrapping his arm around her waist, pulling her in for a kiss, and then he stopped.

'What?' Erica asked, hands on his chest.

'The shadow's been lifted. It feels so much better in here.' Alfie took a deep breath. 'I mean, it smells a bit sugary and it's quite loud, but still. A lot better.'

Erica leaned back to give him a look.

'You felt the presence of that thing and you didn't offer to help?'

'You figured it out in the end.' Alfie leaned in to kiss her but Erica moved away.

'When did you feel the presence? When were you here without me?'

'I'm teaching Jess about her gift. How to hone her foresight.'

Erica narrowed her eyes.

'She only discovered that gift after the witch-finder. How did you know the damn thing was here?'

'Maybe because I'm more a part of your life than you originally thought.' Alfie winked at her and then let his arm fall away. A moment later, Ruby and five of her friends ran into the hallway. Alfie bent in an attempt to be eye level.

'Hello, Ruby. Happy birthday.'

Ruby, overcome with momentary shyness, said nothing and looked at Erica.

'You remember Alfie?'

Ruby nodded.

'He brought you a present.'

Alfie offered the gift to Ruby who took it and said a quiet, 'Thank you.'

'Rubes? Where have you gone? Oh, hi!' Jess swept into the hallway and beamed at the sight of Alfie and Erica.

Alfie straightened and Ruby turned to her mother, proffering the present.

'From Alfie,' said Erica, in case there was confusion.

'Oh, how sweet. Thank you, Alfie. Have you said thank you, Ruby?'

Ruby nodded.

'Go and add it to your other presents. We'll open them all together? Okay?'

Ruby grinned and nodded again, turning back to

Alfie.

'Thank you, Alfie!' she shouted and then she ran into the living room, her friends following closely.

Alfie blinked and then looked at Erica.

'Did that go well? I can't tell.'

'That's really lovely of you,' said Jess. 'Thank you.' Her hair was sticking up in places and there was a brown stain on the sleeve of her dress but Erica didn't want to point any of this out. She probably knew anyway.

'No problem. I hope it's okay. Don't worry, it's nothing fae. Nothing scary. I even asked for advice in the shop.'

'A kid's shop, right?' Erica murmured.

Alfie elbowed her.

He stiffened as Jess's eyes filled with tears and she stepped over, wrapping her arms around his waist and hugging him tight.

'Thank you,' she murmured.

'Erm, it's okay?' Alfie carefully patted her back, staring wide-eyed at Erica for help. Erica just held a hand over her mouth to hold back the laughter. Jess walked away, into the living room, following the children and smiling to herself.

'What the fuck was that about?' Alfie hissed.

Erica couldn't hold the laughter back anymore.

'Poor woman. She's got a house full of five-year-olds, judgy parents and, worst of all, her ex.' Erica gestured to the living room. 'Paul's in there along with Marshall. Imagine. Your ex, your new love and a load of small children in one room. And in the room with all the alcohol are a load of adults who belong to those children.'

Alfie raised an eyebrow and whistled.

'Poor Jess. And why are we here?'

'Moral support?'

They grinned at one another. Alfie took Erica's hand and squeezed.

'Seriously, though,' she said. 'My family will be here soon. We can probably leave then. Mum will sort Jess out better than I ever could in this situation.'

'Rubbish. I'm not leaving this. This is going to be great.'

Erica studied him.

'You want to stay?'

There was an odd twinkle in Alfie's eye.

'Just for the spectacle.'

Erica laughed.

'Can we at least find somewhere quiet?'

'Hang on.' Alfie let go of Erica's hand. 'Stay here.' He wandered into the kitchen and Erica heard him speaking. 'Hello. Hi. Aren't you April's sister? How is she? Oh, good. Excuse me. Sorry, excuse me. Thanks ever so much.'

He returned triumphant, holding two cans of cold beer aloft.

Erica took one and Alfie opened the front door, beckoning for her to join him. They sat on the front door step and sipped their beers.

'So,' said Erica. 'Who's April?'

Alfie snorted into his drink and then wiped the bubbles from his nose.

'No one?' He offered Erica a grin and then shrugged. 'I knew her when she was eighteen.'

'Oh yeah?'

'Yeah. She was fun. But she wasn't you.'

Erica studied the fae sitting beside her, can of beer in one hand, his other behind him, propping him up as he lifted his scarred face to the sun. Would she prefer to be sitting with Rick right now? Would Rick have battled his way through the kitchen to find them drinks?

Erica traced the back of her finger over Alfie's cheek. He turned into it, holding her gaze.

She smiled and leaned forward to gently kiss his lips. Alfie let her, kissing her back but not moving. When she leaned back that charming, easy grin was back on his face.

'What was that for?' he asked quietly.

Erica shrugged, turning away and sipping her beer.

'I dunno. You're not bad looking. And you're kinda fun.' She smiled to herself, feeling Alfie's eyes on her.

There was a long pause, long enough for the smile to fade and for Erica to look back to him. He was still watching her but the grin was gone, his eyes soft.

'What's wrong?' she asked.

'I don't know how much longer I can do this without asking you the big question.'

For a short moment, Erica wondered if he was about to propose. Then, sense and logic came flooding back to her.

'You mean about Rick?'

Alfie nodded.

'I haven't seen Rick in a little while,' Erica said, looking away again. 'I don't know what's going on anymore. With him, I mean. You know, I went looking for you the other day. At the cemetery. You weren't there. But Eolande was. That was an interesting chat.'

'Oh?'

'Yeah. We talked about you.'

Alfie sighed.

'I'm not sure if I like the sound of that. What did she have to say?'

'She helped me think,' Erica murmured, staring down at her can of beer.

'And?' Alfie prompted.

'And...I love being with you. I'm having fun. I'm pissed off that I'm being made to make this decision,' Erica told him. 'And I probably need to speak to Rick. Blah blah blah. I'm sick of it.' She leaned back, stretching her legs out. 'Aren't you sick of it?'

'This feeling? Yeah. I'm sick of it. And yeah, I'm pissed off too. I thought I'd have a little longer with you before he rocked up, winning your heart.'

Erica watched him for a moment.

'You think that's all he has to do to win my heart? Is rock up?'

Alfie looked at her with a fierce keenness.

'Isn't it?'

Erica shivered.

'When we met, I told you my heart is my own,' she said.

'Pretty sure I told you that, but sure, whatever, go on.'

That grin was back and Erica couldn't help but smile.

'And yes, I thought I loved Rick when I first met him.'

Alfie twitched.

'And you certainly didn't love me,' he murmured.

Erica's smile vanished, her chest tightening.

'But things change,' she said slowly.

'They do. When I first met you, I could see everything clearly. My future. Your future. And now, I can't. Now that I have you, the future is blurry. I'm not used to it, Ric. You turn me upside down.'

The tightening in Erica's chest jolted.

'You don't like it?' she murmured.

'Being with you?' Alfie met her eyes and smiled. 'I love it. Because I love you. There was a glimpse of happiness there that I haven't experienced in a long, long time. If I ever have. And I want it back. I love that you turn me upside down. What I hate, detest, with a passion, is the idea of losing you.'

Erica considered him.

'You always said that you could give me up when the time came.'

'Yeah. Well. Things change.'

They stared at each other in silence.

'If I'd never met Rick that time, I'd—'

'—Be mine,' finished Alfie. 'Except that isn't true. Which is why this is so fucked up.' He broke their stare, turning back to face the driveway, lifting his beer to his lips.

'So, I say no to Rick,' Erica started quietly. 'I say yes to you. Then what? What happens to us?'

Alfie shrugged, not looking at her.

'I don't know. I can't see. Maybe we fall madly in love and live happily ever after.'

'Or maybe we have a normal relationship full of arguments and laughter,' Erica pointed out.

Alfie looked at her, frowning.

'That's what I said.'

Erica grinned.

'If I say yes to you, I lose Rick and a future with a husband and child,' she said after another moment's pause.

'You'll have me. And I'm open to marriage. We can have a child.'

Erica searched Alfie's eyes and then smiled, leaning into him.

'You'd hate that,' she murmured. 'You'd have to come live here. Away from the cemetery.'

Alfie slipped an arm around her waist, taking a gulp of beer.

'Worth it,' he said after swallowing hard.

Erica snuggled up to him and breathed in his scent of freshly mowed grass and summertime trees. In that moment, she couldn't remember what Rick smelled of. She closed her eyes and took another deep breath of Alfie.

43

Jess

A scream made Jess blink. She'd been staring at the living room wall. The scream had come from one of Ruby's friends, squealing as Ruby and another girl poked her. All three jumped up and ran through the house, into the kitchen and, judging by the muffled tones of their high-pitched yells, out into the garden.

'Is it six o'clock yet?' Jess mumbled.

'What happens at six?' Marshall asked from behind her. With a surge of relief, Jess crumpled into his arms and held onto him tight.

'They'll be gone by six. Won't they?'

Marshall chuckled and kissed the top of her head

'I bloody hope so. Come on, it's Ruby's birthday. We're supposed to be having fun. And it's nearly time for food.'

Jess stared up at Marshall, her mind already in the kitchen, shoving parents out of the way.

'Is there anything I can help with?' came a shrill woman's voice.

Jess shuddered, put on her best mothering smile and turned to the woman in the living room doorway.

'No, thank you, Evie. Everything's under control,' she replied through gritted teeth.

The woman gave Marshall a long glance and then stalked back into the hallway where a couple of other mothers had congregated.

'She's just trying to help,' said Marshall.

'No. You don't know her,' Jess hissed. 'She's the single mother who's on the PTA and does crafts and takes part in every event while holding down a job and whose child is always immaculate.'

Marshall stared down at her.

'How does she manage that?'

'Fuck knows. I have two theories. One, she made some sort of pact with the Devil. Or two, she can somehow afford a cleaner and a nanny. Which, judging by the rumours of how much her ex-husband earns, could be the truth. But we shouldn't rule out the Devil thing.'

Marshall gave her a squeeze and another kiss.

'Okay, well, I'll go sort out the food.'

'I should help,' said Jess, aware that this was her house and her daughter's party and she'd just spent a good amount of time staring at a wall.

'Why don't you go find Erica?' Marshall offered.

'Because she's out on the front door step,

probably with her tongue down Alfie's throat.'

'Right. So, maybe don't go out there then.'

'No. Bit awkward.'

Marshall smiled down at her.

'You wanna do the food and I'll go mingle with the parents?'

Jess relaxed. What had she done to deserve such a good man?

'Deal.' She reached up and kissed him.

They left the living room just as five children, shadowed by one of the fathers, ran into the room and bounced on the sofa. Jess flinched but turned her back, following Marshall towards the kitchen.

'Jess?'

Jess fought the urge to run out of the front door, leap over Erica and Alfie and keep running. Paul, ex-boyfriend, bringer of Bubbles and father of Ruby, came out of the kitchen, ignoring Marshall and wandered over to her. He had a glass of what looked suspiciously like wine in his hand.

'Everything okay? Is Ruby in the garden?' she asked.

'Yeah. One of the mums is talking about a big group game of something. They're arguing over what it should be.'

'Who's arguing? The mums?'

'Nah, the kids.'

Paul and Jess stared at one another and then both smiled.

'At least they're keeping busy,' he said.

'As long as Ruby's happy. It's her birthday. She should get to choose the games.'

'True.'

There was a pause which turned the air between them awkward and then Jess wasn't sure if she should speak just to fill the silence or wait for Paul to speak. He'd been the one to start this conversation, after all.

'There is something I probably should tell you,' Jess murmured, glancing back at the group of mums behind her. She led Paul towards the stairs. A light breeze from the kitchen made her heart jolt and she instinctively looked up to the landing.

'You okay?'

'Hmm? Yeah. No. I'm fine.' Jess wrapped her arms about herself and allowed herself a small shudder. 'Just tired, I guess.'

'It's a good party,' Paul told her.

Jess gave a small laugh.

'I've hardly spoken to the other parents, the kids have broken up into factions and are arguing over games and I just want to go hide in my bedroom. How is it good?'

Paul smiled and gestured for her to follow him. He led her through the kitchen, past Marshall and a mother nattering his ear off as she helped him to pour crisps into bowls, and out onto the patio. The first thing Jess saw was the burner. She'd emptied the remnants of the burnt book into the bin as soon as the fire had died and the ashes were cold.

She hugged herself, trying to bask in the sunlight rather than feel the shivers.

'Jess?'

'Hmm?' She looked up at Paul who gestured to Ruby and Bubbles playing with a group of other five-year-olds on the lawn. Jess smiled, watching Ruby's grinning face.

'It's a good party,' Paul told her. 'Look how happy she is.'

Jess sighed.

'Right.' She smiled at him. 'Thanks.'

'What's gotten into you recently?'

'What do you mean? Nothing.'

Paul raised an eyebrow.

'You seem really distracted.' He glanced back to the kitchen and Marshall. 'Everything okay in paradise?'

'Yes.' Jess grinned. 'Yeah. Actually, that's what I need to tell you.'

'Oh?'

'Don't tell Ruby. She doesn't know yet and don't tell Erica because I haven't had a chance to mention it yet, actually, don't tell anyone. But we're getting married.'

Paul's expression froze and then fell.

'Oh. Well. Congratulations.'

Jess stared wide-eyed at him.

'What's wrong? You're not going to tell me you want me back, are you?'

Paul laughed, a little too hard and loud for Jess's

liking. He laughed so hard, in fact, that the other parents in the garden turned to look at them and Marshall looked over his shoulder from the kitchen. Jess waited for Paul to stop and then raised a questioning eyebrow.

'I was going to propose to Katy. In a couple of weeks, in fact. We're going away for the weekend to an expensive hotel.'

'Oh. So? You can still do that.'

'You've kinda stolen my thunder.'

'No. The thunder is stolen by the second person, Paul. You'll be stealing my thunder. But I don't see why that's a problem. Except, maybe, for Ruby.' Jess looked over at her daughter, blowing bubbles with her friends as the dog barked at them, tail wagging furiously. 'Both her parents getting engaged at the same time might be a bit much.'

'She's only five. Maybe she doesn't have to know yet.'

Jess eyed Paul.

'I don't know about you, but I want my daughter to know that Marshall is going to become her other father. And I would like her to know that she's getting a second mother. Katy does realise that, right? That she'd become Ruby's second mother?' Jess wasn't sure how she felt about that, never mind Katy or Ruby, but it wasn't as if she had much choice in the matter.

Paul was obviously thinking the same thing as he narrowed his eyes at her.

'I hadn't thought of it like that.'

Jess cocked her head at him. Of course he hadn't. That pretty much summed up his definition of fatherhood.

'We have to sell it to her right. She's getting an additional mum and dad. Our family is growing.'

Paul glanced back at her from Ruby.

'You're not pregnant?'

Jess turned on him.

'Why? Because you think the only reason Marshall would marry me is if I'm pregnant?' she hissed. 'No. I'm not pregnant.'

'Of course not,' said Paul, raising his hands in submission. 'Why would I think that? I didn't marry you when I got you pregnant.'

'Thank god.'

There was a pause as both ground their teeth, watching their daughter giggle with her friends. Jess sighed.

'This should be a happy thing. Ruby's growing up and she has all of us here to enjoy it with her. Her family's getting bigger, that just means more people to love her. That's what we need to focus on. Go get engaged, Paul. I'll do the same. And we'll carry on as we are. Yeah?'

Paul worked his shoulders and then nodded.

'Yeah. You're right. We need to focus on her. That's what's important.'

Jess watched him, waiting for him to say something stupid but he seemed to be done talking.

'You're still having her next weekend, right?' Jess asked, turning back to Ruby.

'Yup. Got a birthday weekend all planned out. Pizza, movies and fort building.'

'Fort building?'

Paul shrugged.

'I asked what she wanted to do. She said she wanted to build a fort.'

Jess grinned.

'I wouldn't mind a fort,' she murmured. 'Somewhere to go hide in.' She glanced back towards the house. 'Although I have a feeling if we had a fort, Erica and Alfie would be in there right now and I wouldn't want to know.'

'That the guy Erica's sat on the front door step with?'

'Hmm.'

'What's up with him?'

'What do you mean?'

'He's...I dunno. He's a bit...weird.'

Jess laughed.

'You have no idea.'

Paul studied her.

'But you're okay with him being around our daughter?'

Jess exhaled slowly, feeling the muscles in her body relax despite the fact that her house had been taken over by screaming, happy children and a bunch of adults who were raiding her alcohol stash.

'Yeah. You know what? I can honestly say that

every man I've introduced Ruby to recently, I would trust them with her life.'

Paul gave her a strange look and then went back to watching their daughter.

'We'll have to chat about wedding dates,' he murmured. 'Don't want them being too close together.'

Jess looked at him and grinned.

'I have a feeling that'll be more important to Katy than me. Do whatever you want, Paul. We'll work around it.' She patted him on the shoulder and turned to go back into the kitchen.

The woman was still chatting to Marshall and he gave Jess a desperate look as she stepped inside. Jess tried to place the woman.

'Hi, Lucy,' she said. Of course, Lucy was Charlotte's mother. Charlotte was the little girl with dark brown hair tied back with a green ribbon. Jess made a mental note to award herself a glass of wine later for remembering that.

'Hi, Jess. Great party,' said Lucy, looking sideways at Marshall. 'I was just helping with the food.'

'Oh, thanks. That's lovely of you.' Jess was about to suggest that she take over when a commotion came from the hallway and Minerva stormed into the kitchen.

'Where's the birthday girl?' she cried, looking from Jess to Marshall to Lucy. She squinted at Lucy.

'In the garden.' Jess pointed behind her.

With what Jess could have sworn was a cackle, Minerva pushed her way through and outside. Behind her came Esther and John, who already looked shell-shocked.

'Sorry we're late,' said Esther, placing a carrier bag on the worktop. She beamed up at Marshall. 'Now, what can I do?'

'It's done, Esther,' said Marshall, flashing a smile at Lucy who grinned back. 'You can grab a drink and go have a sit down.'

'Oh no, no thank you. Sit down? When there's a birthday girl around? I don't think so.' Esther went to follow Minerva into the garden, squeezing Jess's arm as she passed.

'I'll have a drink,' said John.

Marshall grabbed him a beer and another for himself and led John out into the garden. Lucy made her excuses and followed.

Jess found herself alone in her own kitchen. In a small moment of panic, she wondered whether to grab the chocolate or the wine first.

'Is it food time?' Erica asked, leading Alfie in.

Jess looked up and hurriedly crunched on the handful of crisps she'd rammed into her mouth. Unable to chew fast enough, she nodded and gestured at the bowls and plates of food.

'Help ourselves?' Erica offered.

Jess swallowed and nodded.

'I just had a chat with Paul,' she murmured, sidling closer to them.

'Oh dear,' said Erica.

'Don't tell anyone but he's going to propose to Katy,' Jess whispered. 'That's his girlfriend,' she added to Alfie.

He shrugged.

'I assumed.'

'How do you feel about that?' Erica asked carefully.

'Well, he's annoyed because he reckons I've stolen his thunder. Don't tell anyone. No one. Not even Ruby knows. But Marshall asked me to marry him.'

Erica let out a squeal and then slapped her hand over her mouth. Alfie stifled a laugh.

'Congratulations,' he told Jess.

'Thank you.'

Erica silently moved closer and wrapped her arms around her friend.

'So you don't give a shit about Paul getting engaged?' she asked, holding Jess tight.

'Nope. I have everything I ever wanted right here.'

They grinned at each other.

'You've only been together a few months. Isn't it a little soon to get engaged?' Erica tested.

'My mum once told me that when you find the right person, you'll know. Yeah, getting engaged so soon is probably crazy, but it's Marshall, and I just know.'

Jess and Alfie exchanged a private look. Erica's

eyes went distant for a moment and then refocused on the food.

'So, we help ourselves? Now?' She reached for a slice of pizza.

'Shouldn't the kids go first?' Alfie asked, peering into the garden.

'No,' said Jess and Erica simultaneously.

'No,' Jess continued. 'Adult fingers before sticky fingers.'

Alfie grinned.

'What a motto to live by.'

44

Rick

Seeing Erica and Alfie sitting on the front door step, sipping from cans of beer, Alfie's arm tightly wrapped around her waist, had made up Rick's mind. He'd thought he'd known when he'd set out that morning to find her, but it turned out he'd just been guessing. Another sleepless night spent in his car, lying on his back in the cramped back seat, staring up at nothing, his thoughts whirring.

What did he want?

He wanted warmth and a proper bed. He wanted a shower. He wanted to be able to live a normal life not wondering if his boss was waiting around the corner to drag him home.

He hadn't remembered going on a date with that woman at first but he'd woken that morning with a new memory, a blonde woman in his bed and his heart full. This woman, and her name was a vague blur still, seemed to have replaced Erica in his timeline. If Rick went back to his own time now, would he forget all about Erica and find a new loving wife waiting for him? Maybe it wouldn't be such a bad life.

But it was a life he didn't want.

Did he even want a life with Erica anymore?

That was the question he found most troubling. He still loved her and, for some unknown reason, he still remembered her. Did that mean something or had his trainers been wrong about memories vanishing as the timeline changed?

There were too many questions and so many of those questions didn't help his current situation. He had to focus.

What did he want?

He wanted Erica. But that was his default answer.

What did he want? Right then.

Freedom.

Freedom from his boss, from his job, from being a husband and a father. Those romantic rushing feelings of first meeting Erica had been over too soon. The giddy excitement overwhelmed by work stress. He wouldn't get another chance at that and this meeting with Erica hadn't exactly gone to plan.

That was what he wanted. The giddy excitement, the rush, the fun, the adventure. Not necessarily with another woman. He still wanted Erica. There was no question in his mind that she was the one for him, but maybe there was less of a rush this time.

He glanced down at the device on his wrist.

He had all the time in the world.

That morning, he'd driven to Jess's house and watched guests arriving for Ruby's birthday. He'd smiled at the children, skipping up the driveway, memories of attending Ruby's birthday parties flashing before him. There would be pizza and crisps and squash. Alcohol for the parents, within reason, and lots of jelly and ice cream, followed by a large birthday cake that Jess could carefully slice up and place into party bags. What the guests didn't know was that Jess always ordered two cakes, one for the party and one for the quiet family gathering that followed.

Rick remembered his first time at one of those family gatherings. How welcome they'd made him. How much they'd laughed.

It was a jolt to see Erica sitting with Alfie and the sudden knowledge that it would be Alfie attending the gathering this year. Would he be welcomed into the family? Would he share their humour? Would he help Marshall set up the barbecue?

Yet, somehow it was also expected and even a relief, to see them together. It made his decision complete, although watching him touch her, watching her laugh with him was like being punched.

He knew, deep down and without question, what he had to do.

45

Jess

Jess woke the following morning with a headache to find the bed empty.

'Marshall?' she croaked, sitting up and listening. She flopped back onto the bed as she heard Ruby's high-pitched voice and Marshall's deep rumble coming from downstairs.

'God bless that man,' she murmured to the ceiling. Although it should have probably been 'Goddess' now. What would Minerva say? 'I don't know what I did to deserve him, but I'm so glad I did it.'

She got back up slowly, wrapping a dressing gown around her and disappearing into the bathroom before attempting the stairs. Bubbles rushed at her before she made it down and Jess stopped, closing her eyes and holding her hands out in a vain attempt to stop the dog crashing into her.

'Morning, Mummy!' Ruby shouted.

Jess held a hand up to her daughter as she walked into the kitchen, Bubbles bouncing in front of her.

'There's no need to shout. Please.'

Marshall grinned and went to pour her some coffee.

'You didn't drink that much yesterday,' he said.

'It's the small child birthday hangover. You don't have it?'

'Oh, is that was it is? I was wondering if I should call the doctor. But then coffee seemed to help.' Marshall handed her a steaming mug and she took it gratefully, sitting at the table.

'Why on earth are we up so early?' she asked. 'Oh, no, wait, I remember. You turned five. You're not fifteen yet. Can you imagine?' she said to Marshall. 'When she's fifteen. The lie ins we'll get.'

Marshall grinned and gave a contented sigh at the thought.

'Mummy! Look!' Ruby outstretched her arm, her palm up and in the centre sat a tooth. She grinned, showing off the gap in her mouth.

'Oh! It waited until you were five. That was thoughtful.' Jess scooped Ruby up into a hug. 'Keep it safe. You can put it under your pillow tonight for the tooth fairy.'

'I told her she looks like a pirate. She just needs to plug that gap with a golden tooth.'

Ruby looked up at Jess and pulled her best pirate face.

Jess laughed.

'If only the tooth fairy could afford to pay you enough for a golden tooth.'

Marshall cleared his throat and there was a strange pause. He smiled and looked down at Ruby. The two of them shared a look. Jess narrowed her eyes, sipping at her coffee. It was definitely too early for them to be sharing secret looks.

'What's going on?' she asked.

'Can we do it now?' Ruby whined pleadingly.

'I dunno, Rubes. I don't think Mum's awake enough yet. It's a bit early.'

'Mummy! Wake up!' Ruby climbed onto Jess's lap and bounced.

'Okay, all right, all right, I'm awake, I'm awake, stop. Please. Stop.' Jess grabbed Ruby and tried to make her still. Ruby giggled and then gave an extravagant gesture for Marshall to continue.

Marshall searched Jess's eyes and something in Jess shifted. Just what was going on?

'You know, we've been through a lot recently,' he said, his voice soft.

'You're not kidding.' Jess sipped her coffee again, around Ruby.

'And I know it's not possible to just go through this stuff and then go back to normal.'

Jess looked down at the table. That was true.

'So,' Marshall continued. 'I reckon we just have to stick together and make a new normal.'

'A new normal?' Jess put her mug down and

eased Ruby off her lap. The girl slid onto the floor and climbed up onto her own chair, looking between Marshall and Jess as she kicked her legs.

'Yeah.' Marshall glanced at Ruby. 'Like, doing something special after every...incident like this one. And the one before. What do you think?'

'Oh. Yes. That sounds like a great idea. Right, Ruby?' Jess smiled, relaxing back into her chair. 'We'll do something special every time I finish a scary job. Perfect. It'll give me something to look forward to when everything's a bit...you know, terrifying.'

'Exactly. We can go away for the weekend. Or visit the beach. Or get take out. Or something. Depending on what the job was like.'

'Otherwise known as blowing the profits,' Jess suggested.

Marshall shrugged.

'It'll only be for the big, scary jobs. Not the bread and butter ones.'

'Fair enough.'

Marshall and Ruby shared another smile and Jess leaned forward. Whatever this was, it wasn't finished yet.

'So, the way I see it, you just finished two big, scary jobs. The scary thing in the woods,' said Marshall, glancing back to Ruby, choosing his words carefully. 'And then removing the spirit from this house.'

The demon and the poltergeist. Jess sighed,

looking down into her coffee. What a couple of weeks it had been. It would be nice, she put out into the universe, that if they had to go through these things, they could be better spaced out.

'When I first met you, I just thought you were this incredible, beautiful, clever, sweet woman who took my breath away,' said Marshall.

Jess snapped up to look at him.

'Turns out you're so much more than that,' he continued. 'You protect us, all three of us.' He gestured to the dog. 'You go out of your way to look after everyone, Jess. You make me so incredibly happy, you both do,' he added to Ruby. 'And I hope I do a good job of looking after you because I want to make you as happy as you make me.' Marshall pushed his chair back and stood up. Jess watched, her breath coming short as Marshall walked around the table to her.

'All I ever wanted was a family,' he murmured, just to her. 'And you and Ruby and Bubbles have surpassed any dream I could have had. I want to look after you all and make you all happy. I want to protect you all. I want to protect you, Jess, from the things you've faced down, the things you've beaten, the things you've seen so we didn't have to. And I want so much more with you.' Marshall lowered himself onto one knee.

Ruby bounced in her chair, her hands over her mouth.

Jess couldn't move. She faced Marshall, watching him, his words swirling around her head bringing a sense of warmth and sunshine with them.

Marshall pulled out a small velvet box and opened it in front of her. The diamond actually managed to twinkle in the morning light shining through the window.

'Jess Tidswell. Will you marry me?'

A tear rolled down Jess's cheek as she nodded.

'You know I will,' she whispered, folding forwards towards him. She stopped short of wrapping her arms around him as Ruby leapt up and roared, hands in the air.

Marshall, beaming, pulled the ring from the box and slid it onto Jess's finger. She stared at it for a moment, dumbfounded, and then she leapt up and wrapped her arms around his neck.

Marshall managed to stand, lifting her up and holding onto her tight.

'I love you so much,' she whispered into his ear, kissing his cheek.

'I love you too,' he muffled into her hair. Lowering her to the ground, Marshall kissed her hard.

Ruby ran around them, shouting and yelling, while Bubbles stood in the corner and barked, unsure of what was going on or how to be a part of it.

Jess bumped her nose against Marshall's, unable to keep the grin from her aching face. He wiped a tear from her cheek with his thumb.

Jess watched Ruby and Bubbles and laughed. Crouching down, she scooped Ruby into her arms and hugged her, reaching out an arm to the dog who ran towards them, eager to finally have a part to play. Marshall crouched beside her and managed to envelop all three of them in his open arms.

After a moment, they fell apart from one another and Jess wiped her eyes, glancing down at the diamond on her finger.

'Well. I think every day should start like this. We need to celebrate.'

Ruby cheered, punching the air.

Jess ignored her first instinct, to see if Paul could take Ruby for the day so that Jess could take Marshall to bed. No, they had to celebrate as a family first.

'Pancakes for breakfast,' said Marshall. Ruby squealed her agreement. 'Then everyone in the car. We'll take Bubbles for an adventure somewhere fun with lots of grass and smells. Bacon sandwiches and coffee for lunch, then back home for birthday cake. How does that sound?'

'Yes!' Ruby screamed, dancing around the kitchen.

'Don't forget, we've got our little party tonight with Erica's family,' Marshall reminded Jess. 'We can tell them then, if you like. Have some champagne.'

'Perfect,' she said. 'Just like you.' She kissed his

lips.

'I'll remember you said that. In fact, can I get that in writing?'

Jess laughed, wrapping her arms around his waist and pushing her cheek against his chest as she watched Ruby dance.

'Right! Pancakes!' Marshall declared. 'Ruby, you give me a hand. You, go get dressed.' He kissed Jess and then smacked her behind as she walked away.

Jess ran up the stairs, giggling to herself.

Once in her bedroom, she sat on the bed and allowed herself a moment to study her engagement ring. Without thinking, she lifted her eyes to look out the door, across the hall to Ruby's bedroom.

The last two weeks had been filled with terror and doubt. It had felt longer than two weeks. Surely, a year had gone by. If not a year, then months. How could so much have happened in less than a month?

At the back of her mind, the demon's eyes watched her and in front of her, Ruby's bedroom door stared back at her. She blinked and shook her head.

'You have no power over me,' she whispered to them. I'm stronger than you, and I'm going to learn more. I'm going to get stronger. For my daughter and my soon-to-be husband and my friends and my dog and myself. I'm going to learn how to see you coming. I'm going to learn how to defeat you. If we ever meet again, you'll be quaking in whatever demons wear instead of boots. And you, she told the poltergeist, you wouldn't dare come back here. Back to this house of witches.

Smiling, body tingling, heart pounding, Jess shrugged off her robe to find suitable dog adventuring clothes as the sound of happy chatting and clattering pans came from downstairs.

46

Erica

Rick sat beside Erica on the bench and looked out over the park.

'Sorry I'm late.'

'It's okay. You're not that late. I like that you chose to meet here,' Erica said gently. It felt a little final, meeting where they'd first parted. Where they'd first kissed. Was this part of his plan?

They sat in silence for a moment, listening to the birds singing, watching families wandering past.

'Are you going to ask me to choose?' Erica murmured.

'My boss is here,' Rick said. Erica turned to him.

'What?'

'My boss. DCI Burns. He's here and he's looking for me, to drag me back to the future.'

Erica stared ahead.

'Shit,' she murmured.

'Yeah. And that's not all. I saw myself on a date

with some woman I didn't recognise.'

Erica turned to him again, frowning.

'Excuse me?'

Rick met her gaze and gave an apologetic smile. Erica blinked as she worked her way through what he'd said, her gut twisting in a strange, unfounded jealousy.

'So,' she started. 'You're saying that you, present day you, has gone on a date that you, future you, don't remember. Are you... Does that mean you're cheating on me? No. You don't want to be with me anymore? I don't understand.'

Rick shrugged, an infuriating move, and Erica had to resist the urge to hit him.

'Me neither. None of this makes sense. I'm in love with you. I'm still in love with you. But you're not my future anymore. I shouldn't remember you, but I do. My past has changed, I'm dating someone I don't know. How does that work? At first I wondered if we were even the same person anymore and then this morning I woke up with a memory of the date. What's that about? Why the delay? Am I going to start forgetting you?' Rick sighed. 'I don't want to forget you.'

Erica shifted on the bench and crossed her arms. Would it be such a bad thing? To forget Rick.

'I don't know what to say.'

'It's okay. You don't have to say anything. I went looking for you, when I found all of this out. I went to the cemetery but you weren't there. Alfie was there and he actually made a lot of sense. Annoyingly.' Rick smiled. 'And he gave me an option. I know he's just trying to get rid of me so he can have you, but like I said, he made sense.'

Erica was frowning at him.

'What's going on Rick? Just tell me.'

He searched her eyes. She'd somehow forgotten how bright blue his eyes were, how soft and somehow knowledgeable. He knew things she could only dream of.

'I'm not going to ask you to choose between us,' Rick told her. 'I love you, Ricci. Whatever present day me is up to, I want to be with you. I'm going to end up with you. I know we're meant to be together. But, I know now that we're not meant to be together yet.' Rick smiled. 'I didn't like my life before this. I mean, I enjoyed work but not the politics. I love you, being married to you, having our child, but I hated where we lived. I hated our day to day. It always felt like something was missing. And now we've been given another chance. Both of us have. And I think we should both grab that chance.'

'What chance?'

'To do something more before we come back together.'

Erica stared at him.

'You don't want to be with me right now?'

Rick smiled and took her hand in his, running his thumb over her skin.

'You don't want to be with me right now,' he said

softly. 'You want Alfie. Any idiot can see that. And you should be with Alfie. He'll look after you, keep you safe, make you happy. Until I come back. At which point I will endeavour to sweep you off your feet and make you even happier.'

Erica couldn't help but smile.

'You want me to stay here with Alfie?'

'Well, I don't want you to, but if that's what will make you happy, then yes.'

'And what about you? What are you going to do?'

Rick dropped her hand and dug around in his pocket. He pulled out the pocket watch that Alfie had given him and held it up so Erica could see it.

'Alfie said this would tell me when it was time to come back and find you.'

Erica studied the watch and its intricate golden cogs ticking away the seconds.

'Do you trust him?' she asked.

'Do you?'

Erica turned back to those blue eyes and in that moment she didn't know.

'I trust that he wants you to be happy,' Rick continued. 'And I believe that I can make you happy.'

'So, your plan is to go away and come back when I'm ready? Or when Alfie stops making me happy, or whatever?'

'Pretty much, yeah.' Rick pocketed the watch.

'Where will you go? What about your boss?'

Rick grinned and took her hand again.

'Anywhere I like.' He lifted his sleeve and showed her his time travel device. 'I'm going exploring. To all of the places and times I've ever wanted to.'

Erica watched his eyes light up as he spoke even as her heart seemed to drop.

'Okay.' The word didn't come out properly and she cleared her throat. 'That makes sense.' She didn't have to choose between them, she didn't have to make any decision and yet it still hurt. 'Isn't that breaking the law? Otherwise everyone would be doing it, right?'

'It's complicated,' Rick admitted.

In the pause that followed, Erica squeezed his hand, gripping onto him. He tilted his head thoughtfully at her.

'You can come with me.'

Erica looked out over the park, trying to imagine travelling through time with Rick.

'I can't. I can't leave my family. Jess is getting married. And I want to see what happens with the business.' She turned back to him. 'I can't just up and leave right now.'

Rick smiled.

'But you might later. One day.'

'One day,' she agreed, her stomach tingling with the first stages of excitement. Still, she couldn't let him go. 'What if you forget me?' she whispered.

Rick leaned into her, placing an arm around her.

'Will you forget me?' he murmured, his breath

lifting her hair.

She shook her head.

'I can't.'

'Same.'

Their noses brushed against one another.

'I hate this,' she told him. 'I hated having to choose and now I hate the idea of you leaving again.'

'I'll come back for you,' Rick told her, their lips almost touching.

'You better do,' she breathed, leaning forward and pressing her lips against his.

When the kiss broke, she pulled away.

'I really hate the idea of not being able to contact you,' she said. 'What if something happens? What if that watch doesn't work?'

'I'll keep an eye on you.' Rick winked at her.

'How?'

Rick waved his wrist.

'I don't admit to being an expert on why it works but I know how it works. And I *will* be back for you. Do you trust me?'

Erica nodded.

'Without question.'

Grinning, Rick leaned in and kissed her softly.

'What about your boss? Will he follow you?'

'I doubt it.' Rick leaned back.

'And if you disappear in time?'

Rick twitched.

'You don't have to worry about that.'

'Why? Because you'll be worrying about it?' Erica sighed. 'You can't come back to me if you're in prison, Rick. If you go back now, maybe everything will be okay.'

'If I go back now then I'll never see you again.'

Erica looked back to him and bit her lip. He brushed her hair behind her ear.

'Please don't worry about it,' he added. 'Please. Just go, have fun with Alfie, but not too much fun. Build a business, have fun with Jess. I'll be in touch. I'll be thinking of you. And when you're ready, I'll be back.'

He kissed her again and this time, Erica held his head in place so he couldn't pull away. When she released him, she pressed her forehead against his.

'When do you have to go?'

'Now.'

'What?' Erica pulled back. 'Now? Right now? Why?'

Rick gave her a frown.

'I have to go some time. Why not now?'

'Well...we could...' Erica stopped. They could what? It was hard to deny that she enjoyed kissing him. There was just something about him, something that made her want to be alone with him. Alfie popped into her mind with a guilty twist.

Rick smiled sweetly and kissed her again.

'You have no idea how much I'd like that.'

Then why couldn't they? Why shouldn't they? Alfie would be hurt and angry, but he'd understand, wouldn't he? Erica sighed. She couldn't do that to him. She couldn't hurt him like that.

'Make sure you do come back to me,' she told Rick.

'Always.' Rick kissed her hard and then kissed the back of her hand before letting her go. Standing and throwing his backpack over his shoulder, he took one last look at her as her insides clawed at her. 'I'll see you again, when we're ready. Stay safe, Ricci.'

'You too,' she murmured. 'See you soon.' She wanted to jump up and go with him. She clenched her hands into fists, gripping her own top to stop herself from moving.

Rick took one last look at her and then turned the device on his wrist.

'Check my car,' he said, throwing keys which landed in front of her. 'I love you, Ricci.'

There was a flash of light and Erica lifted her arms to shield her eyes. When she blinked away the blocks of colour, Rick was gone.

Erica gave a deep sigh and looked down at the keys. With a groan, wondering if she'd made the right decision, Erica picked up the keys and made her way to the small car park, past her Mini to the rental car. It opened with a beep and Erica climbed in, sitting in the driver's seat. The vehicle smelled of Rick. Her eyes welled as she searched through the car. It was clean and empty. She tried the glove compartment and found a small bag. Sniffing, wiping at her eyes, Erica pulled out the bag and looked inside.

With a laugh, she tipped out Rick's police warrant card, a ring and a small envelope. The ring was a plain silver band. Erica studied it before opening the envelope.

Ricci
Please keep my warrant card safe, to remember me. I'll be back for it.
The ring is my promise.
One day, I'll come back to you and if you want me to, I'll replace it with a wedding ring.
All my love
Rick

Tears dripping down her cheeks, Erica gathered it all together back into the bag, climbed out of the car, chucking the key onto the driver's seat and slamming the door. She went to her own car and took out the ring, sliding it onto her left ring finger.

Then she swallowed down on a sob, started the ignition and began the drive home.

***

Erica and Jess return in
Bewitching
available from your favourite book place and at
www.jenice.co.uk

Join us in the woods

for news, early access and freebies at

www.jenice.co.uk

If you enjoyed this book

Authors love getting ratings and reviews. It's one
of the best ways to support authors you enjoy,
along with telling all your friends.
I would really appreciate it if you could leave a
rating or review wherever you get your books.